THE MARRIAGE SABBATICAL

Also by Lian Dolan

Lost and Found in Paris

The Sweeney Sisters

Elizabeth the First Wife

Helen of Pasadena

THE MARRIAGE SABBATICAL

A Novel

LIAN DOLAN

WM

WILLIAM MORROW

An Imprint of HarperCollinsPublishers

HarperCollins books may be purchased for educational, business, or sales promotional use. For information, please email the Special Markets Department at SPsales@harpercollins.com.

FIRST EDITION

Designed by Kyle O'Brien

Library of Congress Cataloging-in-Publication Data

Names: Dolan, Lian, author.
Title: The marriage sabbatical : a novel / Lian Dolan.
Description: First edition. | New York, NY : William Morrow, [2024] |
Identifiers: LCCN 2023009529 | ISBN 9780063270619 (hardcover) | ISBN 9780063270626 (ebook)
Subjects: LCSH: Marriage—Fiction. | LCGFT: Novels.
Classification: LCC PS3604.O427 M37 2024 | DDC 813/.6—dc23/eng/20230306
LC record available at https://lccn.loc.gov/2023009529

ISBN 978-0-06-327061-9

24 25 26 27 28 LBC 5 4 3 2 1

For Berick

THE MARRIAGE SABBATICAL

Chapter 1

Portland
August

"Why did I say yes to this?" Nicole Elswick stood in the bathroom of her Portland home, wrapped in a towel and dread, waiting for her turn in the shower. "I liked it better when we never talked to our neighbors."

"This is your fault. You had to comment on their seasonal wreath collection. We could have kept nodding and waving at them from across the street without any actual conversation," her husband, Jason, responded, stepping out of the shower wrapped in his own towel. "That worked for a lotta years."

"I know. Weak moment." Normally, Nicole was all too happy to hightail it into the house rather than stand in the driveway chatting up the neighbors. She worked in retail and was forced to be pleasant to people all day. It was a chore, the one part of her job she struggled to do well. Why shouldn't she be her true self at home, preferring quiet to interaction? But the stay-at-home orders over the last few years had forced them to interact with others on the street, sometimes out of sheer boredom, a new phenomenon on their normally chilly but polite block. And once that genie was out of the bag, you couldn't go back to pre-pandemic behavior.

Today, as she pulled a few weeds in the front yard as a stress reliever, she had on her friendly face, and the shiny couple in the Dutch Colonial took that as an invitation to cross the road. The couple always looked like they were dressed for the wrong city, preferring brights to neutrals, new to well-worn, and not a Birkenstock in sight. A high-energy exchange about what they'd been up to ensued, even though she'd never really cared about what they'd been up to in the past. Twenty minutes later, she was agreeing to an impromptu paella dinner in their backyard that night. "The husband said the wife can really cook. And she promised a lot of sangria."

"What are their names again?" Jason, who could quote entire passages from books he read in college, was terrible with names. Or at least, that's what he claimed. Nicole suspected it had more to do with priorities than a memory issue. It seemed to be the names of her connections, not his, where his memory lapsed the most frequently.

"Jen and Rich. She's in medical sales; he's in real estate. They moved here from Phoenix. They hate the weather but love the airport. Apparently, they travel a lot for work. No kids, no pets. She's about our age; he seems to be about ten years older." Though what did "our age" even mean anymore. The other day at the coffee shop, the woman next to her rolled her eyes at the young barista for checking her phone between orders, whispering that people of "our generation" would never do that. The woman was seventy, at least. At forty-seven, Nicole didn't really feel any kinship with her. Surely they weren't the same generation.

"Of course, Jen and Rich."

"Do you think people say that about us? *'Of course, Nicole and Jason.'* Like we're exactly what people expect. Nothing to see here, just . . . Nicole and Jason. Been married for twenty-three years and have all the cultural markers to prove it. A house, two kids, an electric vehicle."

"I hope not. I mean, look at us. I've got this tattoo now and you have that purple stripy thing in your hair. I think we still surprise people." Jason flashed the inked Soundgarden lyric on his forearm and they both laughed. He saw that as an opening. "Hey, we could celebrate the kids being gone by, you know . . ." He nodded his head toward the bedroom with a hopeful grin.

"You know I'll feel better when they both land safely." In the last twenty-four hours, both their children had boarded planes for study abroad programs on different continents. Jack was on his way to Tokyo and Chelsea to Sydney. The children were eighteen months apart, but both were now college juniors, thanks to a few semesters off for Jack, who wasn't a fan of remote learning.

It was the start of a year of adventure for all of them, and she was going to have to get comfortable with the distance—but Nicole would feel better when she got a message that they'd arrived safely and were in the custody of the adults who directed their respective programs. They'd been living on top of one another for the better part of the last three years and now that they were finally gone for good, she was on edge all day, gritting out the change as was her way. Maybe that's why she was nice to the neighbors, as a coping mechanism.

"They're going to be fine," Jason said, reiterating the words he'd said a million times about their children during the last two decades. No matter what the issue, from ear infections to bad grades to panic attacks, he repeated the same phrase. They weren't always fine, but they were eventually fine—which validated his point of view but left Nicole to do the worrying on her own.

"It's been a while since we had the house to ourselves," he said, kneading her shoulders as his damp skin rubbed against her dry skin. She loved the way he smelled right out of the shower, a combination of fig and clove from his bodywash. He still had a full head of hair and enough interest in sex for the two of them, which had carried them through some lean years. He was also easy to please and that helped, too. "Plus, it would be our secret from Jen and Rich. Straight from the sheets to their backyard. Keeps us surprising." He bent to kiss her neck, his go-to move that still worked.

If we do this now, then we won't have to do this later, thought Nicole. She knew she'd be emotionally exhausted after a day of airport drop-offs and then dinner. She brushed her hand across his bare chest, sweeping down to his abdomen, her go-to move. He responded immediately. "Okay," she said, leading him to the bedroom, but keeping her towel on to hide the pandemic pounds she had left to shed. "But let's make it fast. I have to blow-dry my hair."

The paella was awful, inedible really. The neighbors were a chore as well, but not as dreadful as the paella. Jason had to avoid making eye contact with Nicole when Jen set the big copper pan down in the middle of the table, revealing a pile of bright yellow mush with a few mussel shells peeking out. Not exactly the saffron-infused crispy rice dish of his dreams. He wanted to lean over to his wife and ask her if paella was supposed to be this wet but managed to restrain himself because he knew he'd never recover if he did. Nicole could sense his smirk, because she shook her head slightly, warning him off.

The burden of being a foodie with professional credentials was the frequency with which Jason had to lie to civilians outside of the business, assuring them that their creations were delicious. For twenty-five years, he had worked for and then run a small publishing company called Stumptown Press, which was credited with creating the zeitgeist for the Portland food scene and then all things Portlandia through cookbooks, design books, even coloring books. His career flourished from a local success to a national role once Stumptown Press was acquired by Kincaid & Blume Publishing, but locals still thought of him as the Godfather of the Food Scene. He'd eaten, and often discovered, the best food the city had to offer, turning chefs into stars through books and eventually TV appearances, product lines, and other endorsements. Jen's paella was not going to make her a star.

"Look at that pan," he'd managed to say, as the cook waited for her compliment.

For a good hour, Jason pushed the soggy rice around the plate while Rich topped him off repeatedly, first with sangria then moving on to Rioja. Rich dominated the conversation as only a guy who thinks his life choices were the *best* choices could. He was his own PR department for Rich Inc., a corporate real estate guy who was really killing with his hot second wife and superior wireless stereo system. Jen was happy to play second fiddle and clearly enjoying her man's performance. Because the couple had no children, they didn't even feign interest in Nicole and Jason's kids.

Instead, most of the conversation centered around their demanding but lucrative careers with a lot of business travel and the kind of perks that Jason thought had gone out with the global financial crisis: Super Bowl tickets, vacations in Hawaii, extravagant corporate holiday parties at hotels. Jen would pipe in occasionally, name-dropping an expensive restaurant in Vegas or the pop star that entertained at the sales meeting in Tucson. Jason managed to engage with his own brushes with fame, fueled by a touch of resentment and a lot of Rioja.

None of it was fascinating, but the nonstop storytelling relieved Nicole from carrying any of the burden of conversation. Jason could see that she had checked out completely, like a phone on low power mode conserving her energy life. A lengthy discussion about conventions in the good old days left her on the outside. While Rich, Jen, and Jason had jobs that had them earning executive-level status on airlines, she had given up that life years before when her children were born back-to-back. She stepped off the management track at Needham's, the Northwest's premier department store, in return for flexible hours and more time at home. Jason knew conversations like this one reminded her of the career she walked away from, one that she mourned, even though she would swear she didn't.

By the time they retired to the outdoor firepit for dessert, the dinner table was littered with wine bottles and about ninety percent of the paella remaining. Jason hoped the dessert was edible enough to soak up some of the wine. Mercifully, a cheese and fruit platter arrived as Nicole, who'd switched to sparkling water hours earlier, whispered to Jason, "Fifteen more minutes."

Jason, making a meal of almonds and manchego, took that as a prompt to steer the conversation in a different direction and end the evening with a mic drop for his ego before they exited. Maybe his time at Stumptown didn't include rounds of golf with actual PGA pros, but he did have one perk in his future. "Did Nicole tell you about our sabbatical?"

Nicole turned to him with the frozen smile of a wife who was planning murder later, after the cheese course. But Jason had committed now, so he carried on. "In a few weeks, we're headed off on a yearlong trip. My company gives a paid sabbatical after twenty-five years of service. And, believe me, I have earned it. A year fully paid. We're traveling to Patagonia, you know, that spectacular mountain region split between Argentina and Chile? Then we'll stay in Nicaragua for six months to learn to surf. I'm also going to finish the book I've been working on."

Ignoring Nicole's body language, he proceeded to fill out the details of their plans: their house would be rented for a year through an executive relocation firm to a family of five at a fee high enough to fund the year; the first half of the trip would include a guided tour through Patagonia on motorcycles with a small group, taking them four thousand miles through mountains, rainforests, fjords, glaciers, and the Strait of Magellan, finishing in Tierra del Fuego; by New Year's, they'd be in Playa Maderas, Nicaragua, a low-key surf town on the edge of a jungle in a rented hut; and in May, they'd meet their kids in the Philippines for family travel time. Then he wrapped up triumphantly. "It's going to be quite an adventure."

Nicole noted the many details that Jason had left out. Like how the trip was inspired by the sudden death of his college friend Charlie three years before in a single-car accident after he had worked a long twenty-hour shift in the ER. Or how the whole plan had been his dream trip with Charlie—and now Nicole was a reluctant substitute. Or the fact that he turned fifty last year and never celebrated because of the pandemic and had been a big ball of uptight since. He certainly failed to mention that the book he was "working on" was a pile of notes he scribbled over twenty years because he was terrified to write anything of his own. She kept those thoughts to herself. The less said, the sooner they could leave.

Jen spoke first, turning her tipsy attention to Nicole. "Wait a minute. You're going on a motorcycle trip in the Andes, then learning to surf? I would not have pegged you for that type! I'm shocked! Aren't you, Rich?"

If Rich was shocked, he retained enough decorum and sobriety to pretend he wasn't. "I'm impressed by both of you! I didn't think it was safe enough to travel to South America. We need our creature comforts, so we'll stick to Florida if we want south of the border adventure. Right, honey?"

Jen nodded, adding, "You seem like the type that would prefer a nice long vacation at the Oregon coast, drinking coffee, reading books, and storm watching. I know I would. I mean, I'd get bored in a weekend, but I bet you wouldn't."

Nicole had been bullied by girls like Jen—girls *named* Jen—her entire life. Girls who were a little bit better at school, a little bit more confident in crowds, a little bit cuter by the standard definition of beauty. The type of girl who could shop at the mall while she had to work at the mall. Girls who only had two parents and one house while Nicole had parents and stepparents and other assorted adults in her chaotic homelife, moving from house to house. Why the Jens of the world bothered with her, she never understood. Maybe because she was an easy target, with her bobbed brown hair, pale skin, and her classic but simple wardrobe. A person who'd rather blend in than stand out was somehow threatening to the kind of girls who had to be the center of attention all the time. But they always found her, those Jens, pointing out her flaws with gusto. She wished at her age that they wouldn't get under her skin, but they did. They still did.

The truth is that Nicole would rather be curled up on a couch, drinking coffee and reading books. She wasn't a fan of the Oregon coast, too cold and foggy, a dreary beach experience. Sand, in general, was an issue for her. But a cozy mountain house with a fire would suit her fine. Or a cool loft in SoHo. Or a modern lake cabin in Minnesota. Really almost anywhere but where she was headed. She was dreading this trip, everything about it from the location to the language to the physicality. And it was only hitting her right now, with the kids finally gone and the clock ticking down to the departure date: she did not want to go.

But she couldn't tell Jason. It was the only thing he'd been excited about in years. He needed this sabbatical—to grieve for his friend, to make peace with his choices, to do what he wanted to do for twelve months after decades of putting others' needs before his own—so she had to go and make the best of it. But there was no way that Jen would get to know any of that.

"I think I'm more excited than Jason," she lied. "And what a way to recharge everything by plunging into the unknown. Our senses, our creative lives, our relationship, and who knows what else. I think the whole experience will keep us on edge, in a surprising way. Don't you, Jason?"

He beamed at her, a drunken beam, but one filled with pride. He poured himself another swallow of wine and toasted, "Here's to keeping marriage surprising!"

Rich and Jen whooped in agreement and then exchanged a long look at each other, like they had a secret about to burst out into the night air. "You know, you don't need to leave the country to keep your marriage surprising," Rich tossed out like a conversation grenade.

"Oh, Rich, do you think they can handle this?" Jen giggled, now perched on the arm of Rich's Adirondack chair, bracing herself to stay upright, completely unaware that a good portion of her right breast had freed itself from her batik maxi dress and was exposed for all the world to see. Or maybe that was her intent. "I mean, we don't want to scare our new friends."

Jason had consumed enough alcohol so that he wasn't tracking where this confession was heading, but Nicole felt panic rising in her chest. *Please don't tell us about your S&M dungeon. Please don't tell us about your S&M dungeon.*

"They can handle it! Look, this guy's got a tattoo!" Rich said. "We're all adults here. No judgment, right?" That phrase alone was enough to make even Jason start judging immediately. Nicole had started judging these two the minute she spied the large photographic portrait of themselves over the mantel. Being an adult was not an automatic reprieve from judgment, but Rich plunged ahead regardless. "Listen, we have this thing called the Five Hundred Mile Rule. It's simple: when we're more than five hundred miles apart, anything goes, no questions asked."

"It sounds so naughty when you say it like that!" Jen cooed, reaching over for a chocolate truffle and exposing her other breast. "I mean, it is kind of naughty, but it does spice things up!"

Jason had taken a moment to catch up, but now he was putting it all together. Thanks to the Five Hundred Mile Rule, this guy in the khaki shorts and goofy Hawaiian shirt was getting more action than he was. And he was so totally unashamed about it that he was boasting to the neighbors, people he would see every morning pulling out of his driveway. Of course, Jason had been around men who talked about their extracurricular affairs, but not in front of their wives. Or at a dinner party. *Jesus, what is going on here?* Nicole's face revealed her discomfort about every part of this conversation, but Jason had to get more facts on the table. "Anything goes, with anyone, anywhere?"

The neighbors nodded, with Rich adding, "Outside of a five-hundred-mile radius. Keeps it away from our homelife."

"We love what we have here," Jen said, waving her hand around like a car model at the auto show. "We don't want to mess with this life, but we like having our own private lives, too."

Jason was already imagining a Five Hundred Mile Rule how-to guide on a bookstore shelf because that's how his brain worked, even one soaked in red wine. He had a million questions about the logistics of this revelation, but he forced himself to ask one at a time. "And you both agreed to this?" he asked, directing his attention to Jen.

"It only works if you both agree!" Jen answered, flirting like a teenager. "You think I was going to let him have all the fun? No way."

Jason and Nicole exchanged a look, the same look they'd been exchanging since the night they met in 1994. The look that questioned how they ended up with these people.

"Is that how you met? In a hotel bar somewhere?" Jason continued; the curiosity that made him so good at his work overpowered the booze.

Jen was clearly the drunkest of all because she thought this question was hilarious. "Oh, my goodness, no. We met at church! A Christian singles mixer! How funny is that?"

Nicole made a conscious effort to close her agape mouth. This sounded like the opposite of fun to her. It sounded creepy and risky and, honestly, exhausting. First of all, the diseases. And second, the safety of sleeping with strangers in strange places. But really, who had the energy for all this? All her mom friends said that the best part of work travel was sleeping alone in a big bed after ordering room service and watching whatever you wanted to watch on TV. She couldn't imagine the effort it would take her to get "date ready" in some random Courtyard Marriot in Houston. Wasn't the point of marriage that you could stop worrying about your personal grooming for months at a time?

The entire evening's conversation replayed in her head, all the conferences and business meetings that they talked about were really a setup for sex with other people. She felt a little sick, being able to picture Jen work her Most Popular Girl in High School persona at the hotel bar in Chicago or Nashville. Then she saw Rich hitting on women half his age, impressed by his gold watch and Black AmEx. She knew she had to say something or else she'd look like a prude, another opportunity for Jen to bully her. She asked the one question that seemed nonjudgmental. "You said you got married ten years ago. Have you been doing this since the beginning of your marriage?"

"Not as part of our vows." Rich guffawed. "But a couple years in, we realized that there was a part of our former lives that we really missed. You know, having some harmless adult fun. Consenting, no consequences. We love each other and what we have together is special. But it's our marriage. We make the rules."

Nicole let that idea roll around in her brain. *It's our marriage. We make the rules.* Never had it occurred to her that she could make the rules in any aspect of her life. She made her bed, showed up to work on time, and repaid her student loans in advance. She was supportive of her mother even though her mother's life was a shitshow. She raised her children to say please and thank you. She said yes to this dinner because she didn't want to offend these strangers. She never made her own rules, especially not with something as sacred as marriage. Nicole was certain that the only reason she and Jason had the life they had was because they'd followed the rules.

Of course, she'd heard whispers of alleged open marriages from some of the women in her long-standing mothers' group. Tessa had said that "most of the parents" at her kids' private school had some sort of arrangement. (Tessa's own arrangement seemed to include an old boyfriend from her family summer home on Cape Cod who she still saw every year.) Then there were the parents from Chelsea's Academic Decathlon team who let it slip at the after-party for the state championships that they declared Burning Man a "free weekend" for the two of them. That made her cringe then and now. How free could it be with all that sand?

But this Five Hundred Mile Rule was new to her. "Is this like a thing, some sort of organized club or something? Do you have meet-ups?"

"I guess we'd heard about it somewhere. Somebody mentioned it to us and now we're mentioning it to you. We don't overthink it. It works for us, right, honey?" Rich and his bride looked pleased that Jason and Nicole were stunned and uncomfortable. "I can see we've surprised you!"

"Well, if it works for you, that's what counts!" Jason said in the same bright tone he used to compliment Jen's copper pan, sobering up enough to rise to his feet. He was both fascinated and uneasy about the direction of this conversation. Safer to leave than stay, he reasoned.

Nicole felt the need to get away from these people as soon as possible. In a million years, she never would have guessed that the couple responsible for rotating front door wreaths featuring phrases like "Hearth & Harvest" or "Luck of the Irish" would operate under a totally different monogamy code as they did. And the worst part was that she could never un-know this. "This has been quite an evening! An end to a long day for us, so we'll say good night."

"And thank you. I didn't think anything could top that paella, but you sure did! Keep . . ." Jason struggled to find the correct sign-off. "Keep . . . up the good work. We'll let ourselves out."

———

As they made their way down the side yard, Jason said in a very loud voice, "So much to unpack. Let's never go there again."

Nicole laid out aspirin, water, and a cup of tea on the kitchen island while Jason steadied himself on a stool. "Here," she said. "Take these and drink this. Or you'll have such a red wine hangover tomorrow."

"I'll have a hangover regardless," Jason answered after popping the pills and downing the water. "How weird was that? Why would they tell us that? We don't even know them. It's always the people you least expect."

"The people you'd least expect, what? Having more sex than us?"

"We don't know if it's more. But we know it's with total strangers at the airport Hilton," Jason answered. "Those two didn't exactly look like swingers, is what I mean."

"I feel kind of sullied. Like I want to take a shower. Do you think they were trying to recruit us or something? It felt like a setup." Nicole set down two pieces of buttered toast, cut diagonally, with a folded napkin for her husband. "The whole night seemed to be leading to that."

"Orchestrated, that's for sure." He took a sip of the tea, made with fresh ginger and lemon and hot water, like Nicole always used. "So good, thank you." He sounded more sober by the second.

"Eat the toast. I noticed you barely touched the dinner. You'll be hungry in the middle of the night if you don't and then you won't sleep," she said, rubbing his neck a bit, grateful she'd cut herself off from the wine hours ago. "Are we out of touch? I mean, is that sort of thing happening everywhere, and we are not clued in?"

"I like to think I'm clued in." It was literally Jason's job to have his finger on the pulse and anticipate the next big cultural swing. The glacial speed of publishing made reacting to trends impossible but scanning the horizon for new ideas two or three years in the future was exactly what made him so good at his job. He'd been way out ahead of the migration to the Pacific Northwest. He had books in the pipeline to capitalize on the happiness and meditation movements. And when the company's little how-to guide on hygge, the Scandinavian practice of cozy, hit the *New York Times* bestseller list, he scored another promotion. If this Five Hundred Mile Rule was widespread, it would have tripped his radar. "I think they wanted to shock us. I'm not even sure they were telling the truth."

"Who makes up a story like that?"

"I'm in the book business. People make up stories like that every day."

Nicole's phone pinged. It was a message from Chelsea in Sydney. A photo of her in front of an Australian flag with a note: *Made it. Love you.* And then she noticed the text from Jack that had come in an hour before, an almost identical message to his sister's, except the flag was from Japan. "The kids have landed. Chelsea's in Sydney and Jack's in Tokyo." She flashed the photos at her husband, who was polishing off the toast.

"And soon we'll be in Chile."

Her stomach turned. Suddenly, she was exhausted by the day's events. Whatever she needed to say to Jason could wait until tomorrow, until she gathered her courage and he was sober. "I'm going up. Are you coming?"

He shook his head. "I'm exhausted, but I'm going to hydrate and watch TV for a bit. We'll talk tomorrow."

"Love you."

"Love you."

Chapter 2

Portland
April 1994

Jason Elswick was going to go out of his skin. He had heard the news after his afternoon class and his immediate impulse was to flee, to escape the manicured green campus of Lewis and Clark College and find someplace authentic to mourn. A place where he could express his pain without having to explain his pain. Already, the strains of Nirvana echoed around the campus, windows open despite the rain, giant speakers turned outward toward the residential quad blaring the music that defined high school and college for him. How could this be true? How could Kurt be dead?

It was his roommate Charlie Kendrick who told him, meeting him outside his Joyce seminar to break it to him. "I'm sorry, man. I know how much he meant to you." Charlie was a Deadhead, so he didn't share Jason's devotion to Cobain or grunge or loud anything, but he understood having a deep connection to a man and his music. "Can I do anything?"

Jason saw girls on campus who he knew would rather play that lame Cranberries song again and again already crying and wailing as if they'd lost a boyfriend. Oh, for fuck's sake, he couldn't take it. "I gotta get out of here."

"Do you want me to come with you?" Charlie was premed and had barely been off campus for four years except to do research at Oregon Health and Science University Hospital or drive to Eugene once a year to see Jerry and the boys. This was an epic offer. "I can drive."

"No, man. You stay. Don't worry. I won't get messed up. I just need to get out of here." Jason grabbed his backpack, some CDs, and his keys from his room. He high-fived his friend. "Thanks, man."

He got in his beat-up Subaru, not sure where to go, but ended up driving to Satyricon, the gritty, sweaty club in downtown Portland where he'd seen Nirvana twice and every other band worth seeing at least once. He needed to go where he'd last seen Kurt alive. The sketchy Chinatown neighborhood, with boarded-up storefronts, broken glass in the gutter, and drugs on every corner, was the opposite of his privileged campus or almost any other neighborhood in Portland. The grime of Sixth Avenue suited his mood, even though he parked his car a few blocks away to be safe.

As he approached on foot, head bowed in an attempt to shield himself from the rain, there was already a small crowd gathered in front of the club creating some sort of altar to honor their dead leader. He had nothing to offer, no poster or ticket stub or T-shirt like others had left on the bouncer's folding chair serving as the stage for their grief. Some untalented asshole was already strumming his guitar and singing, a poor imitation of the real thing. People passed around joints and pints of whiskey and nodded their heads as if this guy were delivering a musical sermon instead of a lame acoustic version of "Heart-Shaped Box." *Jesus, this isn't any better than those Cranberries girls on campus*, he thought. How could these losers be feeling half what he was feeling?

That's when he spotted her. Tidy, dark-haired, and pale, dressed in a denim button-down shirt, pressed jeans, and a black blazer. She wore a black beret and carried an oversize leather satchel and a designer umbrella, her polished look standing out in a sea of unwashed plaid. She looked more like the women he saw in San Francisco in the Financial District when he went home for break, except younger.

She was crying as she walked toward the club, stopping at the edge of the crowd to survey the scene. Picking her way through the people already dancing in that whirling dervish–style of festivalgoers on shrooms, she approached the makeshift altar.

Jason watched as she attached the handle of her polka-dotted umbrella to the back of the chair with a roll of electrician's tape that she'd pulled out of her satchel. Then she removed the items on top of the chair, laying down a piece of black fabric over the seat. When she reached into the bag again, she carefully removed a stained-glass candleholder featuring the image of Kurt Cobain, distinguishable by his blond hair created by a thousand shards in shades of gold and white. It wasn't some tacky corner store version, but the work of an artist. Did she make it? She placed the glass piece down on the seat of the chair, now protected from the rain by the black umbrella. Next came a tall pillar candle, then she lit the wick. Kurt glowed from the inside.

This girl gets it, thought Jason.

There was a murmuring of approval from the crowd, which numbered in the dozens now. She took that as a sign and proceeded to rearrange the other items from the altar, not only to protect them from the weather but to make more of a cohesive statement. Jason watched in awe as this lovely young woman crafted a memorial out of memories. When she was done, she wiped the tears from her eyes and stood back to look at her work.

Just then, a half dozen drunk or high Nirvana fans blasting a boom box interrupted the moment. They cranked up the music, whipping the crowd into a frenzy, then turned the sidewalk into a mosh pit, screaming the lyrics and slamming into strangers. The mob surged toward the front door, like they wanted to use their bodies to bust into the club. The woman who had just lit the candle appeared panicked, paralyzed by the scene in front of her. She caught Jason's eye with a look that registered as *Who are these people?*

Jason leaped toward her, throwing his body in front of hers to shield her from the aggressive newcomers. He turned to her and said, "Get your candle and let's get out of here. What assholes."

She looked shaken and did as she was told, blowing out the flame and clutching the candleholder close to her as they made their way through the frenzied crowd. Once they were clear of the chaos, he said, "Are you okay? Is your stuff okay?"

"Yes, thanks. That was . . . not what I was expecting."

"I know, seriously. That was not cool," he said, catching his breath. His adrenaline was fired up. He took the girl in at a closer distance. She was beautiful: dark eyes, deep red lipstick. Under the beret, her dyed black hair was in a pixie cut that framed her face and highlighted her cheekbones. She looked young but sophisticated, not like the girls who lived on his hall at all.

"I wanted to be at a place where he had been, you know?"

"Yes, I know. Me, too," Jason confirmed. The rain was getting heavier and she had sacrificed her umbrella at the altar of Kurt. He could tell she was getting colder as her jacket became soaked. "Do you want a ride somewhere? I have my car."

"No, thanks." She shook her head, suspicious at the offer by a total stranger to drive her somewhere. "I think I'll walk. I like the rain. And walking."

"Oh, of course. Right. No, please don't get in the car with a total stranger. I'm an idiot," Jason explained. "I only meant that I think what you did back there was really cool. I'm glad your candle didn't get smashed. I'd like to get you out of this shithole neighborhood to someplace safer. And dryer. I go to school here at Lewis and Clark. And I only want to make sure nobody bothers you. That's all."

She looked at the cute, preppy guy in front of her. Tallish, dark hair wet from the rain, good teeth. She liked his overcoat, maybe a thrift store find or maybe it had been his grandfather's. She took in his well-worn boots and clean nails. He reminded her of the guys who came into the Gap store where she worked and bought three of the exact same button-downs in different colors. That seemed extravagant to her, but they paid like it was no big deal.

He was hardly threatening, probably why he had assumed she'd hop in his car. Truth was, in the fading daylight, she didn't feel safe in this neighborhood either and was worried those drunken mourners from Satyricon might follow her. "I live about a mile from here, if you want to walk with me for a bit," she fibbed, knowing her studio apartment was at least two miles away and she planned on ditching him long before they got to her front door, making an excuse as soon as they crossed Burnside into a better neighborhood.

He thought for one second about the fact that he wasn't keen to leave his car here, but then looked at her, clutching the Cobain candle, and agreed.

"I'm Jason, by the way."

"I'm Nicole."

Chapter 3

Portland
August

Tell him, tell him, tell him. Nicole was giving herself a pep talk. She had to come clean to Jason today, especially after that dinner last night. She'd been up most of the night thinking about Jen and Rich and their ridiculous lives held together by secrets and lies. She didn't want to go down that path with Jason. She had to tell him the truth today.

Of course, they'd had good years and bad; maybe even good decades and bad. There were long stretches of their marriage where the relationship felt more orbital than in sync, with Jason's constant travel and work stress and Nicole's schedule that included so many weekends and holidays, plus her extra hours managing the kids' lives. But with effort they'd managed to reconnect before they drifted completely apart. She felt they'd built something solid on trust and shared goals. Now, that was all in jeopardy because this trip—this epic adventure—that was propping Jason up was sure to tear her down. She owed him honesty. She had to come clean.

"Hey, how was your run?" Jason called out when she opened the back door and entered the mudroom. It was a rhetorical question, really. She'd run almost every Sunday with the same group of women for the last two decades, so the run was always the same. Tessa, Jane, Sarah, and Nicole called themselves the Wolfpack. It was a silly nickname, but it was a special group.

She stripped out of her T-shirt, sports bra, and shorts, tossing them in the laundry. Then she did a once-over with a baby wipe and slipped into a cotton caftan she'd gotten in the habit of wearing post-workout. It made her feel exotic, even in her kitchen in Portland. "Sarah and Ted dropped off Cooper at Whitman and she's a mess. She's really going to struggle with the empty nest because Cooper has pretty much been her full-time job. So, it's like she's out of work now. We told her to get something going that was not Cooper-related before he left for school, but she was all in on Cooper and college apps and dorm decorating. I don't know what she's going to do."

Nicole entered the kitchen to see Jason working the espresso machine and looking pretty chipper, considering his alcohol intake the night before. "You don't look too bad."

"Thank you. I owe it to your tea and toast. Did you tell them about the neighbors?" he asked, a smirk on his face.

"No. I couldn't, mainly because Sarah needed a lot of group therapy. But also, I didn't want to be a gossip." Her goal was to get the image of Rich and Jen out of her head, not conjure it up again and again for the delight of others. "Plus, it gets more disturbing the more I think about it. It's such a cynical way to run a marriage. I don't know how you sustain both lives. Happy married couple by day, Tinder troller by night."

"Oh, I hadn't even considered the apps. What a time suck. I am so glad our generation missed that madness. But I get it. People do what they want to do. As they said, it's their marriage and they get to make the rules. I think a lot of marriages could benefit from that level of freedom."

She puttered around the open kitchen area, stacking the paper she'd read that morning and cleaning up the clutter. Jason's words almost made her laugh. "I'm sure most men would agree with you. At least for themselves. But do they want the same level of freedom for their spouses?"

"I read some stat the other day that said married women cheat at the same rate as men. It's a fifty-fifty thing. Apparently, everybody's a little bored." It was his habit to quote articles or studies in every conversation because he absorbed media on a cellular level. Maybe he did understand the cultural context of what was happening more than her, but that didn't make it right. Nicole studied her husband as he foamed the milk. Was he a little bored? Was she?

"It would make a great book, that's for sure. I sent my team an email this morning to look into this," he said, warming up his favorite handmade mug with a rinse of boiling water. Coffee was his meditation. He gestured toward her to ask if she wanted a latte. She put up her hand as a no. She was already jittery from her morning cup and the lattes Jane whipped up after the run at her house with her professional-level espresso setup. She watched Jason as he poured the milk with confidence and flare. He could give Jane a run for her money with his modest machine. He'd showered and shaved and, standing there in his shorts and soft gray Powell's Books T-shirt, he looked handsome, like a well-groomed version of the boy she'd met outside Satyricon.

Jason had officially gone on sabbatical a week earlier, but it was going to take time for him to disengage completely from the day-to-day work of Stumptown and Kincaid & Blume. He'd left his responsibilities as editorial director to his second-in-command, Olivia Ko. She'd been ready to take over since the day he told her about the sabbatical. She was smart, creative, and both writers and agents loved her. Jason trusted her completely—or he would, once he let go of work mode and embraced a year of recharging. The reason K&B handed out sabbaticals to long-term employees was to prevent burnout and promote fresh thinking, but the catch was that the employees who made it to twenty-five years were the ones who couldn't turn off their work brains. Like Jason.

Part of the reason he picked Patagonia was because he'd be hard to reach there. He knew he had to disengage from technology completely or it would be nearly impossible for him to disengage emotionally. His instructions to Olivia were clear: no contact except in absolute emergencies. He'd given Olivia a code word to text him if she absolutely needed him to check in, otherwise, he'd be off the grid. But he wasn't there yet. "Maybe she can find a journalist working on something similar and steer him or her in that direction. Modern marriage vows sort of thing." He held up his hand and swept it in front of his face, as if he were unveiling a marquee, and then proclaimed, "The New Rules of Marriage."

"As long as Jen and Rich aren't on the cover!"

"I don't know. I kind of thought those pleated khaki shorts were sexy."

Nicole mustered a laugh, then she knew it was time. He was never going to be in a better mood than right now. "I need to talk to you about something." Her tone was more dire than she intended.

Jason looked at her, genuinely worried. "Like something triggered by last night?"

"Yes, but no." Her heart raced a bit at the possibility that Jason thought she might cheat on him. It was laughable. "Not what you're thinking. I have nothing to confess."

"You scared me for a sec," he said with genuine concern. "What's up, Nic?"

"It's about the sabbatical, the trip." She paused and then plunged in. "I don't want to go. I want you to go, but I don't want to go with you." Relief flooded her as she said the words, ones she'd been rehearsing for almost three months, after she studied the map at length for the first time, finally understanding the challenging terrain of Patagonia. The four-thousand-mile route crisscrossed between Chile and Argentina, a good portion of the roads unpaved, from mountainous terrain to rough desert to rain-soaked one-lane roads. Then a cruise during a rough time of year at "the end of the world," or whatever they called that part of Tierra del Fuego. After the physical demands of Patagonia, the itinerary had them staying at a remote beach town at the edge of the Nicaraguan jungle. Add in the cold, the heat, the dirt and sand, the unrelenting wind, and the giant bugs . . . and she knew she was not cut out for adventure, at least not this adventure.

Jason wasn't happy. "We've been planning this for three years. What do you mean you don't want to go?"

"You've been planning it for five years. You and Charlie. Even before he died, you talked about taking this trip. But it terrifies me. I have no business being on a motorcycle in Patagonia, honey. I don't even like being on a motorcycle in the Fred Meyer's parking lot doing the lessons."

"But we'll do the training beforehand in the mountains. You'll get certified. You'll gain confidence." Jason had arranged for a pre-excursion motorcycle boot camp when they hit the ground in Chile. He talked about it as if the instruction in a language she hadn't spoken since eleventh grade was going to magically change her personality type, never mind her upper body strength and balance. Nicole knew better. "There's no way I'd ask you to do this if I didn't think you could."

"I don't want to risk my life for this. I'm sorry. That's not who I am. And you know I'd be a drag if I didn't want to be there. Remember the time we did that hut-to-hut ski in the Canadian Rockies with your family right after we'd gotten married? That was the worst week of my life, of our lives. This is ten times worse than that. Truly, I'd drag you down, maybe literally on some of those mountains." She hoped he understood that she was doing this for him, not because of him. "You're so ready for this and I'm not."

"Okay, so maybe you skip Patagonia, but what about Nicaragua? You can meet me there and then we'd have six months together. Don't you want to do that?"

"Not really. I don't love the beach. My language skills are rusty. There's literally nothing to do in that town but surf and eat shrimp. I know because I've read every review, every word ever written about

Playa Maderas on Tripadvisor, searching for some outlet for my interests. There's nothing. Which I know is great for you because all you want to do is surf and write. You're not looking for distractions. But I don't want to write. I like to go to museums and movies and shop for textiles and glassware. I feel like I'll be sitting around watching you surf and then watching you write. I'd go out of my mind. And again, drag you down."

"You could volunteer?" he suggested, even though he'd barely spent a single minute volunteering in his entire adult life. He donated money, but not time or talents, as they say in the volunteer industrial complex.

"What? Show up in the jungle and say, 'Put me to work'? I feel like I've spent the last twenty years volunteering at the kids' school and nonstop mandatory programs through work. I'd like a break from forced do-gooding."

"I don't know what to say. Are you asking me to call this off?"

"No! Absolutely not. You should go do the sabbatical you've dreamed about and planned for. You deserve that. I don't want to be a burden on your dream," she explained, pouring herself a cup of coffee she didn't want to compose her thoughts. This would be the tough part. "But I would also like to do what I want. It's been a long haul for twenty-three years and these last few with the kids at home instead of college really wore me down. Then losing my job and trying to figure out my next steps. I'm exhausted. I'd love a year to do what I want, to have no responsibilities except my own. Honestly, a year of not making dinner every night would be a dream. Talk about freedom."

"Oh, so this is about dinner? Great, Nicole." Jason started to get angry. There was an edge to his voice. "You can't stay here, in the house. It's rented and we need that income to finance our trip. I guess it's 'my trip' now."

He was right about that. The Galvez-Riley family was scheduled to arrive in two weeks, expecting a semi-furnished three-bedroom, three-bath house with detached guest quarters for the year. Nicole knew they barely had enough time to pack up all their belongings, get them to storage, and super-clean the house before the tenants arrived. There was no getting out of the contract now. "I know I can't stay here."

"I assume we'll have to pay for the Patagonia portion even if you don't come," he snapped, as if all the logistical realities were hitting him at once. All the reservations they had so carefully set up would have to be undone, like canceling a wedding. "That's not cheap, Nicole."

Jason had splurged on a top-rated tour company for the first four months, with the promise of new BMW motorcycles, luxury lodging when available, and a four-night cruise through the Strait of Magellan to wrap up the entire experience. He was right that it wasn't cheap. But even the promise of all those privileged perks didn't tempt Nicole. All she saw was wind, cold, and the possibility of falling off the side of a mountain on her fancy motorcycle. "We won't have to pay for Patagonia. I checked with the tour company. We'll lose the deposit of a few hundred dollars, but the balance is due this week and we won't have to pay that if I cancel tomorrow."

"You checked? Like you've been planning this?"

"Obviously, I didn't wake up this morning and decide to blow up our plans."

"What else have you checked on?" Again, his tone was sharp, frustrated.

"Please, let's not escalate this." She had taken enough customer service training classes over the years to know the language of conflict resolution. She used it frequently with the kids, but rarely on her husband.

"This is coming out of nowhere, Nicole. Why did you wait so long to tell me?"

Because the last few years have been a slow-moving nightmare, she wanted to scream. The pandemic, the remote learning, the politics of all of it. Her parents refusing to get vaccinated and railing against the government because they had to for their jobs. Jason's parents, both doctors, on the opposite end of the spectrum, practically donning hazmat suits at Christmas and railing against people like Nicole's parents. The stress of Jason working from home while she was forced out of her retail job early because the entire industry was imploding. The constant protests in downtown Portland that fascinated her son, drawing him into the action. And, of course, there was sourdough weight gain, the perimenopause sleepless nights, and making dinner every fucking night through it all.

It wasn't until she put her two children on international flights that she realized this sabbatical was going to happen for real. Maybe she was wishing the world would cancel it, like it had so many plans in the past few years. But no such luck. She had to be the one to pull the plug. "I'm sorry. It seemed so far away until it wasn't. Suddenly it was here."

Jason paced around the living room. He was trying to control his rage as best he could, but he was furious. "I can't believe you're making me go alone. Nine months by myself in foreign countries is not what I wanted."

"You know this trip is the one you and Charlie wanted to take when you turned fifty. And then Charlie died before you both got there. I'm not Charlie. I'm your wife who hates wind and sand and is terrified of motorcycles and big waves. I wanted to support your sabbatical because I love you and want you to have the trip of a lifetime, but you know you'd rather be going with Charlie than me. At least admit that."

"That's a false equivalency." Jason would never admit that because that would give Nicole a tiny wedge to drive home the rest of her agenda. Also, because it was true.

He had no idea how to mourn his friend who was the man his parents had wanted him to be: a doctor; a humanitarian who volunteered time in underserved communities; a husband to Clare, who came from a socially prominent family with money. He missed knowing Charlie was out there in the world saving lives. Jason felt noble by association. And he had no idea what to do with his anger when he finally accepted Charlie wasn't coming back. A stupid single-car accident was not the kind of hero's death he deserved. But admitting all that to Nicole was losing control of his narrative and he wouldn't risk that. "You really don't want to do this?"

"No, but I want to do something similar, in that it's a desire I've had. But not this."

"What? What is it you want?"

"I'd like to go to Santa Fe for the year and study silversmithing."

Jason laughed and waited for the punch line, but none came. "Are you serious?"

"Yes. Remember, I used to create art, not just fold T-shirts and arrange merchandising walls. Stained glass, graphic design. The jewelry I started making during the last few years is very satisfying, and my friends love it." About three years earlier, Nicole had scored a trunkful of jewelry-making supplies at an estate sale—everything from soldering tools to hammers to something called a pickle pot. And a million beads of all shapes and colors, along with silver thread and leather strips.

At first, she focused in on the beads, because stringing beads was something she'd done as a kid at YMCA camp and continued in high school, making earrings for her friends and to sell at fundraisers for the theater department. The quiet concentrated work suited her.

She'd spent long hours during the pandemic in the attic turning out bracelets and necklaces, at first as therapy after losing her job, but then it became a creative outlet she didn't want to abandon. Eventually, she wanted to learn how to use the other tools, so she turned to YouTube to watch and learn from silversmiths across the country who shared their how-to videos. In the attic with the windows open, she had made some initial forays into soldering, shaping and polishing silver into misshapen rings and bracelets. She wasn't a natural, but she found the focus and slightly dangerous process to be meditative, a welcome respite from stress.

Now, she had an idea for a product line, but she needed to learn the craft. Jason had his book and she had her jewelry. "I have an idea for a line of silver cuffs—you know, bracelets—but I need to learn how to hammer silver first. There's a program in Santa Fe I'd like to take."

"Wow, you've really thought this through. Sounds like you've been planning this for a long time." Jason tried to lighten his tone, but it remained accusatory.

"Remember when we were looking for motorcycle schools in the US where I could go to improve my skills? Well, there was one in New Mexico that looked good. And then I started thinking about how I'd like to go there without the motorcycle bit. I did some research, went down a total rabbit hole about all things Santa Fe. One thing led to another and then I applied to the program." It felt great to finally tell him.

"You applied to a program without telling me? I don't know how to react to this." Fear was one thing, duplicity another. "How do you even know what silversmithing is?"

"The internet." Nicole jumped at the opportunity to use the argument she'd been rehearsing. "We're both doing the same thing: something we've wanted to do. You're doing this epic trip and finally working on that novel. I want to get back to doing hands-on creative work. It's the same thing. Except we'll end up doing it in different places."

"And we can afford this? Me doing my thing and you doing yours?" he asked, knowing that his wife was the one who did all the financial planning on a micro scale, while he approached it from a macro perspective. Nicole knew the numbers while Jason understood the goals.

"We should be able to. The cost of the program is less than half the price of the Patagonia portion of your trip and that includes a generous budget for materials. And I can work part-time in Santa Fe to make up a portion of my rent. There are a million shops, I'm sure one of them needs sales help. Housing may be a little more expensive, but I'll cover the extra."

"That's not what I mean. We've never divvied money up like that. And I'll still have my salary. I know we only have another year of college tuition to pay and maybe grad school for the kids. I don't want to blow everything we've worked hard to save."

"I don't either. You know that." And he did know that. Nicole hadn't come from money like he had. She treated every dollar like it mattered, not cheap, but careful. She didn't take her comfortable life for granted. And she'd never learned to be extravagant. She still considered herself to be a girl who worked at the mall to pay for college, even though that was decades ago.

There was a long silence as everything set in. *Is this really happening?* Nicole thought. *Is Jason going to South America and I'm going to Santa Fe?* It was exciting and terrifying. Mostly, she was relieved, so relieved that she wouldn't have to get on that motorcycle. But she could see her husband didn't share her excitement. "What are you thinking?"

"Is there someone else? In Santa Fe? Is that what's happening?" His face could not have been more serious.

"Oh my God, no. No. Never." And that was the absolute truth. In retail, most of her coworkers were women and gay men so there'd never been any temptation despite the long hours. She couldn't remember a time in the last decade when she'd even shared a flirtatious moment with another man, except for that one dad who'd rubbed her back a lot at the summer camp fundraiser, an experience that was more creepy than tempting. "Santa Fe is one hundred percent about me. I need to recharge, get inspired. It's something I want to do for me. It's been so long since I've been able to do something for me."

"I know the feeling," he snapped. "Then I guess this is going to happen because I can't force you to get on a plane with me," he conceded and then there was silence for a long while.

"I'm sorry," she said out of habit. Yes, she was sorry she hadn't been honest from the start, but she wasn't sorry that she was bailing.

"Being alone on this trip is different than being with you on this trip," Jason said, moving back over to the espresso maker. "I'm going to need some time."

Nicole nodded. "Of course."

Jason made himself another latte and then walked out of the kitchen without a word.

Chapter 4

Portland
June 1997

"Do you have this in a forty regular?" the voice asked. Nicole was arranging ties on a table in the men's department of Needham's at their flagship downtown Portland store. She loved working here, with the white marble floor, the warm lighting, and the live piano music in the air. Normally, she worked in women's accessories, but today she was filling in for her friend Oscar while he was on vacation. Menswear wasn't really her area of expertise, but she was a quick study and she knew what she liked to see on men. She turned to address the questioner.

It was him. Jason.

"Oh, it's you."

There was a tilt of the head from the man in the blue jean jacket and then recognition. "You're the girl. From the night Kurt Cobain died."

"Yes, I'm Nicole. You're Jason, right?" Nicole hoped her voice sounded like a question, even though she knew absolutely that this guy's name was Jason, that he wanted to be a writer and disappointed his doctor parents with his choices, that he loved the San Francisco 49ers, black Labs, and Raymond Carver. Nicole remembered his laugh and his smile and his kiss. She'd thought about him almost every day for three years.

When she was alone in bed, she'd let her mind wander back to the night they'd spent together after that terrible news. She'd planned on ditching him before they got to her apartment, but instead they kept talking and talking—first about Kurt and then about themselves. Everything about themselves. They drank tea and ate Thai takeout. Later, he'd run out to buy a bottle of wine and they drank that, too. And they listened to the *Nirvana Unplugged* album again and again. Exhausted, they'd fallen asleep fully clothed on the double bed in her studio apartment. And when he kissed her as he left in the morning, he explained that he was graduating in a few weeks and then heading to Europe for six months with his friend Charlie and there was no sense starting up something. And she remembered what he'd said right before he kissed her: *I probably won't see you again, but I'll never forget this night.*

"How are you?"

"I'm good." Jason was terrible with names, but not with faces, and he could pick her face out of a lineup at a half mile away. He had had many memorable nights since leaving her apartment on that rainy morning in April three years before, but none that made his skin warm from the inside like the twelve hours he'd spent with Nicole. He recalled every detail. Her tiny, tidy apartment filled with flea market finds instead of cheap student furniture. The way she changed out of her work clothes into a silk kimono and leggings and wrapped her legs under her as she sat on a big pillow on the floor. The tea she made from lemon peel and herbs and how she put the takeout on china instead of eating out of the box. Her life story about getting out of Corvallis to the big city of Portland, paying for her own education by working at the Gap because her divorced parents were more invested in their "new" families than their "old" family, which consisted of only her.

Mainly, he remembered how she smelled. She said it was Coco by Chanel because it was the only thing from Chanel that she could afford. Why had he not looked her up when he came back to Portland? It felt like too much water under the bridge after Europe. Or maybe because he was twenty-three and he'd made a lot of mistakes then.

But here she was, standing in front of him, looking older, more grown up, beautiful. Her hair, which had been goth black then, was now a softer dark brown, still short and flattering. She was in a black suit with a charcoal-gray T-shirt under her jacket and small silver hoops in her ears. Her name tag said *Nicole* and below that *Sales Associate*. She smelled the same. "How are you?"

"I'm good, too. I graduated in December and was accepted into Needham's retail merchandising training program. I start in a few weeks. Until then, I'm working on the floor here." Nicole glanced over at the older gentleman behind the counter, her manager Richard. She wanted to stay on his good side because he was so well respected at the company and she didn't want him reporting her for inappropriate behavior with a customer, as if he could tell that she was paralyzed by this Jason even from a distance.

But she also wanted to find out how Jason had spent every minute of the last three years. From his appearance—the expensive haircut, the crisp shirt, the Cole Haan shoes—he was neither a student nor a starving writer. "Let me check on that suit for you, sir." She winked at him. "I'm going to get your measurements mainly because my boss is looking at us. It's against store policy to fraternize with the customers in the store."

"Is that all we're doing? Fraternizing?" Jason looked straight into her eyes when he said that. She was flustered but recovered enough to measure his arms and across his back. She was tempted to run her hands across the back of his neck but restrained herself. He could feel her breath. And it was making him a little crazy. He turned his body around to face her. "Can we fraternize outside of the store? Like at dinner tonight? Have you been to Zefiro?"

The beautiful, glowing restaurant that Nicole had only dreamed of going into? No, she hadn't been there, but she'd walked past it a million times on her way to Cinema 21. "I think that's within company policy. But to be safe, you can pick me up at my apartment. You know the one. At the same address in Goose Hollow." She gave him a triumphant look.

He admired the subtleness of her slam. "I remember."

"Follow me. I think the Calvin Klein blue suit will be a better cut on you. The one you picked out is for old fat guys. I mean, more mature customers. You can wear something with a slimmer cut. And the look of big shoulders in menswear is over, so it's not worth the money." She managed to steer him across the floor without touching him. "Is it for work or a wedding?"

Jason hesitated then understood. "Oh, a wedding. Best man for my friend Charlie. I don't have a suit-y kind of job." He wanted her to ask him a follow-up question about his life now, but she didn't, keeping her focus on her work.

"Then I'm going to talk you into this linen silk blend jacket, too, because it would look amazing with your eyes. You can wear it to the rehearsal dinner." She lifted the sky-blue jacket with a spring-green stripe off the rack in an elegant move. "I'm not sure what you do for a living now, but obviously, you do it well. You can tell by the shoes. You can give me the details at dinner."

At this point, she could have talked him into leather pants and a Nehru jacket. He was putty in her hands and was going to buy whatever she put in front of him, even though publishing was not as lucrative as almost any other career he could have chosen. "You are a very good sales associate, Nicole."

"I love my job." After a bit of searching, she found the suit she wanted in his size. "Let's go back to the dressing rooms."

Yes, please, Jason thought. Then, embarrassed, he realized exactly what she meant.

She opened the dressing room door, hung the clothes on a hook so he could try them on, and turned to leave. But then she paused. "Whatever happened to your car that night? Did it get towed? Or broken into?"

Another detail he remembered as well, walking back in the early morning to the sketchy neighborhood where he'd left his Subaru overnight, risking a tow so he could stay with her. "Nothing happened to it. It was a miracle."

"I've thought about that car a lot," she said, closing the door. "I'll be back in a minute to check on you."

Chapter 5

Portland
August

"Everything okay?" Nicole stood in the doorway of the garage, watching Jason stack and restack the reusable moving boxes until they met his expectations. The boxes would need to be moved again, but that didn't factor into Jason's determination to make them look neat for now. The storage container pod would be delivered to their driveway this week. Because they were renting the house out for the year and needed to empty the drawers and closets for the renters, they decided to use the opportunity to declutter and clear out years of accumulated clothes, toys, schoolwork, old sneakers, participation trophies—all the debris of modern American life lived with two children. Nicole and the kids had started the process over the last few weeks, but Chelsea and Jack's efforts were minimal, ready to part with almost every piece of childhood memorabilia rather than sort it. She'd been the one to go through the items piece by piece and be selective but sentimental with the first-grade art projects or extensive Build-A-Bear collection. The items that were left were the ones that mattered.

Jason had spent most of the last twenty-four hours packing with a vengeance, clearly working something out in his mind with his usual formula of extreme physical labor coupled with the silent treatment. He'd managed to shut out Nicole and any further conversation about her abandonment while he simmered and plotted. At least, that was what Nicole imagined he was doing. He was also punishing her, though he'd never admit that.

Early in their marriage, she'd tried to coax him into talking, sharing his feelings—constantly asking him how he felt about this or what he was thinking about that. It had taken her about a dozen years and hundreds of *Oprah*s taped on her VCR to realize that she had created a pattern of behavior that wasn't healthy. He was never going to talk to her unless she browbeat it out of him. And most often, what came out after all the questioning was a version of the situation where she was to blame, and he was only trying to make her happy.

One day, after a particularly tough argument over a holiday visit from his parents that had been stressful from start to finish, she decided she was done with the browbeating, done with always being the one to insist on conversation over silence.

Her new approach was to let him work it out in his own way and then ask a single time if anything was wrong, or some version of the question. Her strategy hadn't made him open up with more frequency, but it mitigated her feelings of guilt.

She looked at him arranging the containers of their life in neat towers, ready to be loaded into the pod when it arrived. He was clearly ruminating; his efforts to ignore her would have been impressive if they hadn't been so annoying. She would only ask one more time. "Do you need anything from me?"

Jason paused long enough to take a sip of water from his Hydro Flask. It was a warm day in August and he was sweating from his efforts. Soon, he'd change into his tennis clothes and go play doubles at the park with his regular group, like he did every Monday night in spring and summer when it stayed light until ten. But there was time for a response if he wanted to engage. "I assume you canceled with the tour company?"

She nodded. "Yes, everything was refunded except five hundred dollars." She'd also canceled her flight and the extra life insurance policy she'd taken out on herself one day in July when her anxiety overwhelmed her and she needed to do something positive to calm her brain. But she didn't tell her husband about that. In addition, last night when he had retreated to his office above the garage to "take care of a few things," she'd enrolled in the silversmithing program at Santa Fe Community College and booked a small, inexpensive studio apartment in the middle of the city for two weeks so she could get her bearings before looking for more permanent lodging. She'd also scrolled through social media looking for charming boutiques where she could apply for work once she got there. If only Jason hadn't been so brooding, maybe she could have enjoyed the planning more. "And I can use the credit on the flight for our trip to see the kids in May."

"Oh, are we still doing that?"

"What does that mean? Of course we are." The grand finale of their sabbatical would be rendezvousing with Chelsea and Jack after their programs ended. Together, the family had decided on a trip to the Philippines and Vietnam and then a long layover in Hawaii before they made it back to Portland. More sea and sand and swimming for Nicole, but she was used to being the odd man out on family trips.

Chelsea had wanted to study marine biology since their very first trip to the Oregon Coast Aquarium when she was five. Unlike most children, who grow out of their childhood dreams to become ballerinas or baseball players, Chelsea had maintained her focus on spending her life with sea creatures. To that end, she'd volunteered at the zoo as soon as she was old enough, taken scuba lessons and been certified, participated in wildlife counts and animal welfare efforts, and was now spending a year studying at the Great Barrier Reef. Of course, her dream trip involved scuba diving.

Jack, on the other hand, intended on making as much money as possible in international business, but also loved all adventure sports, from snowboarding to rock climbing to scuba diving. To be with her children, Nicole could stand the sand. But why not to be with her husband? "Why would we cancel the family part of the trip? Besides, we have no house to come home to. It's rented through next August."

"I don't know, Nicole. All I know is that yesterday, I was planning on spending almost every minute of the year with my wife, and now I'm going to be spending it alone while she's off studying silversmithing in Santa Fe. It's not that far afield to assume that you might not want to go to the Philippines either."

"I do want to go to the Philippines and Vietnam. And we can stay in Hawaii all summer if that's what you want. But please don't be angry with me."

"I wish it was that easy. I keep asking myself, why did she wait so long to tell me? We could have planned an entirely different itinerary. We could have gone to London for a year. But it's like you waited specifically so you wouldn't have to go."

Nicole's mind flashed back to the glorious week she'd spent in London, prowling the shops and museums on her own while Jason attended the London Book Fair. She would have loved another trip to the city, but Jason was very emphatic about his needs. "That's not true. You wanted to be off the grid. Disconnected. London isn't disconnected from the book business. It's right in the middle of the book business. You're doing exactly what you want. And I waited because . . . because I was scared to tell you. Not because I had some grand scam going on."

"And you think it's fair that I be alone all year, without anyone?"

"There will be a dozen other people on the tour in Patagonia and the same will be true of the surf camp in Playa Maderas. Plus, that's a small town and you're you. You'll know everybody there after two weeks." Jason could walk into a room of strangers every night of the week without any anxiety. He was drawn to people and people were drawn to him. Nicole had learned so much by watching him over the years. She'd gotten more confident, thanks to Jason, but she could never match his energy. She was the one who would really be alone for the year, not him. "You'll make a new friend every day."

"That's not what I mean, Nicole. I mean, alone at night. Alone, alone. No sex for nine months until we meet up with the kids in our tent on the beach in the Philippines." Jason wasn't exactly pouting, but his tone was borderline immature.

"Is that what this is about? Sex? Like everything else would be fine, except the no sex part?" She really hadn't even thought about that piece of this. That was telling. Probably her deepening peri-menopause, which came with brutal headaches and weight gain. Her friend Tessa had blamed every off moment on perimenopause for a decade and now that Nicole was reaching the end of her estrogen reserves, she understood why.

"That's a little broad, but yes. I mean, I know the Patagonia thing isn't for you. And you're right about Playa Maderas. There's nothing to do there but surf, sleep, and write. But I wanted you with me." Now his voice was sincere.

Nicole thought he was sick of her, so much time together over the last few years. But he sounded like he'd miss her, her body, being with her. Hadn't he noticed her disappearing waistline? "You're going to miss me. For the sex?"

Jason shrugged. "I guess. In part. Obviously, there's more to it than that, but yes, I'll miss sex with another human."

"Let's do the Five Hundred Mile Rule." The words were out of her mouth before she could think twice about them. If giving Jason a sabbatical from their marriage vows for nine months was going to make the difference between his enthusiasm or his punishment, then fine. She was willing to bargain with this chip.

"You're joking."

"I'm not. I could tell you were intrigued when Rich and Jen brought it up. And you said it yourself—that you get it. People get to do what they want to do."

"And you said it was a cynical way to run a relationship."

She thought before answering. There was no way that she and Jason were the same kind of couple as Jen and Rich. Those two were porous; she and Jason were solid. "I guess it depends on the couple involved. It's not a cynical way to run our relationship because we trust each other." She heard herself say the words, but she wasn't sure that was true all the time. She thought about the years when the kids were in elementary school and she felt like they were sprinting through every day: school, work, sports, homework, food, housework, endless to-do lists. They could go a whole week without sharing anything except the logistics of carpool pick-ups. Then, Jason had started to travel regularly for work after his promotion and Nicole had worries. He was a handsome, successful straight guy surrounded by all manner of young women who flocked to publishing. She'd be lying if she didn't admit to middle of the night worries about what happened in the after hours of conferences, trade shows, and celebratory dinners in San Francisco and New York, but she was too scared and too tired to ask. She didn't think he'd ever strayed, and she didn't want to think about it. "We do trust each other, right?"

"Yes, we do. But is this what you want?" Jason could hear Jen's voice echo in his head, about it only working if they both agreed. He was so stunned at Nicole's suggestion that he was playing for time with a few extra questions. He couldn't believe she was giving him the equivalent of a marital hall pass for a year. But did he want her to have the same?

"I want you to have the sabbatical you planned and to get everything out of it that you need. I want you to test your physical limits and see the Tierra del Fuego and learn to surf and finish that book you've been talking about for as long as I've known you. I want you to have a release from your responsibilities and your grief. And if that means that occasionally you sleep with somebody else, I guess I'm okay with that."

"Nic, this is kind of a big deal, to open up our marriage."

"That's not the right term. We'll close it back up after this year. It's not a philosophical change. It's pragmatic, nothing more. I want to stay married to you. I'm not suggesting a trial separation. It's relaxing the rules a bit."

There was a long pause as her husband thought about what she was saying. Then he checked his watch. "I'm supposed to go play tennis. Let's pick this up later." He sounded like he was at work, not deciding the course of their marriage. But that's the way he operated, slipping into his business persona when any situation got stressful.

"Of course, yes. Go!" she said as they went back into the house. She also assumed the everyday dialogue of their lives. "I'm going to pick up dinner at Elephants. Trying to keep the kitchen clean until move out day. Any requests?"

"Smoked salmon salad and the tomato-orange soup." It was the order he'd given her almost every time she asked that question over the last twenty years. "And a chocolate chip cookie."

She nodded, then called out to him as he headed up the stairs to change. "Love you."

There was no answer.

As soon as Jason hopped on his bike to ride to Washington Park, Nicole hopped in her car and headed to Elephants to pick up dinner and a few marionberry scones for breakfast, plus grab herself a decaf iced latte. She knew she had at least two hours before Jason returned home from tennis. She dropped the food in the fridge and headed off on foot to Tessa's, after confirming she was home via text.

Tessa lived a few blocks away in a classic Northwest Portland shingled 1909 house with steep steps leading up to a big wide porch. Tessa and her husband, Peter, had relocated to Portland in the early aughts or, as Jason called it, the Great Onslaught, a decade of unrelenting migration by young couples of all stripes to Portland, Oregon, from every major metropolitan area in the country.

They had moved from Boston, reluctantly at first, but now they were the poster couple for the allure of the Pacific Northwest. Peter was recruited to be the CFO of what was a small tech company that grew into a much larger tech company over the years. Tessa quit her job as a lawyer and had her first baby six months after arriving in Portland and minutes after finishing up a house remodel. A new mother in a new town, she advertised for friends by hanging a flyer in Dragonfly Coffee on Thurman. The flyer announced a new playgroup forming at Wallace Park on Wednesday afternoons. But really, it was Tessa and three-month-old Clayton trolling for playdates.

Nicole had powered through her first year of motherhood with almost no support except for a few work colleagues who dropped off the occasional casserole and a part-time sitter who covered Jack during the evening hours between her departure for her night shift and Jason's arrival home. It had been a lonely year as she struggled to balance her baby, her job, and her insecurity about her new role. She was pregnant again when she spotted Tessa's flyer and knew she needed some actual mom friends. She pulled herself together and strolled Jack to the park for the playgroup. She arrived to find Tessa, who had commandeered several picnic tables and decorated them with gingham tablecloths and fresh flowers, arranging a spread of lemonade, tea sandwiches, and little fish crackers. Clayton was fussing, so Nicole immediately took over, working her merchandising know-how on the table while they introduced themselves. By the time others arrived, the Wallace Park Playgroup table looked like a magazine spread, with other mothers cooing over Tessa's efforts. Nicole took no credit, and she won Tessa's admiration for life. And her friendship.

Jane, a single mother by choice and trust fund, and Sarah, the crunchiest and least likely to wear lipstick, joined the group that day as well. Jane's daughter, Carson, was raised like a tiny adult and spoke in full sentences by age two. By contrast, Sarah's three boys played in the mud and spent hours tackling one another in the backyard while she made rolled oat peanut butter balls or lentil chard soup or some other nutritious treat. As the children grew up, most grew apart, but the four mothers stayed in regular contact and excelled as a collective when needed, like during Sarah's emergency hysterectomy or Jane's brief and disastrous marriage to and divorce from Brianna. The Wolfpack knew how to rally.

But today, Nicole wanted to talk to Tessa, only Tessa. When she pulled up to the gray house with the white trim, she could see her friend on the front porch, two glasses of rosé already poured. Nicole decided to leave her iced coffee in the car; rosé was better suited to the conversation she needed to have.

"You don't want to make dinner for a year, so you told your husband he could have sex with other women? Wow. I didn't see that coming."

By the time Nicole had filled Tessa in on the events of the past seventy-two hours, their first glasses of rosé were gone and seconds had been poured. Tessa listened actively while Nicole spoke, not interrupting, but nodding or adding phrases like "Got it!" or "Really?" to the storytelling. Nicole finished by asking the question, "Do you think I'm making a huge mistake?"

"And I assume you're asking me this because of Scott?" Tessa said without missing a beat.

"Yes. I hope you don't mind. I don't know the details of your relationship with Scott. But I heard you and Jane talking one night at the neighborhood summer party and it sounded like it might fit into the category of something outside your marriage?"

"You mean sex outside my marriage?" Tessa had an amused look on her face, not the slightest bit put out.

"Yes. You know I'm not comfortable talking about this stuff."

"That's why I can't believe you're telling me all this. Or doing it! First, thank God you're not doing that crazy trip. We were all sure you were going to die, and we all wanted to speak at your funeral, so know that you are loved. Second, take a deep breath. Nothing's happened yet. And third, I have a book you should read about the history of marriage that will blow your mind and support the notion that a lifetime of monogamy was never part of the contract before the Puritans got a hold of things and the Eisenhower administration really doubled down on the perfect American family myth."

This was classic Tessa: a multipart answer to a single question, ending with a book recommendation. No matter what issue the Wolfpack faced, from teen anxiety to caring for an aging parent to undiagnosed foot pain, Tessa had a book or an article or a podcast to turn to for information. She was a resource librarian at heart, wrapped in a lawyer's efficiency. "What I learned from this book is that our idea of a love-match marriage with inscrutable fidelity that lasts fifty-plus years is a completely modern construct. That very few couples can attain. Marriage used to be a business arrangement. Or a matter of convenience. Or short-lived because the woman died in childbirth or the husband died in a horrific farm accident. Nobody lived long enough to celebrate a golden anniversary. My point is that history tells us that marriage can be more flexible than you think."

"Is that what you have with Peter? A flexible arrangement?"

"Back to Scott, huh? Here's the deal, as kids we spent every summer living next to each other on Cape Cod. And by the time we were seventeen, that included sleeping with each other. It didn't matter if we had a boyfriend at home or college. It's what we did when we were together on the Cape. It started so long ago, like before email, before texting. We'd see each other in the summer and then we'd go back to our regularly scheduled lives for the rest of the year. He got engaged, it didn't stop. I got married in my late thirties, after having a lot of fun in my twenties, and it didn't stop. Scott is important to me. And I'm important to him. But unless we're together on the Cape, we have zero contact. Almost zero contact. We send each other Springsteen quotes on our birthdays. I'm not pining for him and he's not thinking of me."

"Does Peter know?"

"Probably, but not definitely. When Peter and I met, it was time for both of us to get married and have kids. We accepted that we weren't the greatest love story ever told, but we like each other a hell of a lot. And we love our son and we have a very satisfying life. Do we have a lot of great sex? Nope. We rarely did even back in the day. And now, it's even less frequent. Honestly, much less frequent. But that's okay. I think he understands about Scott. But we never talk about it. And, I know this sounds like justification, but having Scott in my life has made me able to stay married to Peter. That I know he understands. He has never, ever questioned my time on the Cape, and he rarely comes with me."

Nicole tried to wrap her head around what Tessa had described, that she could be involved in two relationships that orbited each other but never intersected. It sounded complicated but simple at the same time. She thought about the discipline involved, to put a forty-year relationship in such a tight box. "What should we do?"

"You know I rarely admit this, but I'm no expert." They both laughed and Tessa carried on. "You should do what works for you and for Jason. But don't compromise on what you want because you don't want to rock the boat. If you need this year, take this year. And by that, I mean, go to Santa Fe and do your thing."

"I feel selfish."

"Selfish? You just gave your husband the green light to sleep with beautiful South American women. Hardly selfish." More rosé went into her glass, but Nicole waved off another pour. Tessa continued, "And please stop with the martyr thing. You've made sacrifices for your kids as long as I've known you. Working early shifts, late shifts, and somehow making it to all those theater rehearsals and games. And think of all the sacrifices for Jason's career. And for your mother, if you don't mind me saying. How many times have you dropped everything to help her get over a breakup or a freak health scare? If this year is important to you, take it. You're so young, not even fifty! A baby. Have some fun."

It wasn't a direct answer to her question, but Nicole let Tessa's comments sink in. "Am I a bad wife because I'm telling my husband it's okay to be with other women?"

"No. You may be the best wife, how about that? Also, you're not the first. And you won't be the last."

"I don't want this to spiral out of control. To lose him."

"Then tell him that. And tell him to be safe. It's also a risk for you, you know. What if you meet somebody in Santa Fe who sweeps you off your feet?"

"Oh, please, I want to make my jewelry, do some hot yoga, and be in bed by nine every night. I won't be looking."

"There's that martyr thing again."

Nicole checked her watch. She wanted to be home before Jason so he didn't know she'd been talking to Tessa. She hoped to God he hadn't been talking to his tennis pals. This could be all over town before they even left the city. "I've gotta go. But please, don't tell anyone about this. If our kids found out, I don't know what I'd do."

Tessa made the zip the lip gesture. "I'm a vault. I won't say anything. And I assume you won't say anything."

"Like you said: it's your marriage."

Jason pedaled his bike into the garage and removed his tennis backpack. He'd played like shit, but he had a lot on his mind. He had zero interest in sharing his wife's proposition with the other three men—a shoe designer, a chef, and a CPA. They'd all met through work projects and discovered a mutual love of tennis and cold beer. Jason had put the group together initially, but now Neil the accountant was the designated organizer, texting to make sure everyone was in town and available. For fifteen years, they'd played a couple of sets of doubles every Monday night during the summer at the courts in

Washington Park and then had one beer at the Blue Moon Tavern. They never stayed for another round, and they rarely saw one another during the winter. They talked sports, work, and money, but they weren't the type of friends that Jason could hit with something like "My wife suggested today that we open up our marriage for a year. What do you guys think?"

Instead, he played lousy, barely said anything at the tavern, and rode home, struggling a bit to make it up the hill on Savier Street. He dragged the garbage and the recycling cans out on the street to kill a bit more time before he had to go inside and talk to Nicole. Lost in his own thoughts, it wasn't until he was at the end of the driveway that he saw Rich, the King of Khakis, doing the same thing. Too late to turn around, Jason gave a wave and nod. Rich was on it, charging across the street after positioning his cans exactly one foot from the curb and three feet from each other. "Hey, great to see you, Jason!"

It was a big opening line for a guy Jason had spent a single evening with. "Rich, how are you?" He hoped Rich wouldn't answer the question.

"We thought you might be hiding from us! Hope we didn't scare you off."

Now it was Jason's turn to not answer the question. "We'd had a long day. Nicole was emotional after saying goodbye to the kids."

"Jen thought I'd overshared. She'll be glad to hear I wasn't to blame for the evening ending early."

Early? Jesus, they'd been there for hours. *I guess when you don't have kids, you can have all-night dinner parties,* Jason thought. He was about to make his excuses when a question came to him. Jason knew this was his only chance to ask it unless he wanted to ring the doorbell and risk interacting with Jen. "Can I ask you something about this Five Hundred Mile Rule? You know, I'm a book publisher and we're always looking for cultural trends that will translate to book format. I've been thinking about what you described the other night." Jason's question was personal, but he wanted to throw Rich off. "Doesn't it bother you that your wife is with other men?"

"And I thought I was the old guy!" Rich attempted to throw a little elbow jab Jason's way but wasn't quite close enough. Jason responded with a confused look, so Rich explained. "You're from a different generation than I am. I assumed you were less conventional."

"Ah, sure. Thanks for that, I guess. But men are kind of hardwired to be protective. Competitive. I'm not sure that goes away in a generation, even if we do carpool and unload the dishwasher occasionally."

"Listen, I made that mistake with my first wife. Thought her life began and ended with me as her husband, defender of her honor, only guy she'd ever been with. I never gave her any credit for having an existence outside of our marriage. I never thought about what she gave up becoming my wife, becoming the mother to my children. I never even considered that she could want more than me. It wasn't jealousy, it was a very limited view on who she was. And she left me for my son's baseball coach. She lives in Tampa and is now very happy with a guy who makes a third of what I make, drinks crap beer, and loves her like she's a whole person, not a possession. I'm a new man with Jen."

Jason was startled by the comprehensive answer. "How so?"

"I understand that Jen doesn't need me to defend her. And she had a whole productive life before me. She didn't have to marry me. She wanted to marry me. But that shouldn't mean she gives up everything."

"That's a very enlightened view of marriage. And women."

"Live and learn, right, buddy? It's all about making up rules that work for you. I understand Jen and she understands me. Plus, sex is just sex. There's a lot more to marriage than that." Rich finished up with a finger gun. "Hey, have a great trip. And if you write your book about the Five Hundred Mile Rule, I get a cut!"

———

Later that night, lying in bed, Jason started up the discussion again—quite possibly the worst location for a couple to have this type of conversation. At least that's what Nicole had read in dozens of women's magazines that advised to have any conversations about sex in a "neutral location" as opposed to the bedroom. Her husband, on the other hand, preferred to converse in the dark.

After talking to Rich, Jason had thought about suggesting they go see a counselor to make up a set of rules, sign some sort of agreement. But never in his life had he sought any kind of therapy, believing that there was nothing a couple of days, some physical exertion, and a few drinks couldn't solve. He wouldn't even know how to start with a counselor, especially about this. Wouldn't someone try to talk them out of this? He didn't need their judgment. Instead, he waited until his wife had turned the light off and popped in her mouth guard and said, "Maybe we should set some rules."

Nicole removed the guard from her mouth, set it on the side table, and flipped over in bed to face Jason. "I've been thinking about that, too."

"Oh, yeah? What are your rules?"

"Be safe. And don't fall in love with anybody." Nicole held her breath waiting for a response.

The seconds stretched out before he said, "I will be safe and there's no chance of the other."

It was the best response Jason could have given. "What are yours?"

"Same. Plus, no pregnancies."

"Understood." Though she wanted to clarify that it wasn't her intention to take advantage of the situation. And though the pregnancy ship hadn't officially sailed, it was highly unlikely with her age and IUD. "I don't think you'll have anything to worry about."

"What does that mean?"

"I'm not interested in pursuing other relationships."

"I'm not comfortable with that. This can't be one-sided. There will be repercussions to that, all on me. If we agree to this, there's no reason you can't be a part of it."

"Would that make you feel better about it?"

There was a long pause. "Yes."

That unlocked a door. As long as they both walked through the opening, everything would be fine, to quote Jason. Balance.

"Never ever tell me about what happens," Jason said. He was very firm on this.

"Same. I want no details." Then she added, "Should we take one more night to sleep on this?"

"Honestly, Nic, I don't want to talk about this anymore. If we are doing this, then we should do this. Not talk it to death."

There was a long silence, then Nicole reached out to stroke her husband's face. He needed a shave, but this was probably the beginnings of his sabbatical beard. She liked the roughness against her palm. "Well. We're not five hundred miles apart yet." She traced his cheek and jawline, then ran her fingers lightly over his chest, again and again. She could feel him relax into the moment. "I love you, Jason. Nothing will change that."

"I hope not."

"Be with me tonight," she said as she turned her back to him and pressed her full body into his. "Please."

He buried his face in the back of her neck, providing a solid wall of warmth for her to absorb. When his hand stroked the curve of her side, up and over her hip and down her leg, she moved her body closer, deeper, tighter to him. He responded with a soft growl, like he always did. He responded in other ways, too. This was their rhythm, who they were together. In this bed. After a few moments, he whispered in her ear, "Turn over. Now."

Chapter 6

Portland
June 1998

"And what does your father do, Nicole?" Jason's mother asked as they gathered in his apartment in the Pearl District, a new real estate hot spot in town. Jason had moved into the loft on Irving Street after his first big promotion at Stumptown Press. With the high ceilings and the exposed brick, he could convince himself that he was living a New York City dream but in a much more affordable zip code. Nicole, who was still in her studio apartment, loved staying at the loft and playing house on her days off. Over the last year, they had created a life that included trying new restaurants almost every week, shopping at antique stores and flea markets to fill Jason's loft with one-of-a-kind finds. They hiked when the weather was good and went to the movies when the weather was bad. Over coffee or beer, they dissected the assassinations of Tupac and Biggie, the movies of Gus Van Sant, and the staying power of magazines. It was love.

It had been an almost perfect year, as the two of them forged ahead in their careers and handled adulthood with relative competency. Friends and colleagues invited the couple to gatherings and parties, treating them as a well-matched set of attractive and fun grown-ups, despite being only in their twenties. Their love bubble had kept out naysayers and intruders.

But now, with the arrival of Jason's parents, the outside world was crashing into their relationship. Dr. and Dr. Elswick were in town for a long weekend for a medical conference. Jason's father, Dr. Michael Elswick, a cardiologist, was presenting a paper and Dr. Sandrine Elswick had come along for the sole purpose of checking out the girlfriend of her youngest son. He'd been very vague on the phone about details other than to say she worked at Needham's and looked like Winona Ryder, details that meant almost nothing to Sandrine, who shopped only at Brooks Brothers and didn't engage in pop culture. She intended to get more information about this Nicole over the course of the evening and wasted no time once Jason had poured a rather wan Oregon Pinot Gris. Sandrine preferred those big oaky California chardonnays, but she was glad to see that at least her son had real wineglasses and coasters. "I understand he works at Oregon State University. Is he a professor?"

Nicole had been prepping for this evening for weeks, maybe even her entire life. Jason's mother was like so many customers who entered Needham's—assuming a shopgirl like Nicole had nothing to offer except fetching merchandise but then leaving the store admiring her taste and restraint. She knew she could handle Sandrine Elswick in the handbag department, so she hoped she could handle her here in the loft. "Not a professor. My father runs the Department of General Services for the university."

There was a blank look on her face, but the other Dr. Elswick piped up. "So, in charge of all the buildings and such? We have a department of general services at UCSF, dear." Both doctors taught at the University of California San Francisco medical school in addition to their private practices. Apparently, Dr. Sandrine Elswick had no idea that it was somebody's job to make sure all the buildings had heat, water, and working light bulbs, among other necessities. "That's a big job at a university the size of OSU."

"It is. He takes care of all the buildings from the football stadium to the science labs. My father loves his work. He went to the engineering school there but likes to say he found his calling in the boiler room where he worked as a student. He's been there twenty-five years."

"And your mother? Does she work outside the home?"

Nicole almost burst out laughing. The idea that her mother could afford to live without working "outside the home" was ludicrous, but she managed to answer. "My parents are divorced. My mother also lives in Corvallis with her new husband. She's in restaurant management." Most of that was true to a degree. Janet Cardone Nash Hardaway Touey had lived in Corvallis her whole life, rarely leaving the city, never mind the state. Her "new husband" was also her third husband and there had been countless other men in between. And she was the assistant manager of the breakfast shift at a local favorite, The Round-Up, a restaurant that served bacon at every meal and vegetables at none. She was eighteen when she gave birth to Nicole and the years after the divorce from Nicole's father were the misspent youth she never had. Her mother's lifestyle made Nicole's high school years more of a caretaking mission than an educational experience. Nicole had told Jason all of this and more, of course, but her survival sense kicked in and she spared his mother the gritty details.

"I see. Good for her, moving on. And your father?"

"My father is also remarried. He and his wife have two little girls."

"Do you see them much?"

"Mom, enough. It's not a job interview," Jason cut in as he put down a bowl of nuts next to fruit and cheese. He'd taken the day off to clean the loft and shop for food and drinks. His mother would be taking notes, he was sure. Easier to impress than to make a statement by not trying to impress. He'd never found any middle ground with his mother, a place where they could both relax and be who they really were. Instead, he was on high alert whenever they were together.

"I'm making conversation," she replied, even though the four of them in the room knew that wasn't true. As a psychiatrist, her job was to ask questions and draw conclusions from the answers. She probably hadn't truly made conversation since grad school. "I'm sure Nicole doesn't mind."

"Of course not. I've lived in Portland full-time since I was eighteen. I only got a car a few months ago, so before that, traveling to Corvallis was tough. But my dad comes here occasionally." Like when he dropped her off at Portland State. Or delivered a new TV for her graduation gift. Or last January, when he surprised her with the used Jetta out of the blue. It seemed like her father occasionally scored a cash windfall and then he'd arrive with bounty, stay a few hours, and return to his watchful wife, Anita. Jason joked that the cash must be the results of payola from contractors who wanted gigs at the university. Nicole assumed it was a hidden bank account situation, to hide his gifts from the new wife, who viewed any support to Nicole as taking food out of the mouths of her girls. She didn't ask questions, like why he could prepay four years of rent to the landlord on her first day of freshman year. She was grateful for whatever she could get from him.

"Not even home for holidays?"

"I'm in retail. I work most holidays. I spend Thanksgiving getting the store ready for the crowds the next day. I usually work Christmas Eve and sometimes even on Christmas Day to prep for the big sale the next day. And on and on. I see them when I can." Nicole was glad she had the chance to set the reality of her work life up. If she and Jason did last through another holiday together, she wouldn't be coming to this woman's house. Talk about joyless.

"So independent," Sandrine observed, like she was suspicious. From what Jason had told Nicole, his mother was a snob in most areas of her life: upbringing, education, real estate, career choice, vacation locations, and cultural events. The fact that Jason chose to live in Portland, work in publishing, listen to music created in this century, and date a girl from a cow town in Oregon who graduated from a state school was not only an act of rebellion, but it also bordered on an affront to good taste.

To Jason's credit, he shut down the judgment. Apparently, it was easier to do for someone you loved other than yourself. "Maybe next trip Nicole can show you around her stores. She does amazing work at Needham's."

"Where you're a salesgirl?" The questions were back. But this one was a softball for Nicole.

"No, I'm a visual merchandiser. I help to create the retail atmosphere in the stores. I do everything from design the shoe displays to stack the Clinique bonus buys to pile up the cashmere sweaters at Christmas. I'm part of the team that decorates and undecorates the stores at the holidays. We have people to design the store windows, but I assist on the installation, dressing the manikins, and touches like that. I cover three stores here in the Portland area, but love working at the downtown store the most. But I started on the floor, selling. My first job was at the Gap at the mall when I was in high school and I'm still in retail."

From that experience she could tell that Sandrine was a size six, about five feet, seven inches, and favored expensive tailored conservative clothes over anything slightly risky or fun. And you didn't have to have an advanced degree to conclude that Sandrine probably kept her shape by restricting calories, as she'd barely sipped her wine or had a single nut while the Elswick men were digging into the appetizers.

"Sounds fascinating," Sandrine said unconvincingly.

"Speaking of fascinating, has Chris told you about his new research? He landed a big grant from the NIH," Jason's father asked, taking the conversation in another direction, away from the mundane careers of Jason and Nicole, back to the acceptable world of medicine. Chris, Jason's oldest brother, was a cardiologist as well, his wife a dermatologist. They had two children and a house in Atherton. Austin, the middle brother, was an ER doctor and his fiancée was as well. For the next fifteen minutes, the father updated Jason on how his talented siblings were excelling in the family business. Not a single question went Jason's way about his work.

Halfway through a description of Austin's latest medical miracle, Jason announced it was time to go to dinner. He'd picked a favorite Italian place over in Sellwood where he'd gotten to know the chef. "We're going to Assaggio. Great wine list. I've ordered a car for the night so we don't have to worry. Leave everything, I can clean up later," he said, even though neither of the doctors Elswick had made any attempt to be helpful.

They watched as the car left the corner of Irving and Thirteenth streets, whisking Jason's parents back to the Heathman Hotel for the night. Tomorrow, they would fly back to San Francisco, back to their house in Pacific Heights, and shake their heads about what their son was doing with his life. Jason exhaled for dramatic purposes as the taillights disappeared around the corner. He turned to Nicole, who looked pale and perfect in her black sheath dress and red lipstick. "Thank you."

"You were not exaggerating. They are tough." Nicole took his handsome face in her hands and kissed his lips softly. She wanted to heal him from the last two hours, where his parents had spent almost the entirety of the dinner talking about themselves, their work, and their next adventure vacation (snorkeling in St. John's) and two minutes on Jason. He looked angry and defeated. She tried to lift him up. "Your mother cornered me in the ladies' room, convinced we were living together because she saw two toothbrushes in your bathroom."

"What did you say?"

"That we ate a lot of spinach and I wanted to be prepared for any teeth emergencies."

"You did not."

"I did. I'm sorry. It was that last story about Dr. Lucy Chow, the world's greatest dermatologist daughter-in-law, saving teenagers from acne and the wives of Silicon Valley from aging. What a hero!" Lucy, in fact, did sound like a decent sort, but Nicole didn't want to admit that to Jason at this minute.

"You could move in and really piss her off."

"No, thanks. I wouldn't want her to think she was right."

"You could move in, though," he said again, this time without bitterness in his voice.

Nicole laughed. "Where? In the corner where you keep your old newspapers? There's not an extra inch in this place." She liked having her own space, her own rhythm in the mornings or when she got home from work, physically and emotionally spent. She loved being with him a few nights a week, but she still wanted a place of her own. "I like things the way they are, don't you?"

He did. But he loved the way Nicole made him feel, like he was good enough, better than good enough. "Yes, things are great. But maybe someday."

It was the first time he'd ever mentioned a future beyond the next weekend.

"Maybe someday," she agreed.

Chapter 7

Portland
August

The house was like a skeleton, stripped of almost everything but the bare bones of family living: a few couches and a dining table and chairs; a hodgepodge of lamps; enough beds for a family of five to fill. All the books, the artwork, and the sports trophies that made the house on Savier Street a home for more than twenty years were packed away in the storage pod, safe for the sabbatical. Nicole had bought new sheets for the beds and towels for the bathrooms and left a bottle of wine and sparkling apple cider in the fridge. She had arranged a vase of garden flowers to brighten the kitchen and handed over the keys to the rental agent.

Jason was making one last check of the garage, inventorying his garden tools one more time in case they went missing.

"I feel like we should sell this place right now," she said to her husband as she walked in through the back door. She gestured toward the eat-in kitchen they had remodeled years before. "It hasn't been this empty since we moved in."

He looked around at the space where he'd spent so many hours reading or hanging out with the kids while Nicole cooked. "Or this clean."

Jason always called the house "the best decision we ever made." They had bought the 1920 Craftsman before the real estate prices got out of hand in Portland, using a modest inheritance that he'd gotten from his grandmother. They picked up the fixer-upper at a manageable price for a young couple. The house was now worth at least fivefold what they paid for it. But at the time, it seemed like they were committing themselves to a lifetime of debt and maintenance. Jason's parents believed in the stock market, not real estate—though their old Victorian in San Francisco was worth a fortune—and made their point of view very clear with comments like "Why would you invest in an old moldy money pit?"

That made him more determined.

Once he left his trendy loft for home ownership, everything else fell quickly into place. He proposed to Nicole on their first night in the new house, popping the question in front of the fire while they drank champagne. They married at city hall a few months later, followed by a party at a Chinese restaurant, ditching a more traditional wedding day once they concluded that their parents were oil and water. As newlyweds, they worked every free weekend on the house, painting rooms or doing yard work or refinishing furniture. By the time they discovered she was pregnant, a surprise for both, the house had been transformed into a living Pottery Barn catalogue.

After their second child arrived, it was time to remodel the kitchen. A few years later, Jason was able to buy out his boss at Stumptown Press with the equity in the house. In the span of five years, he'd gone from a twentysomething slacker to a full-on adult with stainless-steel appliances. And the pace hadn't slowed. No wonder he needed this break. But it all started with the house. "And, FYI, I'm never selling this place."

She'd never want to sell either, preferring to hand it over to Chelsea or Jack, imagining them raising their families here, though it seemed unlikely that either one of them would land in Portland after graduation. Marine biology careers weren't abundant in Portland for Chelsea. And Jack had made it clear that he envisioned himself leading a glamorous expat life abroad for years to come.

Very early that morning, they had arranged a video call with the kids in Sydney and Tokyo to tell them about their new plans for the year. Nicole had been up in the middle of the night, worried about their reaction to the news that their parents were taking separate sabbaticals, convinced they would assume they were splitting up. Jason told her to keep it light and stick to the facts, predicting that as long as their credit cards and cell phones kept working, the news would barely register. And he was entirely correct.

Chelsea was in love with all things Australia. The people, the sunshine, the accents, the geography—but most of all the animals. She was flying so high on life that nothing Nicole and Jason could have announced, save a serious cancer diagnosis, would trim her wings. And Jack seemed to have matured ten years in ten days, speaking with the worldly perspective of a seasoned traveler, not a student wandering around Tokyo trying to figure out how to ride the subway. He applauded them for their curiosity and modern approach. Have fun, they said. Don't do anything we wouldn't do, they laughed. They all agreed to keep in touch by posting on a family photo sharing site that Jason had set up. When they disconnected, Nicole looked at Jason and said, "You were right. They couldn't have cared less."

"The narcissism of youth is a gift."

She thought how true that was, how she and Jason thought they could power through anything, that it was "us against the world." Together, stresses like their parents or their jobs or a global financial crisis would never take them down. They believed that the part in the wedding vows about "for better or for worse" meant that their marriage would be about 98 percent "for better" and 2 percent "for worse." And surely the "for worse" days would come in the distant future as they aged. Those percentages and that timeline had not held, but they were still together.

But would it be "us against the world" if they were five thousand miles apart?

She checked her phone for the time. "Should we go?"

"I can take an Uber." Jason had made hundreds of trips to the airport during their marriage and Nicole had only taken him a handful of times. He preferred a professional driver who could navigate the drop-off without a hitch or any conversation.

"I think I can spare a half hour considering I won't see you for the next nine months." Her tone was light, flirtatious even. Once the decision had been made and the rules had been finalized, something changed in Nicole and Jason. There was a playfulness in their conversations, a lightness in their demeanor. They both felt it. It wasn't exactly like being newlyweds again, but close enough. The empty nest, the new rules, a sense of why not permeated their relationship from the bedroom to the checkbook.

In the last week, Jason had accomplished more items on his personal to-do list than he had in years, including turning in his car early on the lease and selling the old beat-up Honda Civic that the kids used. Why have cars sitting in the garage, he'd explained to Nicole. He had no idea shedding all the payments and registrations and smog checks could feel so freeing. He'd joked to Nicole that she should sell her car and go back to walking everywhere like she did when they first met.

For Nicole's part, she sold a closet full of her work clothes on Poshmark, convinced that part of her life was over. *I'll never need to wear a black DKNY blazer again*, she texted the Wolfpack. (She kept one just in case.) She pared down her shoe collection, her magazine collection, and her repository of beauty products. Everything she needed in Santa Fe, from jackets to boots to coffee mugs, compressed in two large roller bags, a duffle bag, and a plastic tub. Her whole life for the next nine months would fit in the backseat of her Volkswagen Tiguan and it felt exhilarating. She had enough room in her car to take Jason and his gear to the airport and she wanted to do it.

She wanted the big goodbye kiss.

"All right, let's get this show on the road," he said, before hauling his luggage out the front door and down the steps while Nicole locked up.

There had been almost no conversation in the car en route to PDX. Instead, they let the sounds of a random Elliott Smith playlist fill the car, which took them back to the hours they'd spent flipping through albums at Django Records, now shuttered like so many other landmarks that defined their early relationship. Jason had even published a small but beautifully designed guidebook to Elliott Smith's Portland after his death, writing the copy himself and working with a talented graphic designer. Over the years, the letterpress-printed gem became a treasured collectible among a certain sliver of locals. The music made him nostalgic, not sad.

When Nicole pulled up to the terminal, they both sat for a long moment in the front seat, absorbing the moment. Then she turned to him. "I love you, Jason. Please take care of yourself and have an amazing time."

He hated that in that moment he thought of Rich the neighbor and not somebody deeper, more profound. But it was the Khaki King's words that came to mind as he said to Nicole, "I love you, too. I hope you rediscover what you've been missing."

Then she got her kiss. It was sweeter and softer than she'd imagined.

Jason sat at the bar at Deschutes Brewery in Concourse D, waiting for his flight to Chile. Twenty-four hours from now, he'd be in a completely different world, so he wanted to savor the last few minutes of familiarity. Normally, he didn't drink when in the travel zone, always too pressed to relax when he traveled for business. He used the hours in the air to work, catch up on the parts of his job that took concentrated effort, as opposed to shooting off emails and dipping into conference calls. And he couldn't even remember when he and Nicole had boarded a plane for pleasure, as the travel industry liked to say. Was it for his parents' wedding anniversary in Hawaii? Probably. And that was four years ago.

This morning, as he packed his carry-on bag, he'd told himself that he was going to use the sixteen hours in the air from Portland to Dallas to Santiago to work on his book, the novel that was nothing more than an unfinished outline that had been sitting in a computer file since 2003, when everyone in publishing was looking for the next *Da Vinci Code*. He was sure he had it in him, but he had never found the time. He knew that was the excuse of every never-published author: not enough time. Jason had convinced himself that his excuse was legit, though. And it wasn't like he had given up on his idea of a thriller based on the Iran–Contra affair scandal meets Indiana Jones. The mash-up of a brash archaeologist in search of hidden artifacts, violent drug cartels, a rogue CIA operative, and some South American dictator and his guerrilla armies had the makings of a good thriller. He'd been stashing away relevant articles and research for years. Now, he had the time to pull it all together while traveling through South America.

But the minute he made it through security, he knew he was never going to open his laptop. He gave himself permission to not work on his book for one more day. Instead, he bought some paperback thrillers at the Powell's kiosk, plopped himself on a bar stool, and ordered an IPA. He was struck by the idea that he literally had nothing specific to do and no one to report to for the next nine months. It had taken everything to get him to this place in life where he could do what he wanted to do on his own schedule. Any apprehension slipped away. Maybe not having Nicole with him was the second-best decision they'd ever made, next to buying the house. He'd have a chance to rediscover what he was missing.

For sure, he was missing Charlie. Nicole was right about that, too.

As he sat at the bar, sipping his beer and watching the crowd, he twisted his wedding ring, a habit he'd had for years. He considered taking it off for a second but decided against it for now.

He'd know when and if the timing was right.

Chapter 8

Portland
August

Tessa made a showing of popping the prosecco, whooping as she poured the bubbly into four glasses and handing them out to the Wolfpack, toasting, "To Nicole! To new adventures!"

Jane, Sarah, and Nicole raised their glasses in friendship. They were standing on the back porch of Jane's beautiful modern home perched on the side of Thurman Street, a stunning view looking north to the Willamette River. Nicole was spending her last night in Portland in Jane's guest suite because Jane had absolutely insisted, not taking no for an answer. If Nicole had had her way, she might have booked a hotel out by the airport and holed up for a night by herself, gathering her strength for the fourteen-hundred-mile drive from Portland to Santa Fe. Quietly slipping out of town was appealing.

Jane had promised grilled salmon and an early night, so Nicole agreed. But the way Tessa was pouring the drinks, she had her doubts about the early night. Still, she was glad to be surrounded by the support. She would miss these women, though they assured her that a girls' weekend trip to Santa Fe was already in the works. It seemed that Sarah, new to the empty nest, had taken up event planning with the same zeal she'd used to make jam, fundraise for Little League, and get her three boys into college. Nicole had already gotten texts about possible dates in December.

Sarah was back on it tonight, shouting over the chatter, "We want to see those Christmas farolito things that are in every photo of Santa Fe!"

Somebody has done some pre-drinking before cocktail hour, Nicole thought.

"Yes! And I want at least one of those giant ropes of dried chile peppers. Remember those from the eighties when everybody hung them up in their kitchens, like we even knew how to use chile peppers in Boston," Tessa added.

"They're called ristras. And I think they're really for decorating and good luck," Nicole corrected.

"Oh, look at her. Miss Santa Fe already!" Tessa fired back.

Nicole took the ribbing. As much as she loved these women, she wanted a little time to get her feet under her in Santa Fe, be on her own. At least she'd successfully pushed out the visit as far as she could, responding with vague wishes to get settled and to figure out the lay of the land. It was agreed they'd come the second weekend of December and by then, she hoped she'd be less anxious about seeing old friends in a new context.

But here, on this beautiful August night, surrounded by evergreens and evening skies, she was grateful for this group of women. *Make the most of this moment,* she told herself consciously. She raised her glass a bit higher and responded with vigor, "To new adventures."

During dinner they peppered her with questions about her new plan. Where would she live? ("For the first two weeks, I'm splurging on a vacation rental while I look for a small place to rent that's walking distance to the city center.") When does class start? ("Almost as soon as I get there. I'm all registered online, so I'll hit the ground running. It's about twenty hours of class work a week including studio time.") Why Santa Fe? ("Why not? I've wanted to go there for years and the more I investigated the area, the more I wanted to be there.") The last answer wasn't true. She'd never thought of Santa

Fe or the entire state of New Mexico until Jason had mentioned that motorcycle school. The Southwest hadn't registered in her psyche until recently, but it sounded more romantic if it seemed she was fulfilling a lifelong dream, not a whim born of fear and panic.

Plus, the questions made Nicole feel like a rock star. Her friends seemed to admire her choices. They called her courageous and brave for striking out on her own. For months, she'd felt afraid and embarrassed that the trip to Patagonia was so intimidating. But now, she was beginning to see that this year might be about learning more than how to solder and hammer a silver cuff.

"I can't explain it. But every time you say the word *silversmithing*, I envision Paul Revere as your professor in one of those tricorn hats," Tessa said, as the only New Englander among them.

"I can't wait to see your designs!"

"You'll have to. The cuffs are just lines on paper now. I need to learn how to execute them in metal."

"Won't you miss Jason?" asked Sarah, who checked in with her husband, Ted, a dozen times a day by mutual agreement. Sarah missed Ted when he was sitting in the other room.

"Of course, but—"

"They'll be some hot texts, I'm sure," Jane interrupted. "And really, what's better than that?"

Tessa gave Nicole a head tilt and raised eyebrow, acknowledging their secret. *Shit*, Nicole thought, *I never should have told Tessa.* "Jason's going to be out of service range for most of the first four months. And he has this notion that the kids should emulate his backpacking trip to Europe in the early nineties with no cell phone, no email, and very little parental contact."

In fact, Jason had told Jack and Chelsea, "We were gone six months and never called our parents. Sent a few postcards. That was it." The kids seized upon the idea of a less monitored life. Nicole was a reluctant participant. She didn't want to nag them or deny them the opportunity to be adults. But she was curious about their lives and wanted to be included. Still, she agreed to very limited contact in the spirit of independence.

With the Wolfpack, she didn't want to go into too many details about the plan that they'd cooked up, knowing the level of constant communication her friends had with their spouses and/or offspring. Sarah never put her phone down, even stopping mid-run if she got a text from one of her boys. Jane's daughter, the most mature one in the bunch, pinged her mother a dozen times a day. Even Tessa, who was the least attentive parent, kept her phone on the table at every meal. She knew they would never understand Jason's directive on minimal communication. In the Elswick family, everybody wanted space, especially the kids. "Jason and I will be emailing once a week. No texts except in an actual emergency. Saving ourselves for emails. The kids wanted less contact, more independence, so we're doing a photo sharing site and Zoom call at Christmas. But otherwise, trying to do our own thing."

Tessa jumped in. "Let's face it, aren't we all a little sick of spouses after this pandemic? Even you, Sarah. You can admit it."

"I think this whole experience has made Ted and me closer," Sarah said.

"How is that possible?" Tessa asked rhetorically. Secretly, they were all a bit envious of how Sarah and Ted were in sync at all times, a couple who not only loved each other but looked like they were in love with each other. Not that Nicole, Tessa, or—God knows—Jane would want to be with a guy like Ted, but the relationship was something special. It was the sort of marriage that Tessa claimed didn't exist, long-standing and romantic.

"Had Brianna and I not gotten divorced in 2019, we'd both be dead or in jail by now. There's no way we'd have made it through lockdown." The group laughed, knowing it was true. The Jane/Brianna relationship was brief, brilliant, and then broken. Jane was not meant to be anybody's "better half." She was complete all on her own.

"I'm not sure I could spend that much time away from Ted. I'd be lonely," Sarah said. "But you won't be lonely, Nicole. You like being alone." Though it might have been true that Nicole was the least social of the foursome, the words sounded harsh. Also, because Jason was the spouse who spent the most time traveling for business, it came off as accusatory. Sarah recognized that right away. "I'm so sorry, I didn't mean it like that."

Nicole was all largesse. "No apologies necessary. Jason and I are used to being apart for a week or two at a time. And I do like being alone, but I worry about being lonely. I hope I connect with some of the other silversmiths." She looked in Tessa's direction.

"Bring one of those Revolutionary War hats! Icebreaker!" Tessa teased.

Sarah popped up. "We have lovely parting gifts! Not too many because I think you made it very clear your car was full in many, many texts."

"Trying to prevent you all from buying me a new dog or yurt or something wildly impractical," Nicole countered.

Sarah handed her a small but heavy gift bag. "We agreed this was the only additional item you might need to pack."

Nicole lifted the bag comically. "It's so heavy."

"Lots of batteries," Tessa quipped.

Nicole unwrapped the box, but she didn't need to. She knew exactly what was covered in silver paper: a vibrator. "This is so thoughtful, I might cry." And there was laughter and whoops.

"Now you really won't miss Jason," Jane said, rising to clear the plates. She ran a tight ship at her house, so maybe it would be an early night after all. When the Wolfpack met for coffee in Jane's gourmet kitchen with the pro-level espresso machine after running on Sundays, the event lasted exactly sixty minutes. Jane made it clear when it was time for everyone to go. She wanted to get on with her day and to meet her other friends, of which she had many. Her activity suggested that the evening was over. "Anything else I can get you, Nicole? We were going to get you a cake, but I didn't want to be stuck with extra cake because menopause, so no cake. I have dark chocolate squares if anyone wants one. They are wrapped to go."

More laughter. Then Nicole piped up. "There is one more thing I'd love."

"Please don't say a picture, because this dress makes me look like a tent," Sarah said.

"Not a photo, although I think you look gorgeous," Nicole assured Sarah, then turned to Jane. "I want you to make me a blonde."

Jane's face lit up. While most of America had spent the years 2020 and 2021 baking sourdough bread, Jane had dedicated herself to learning how to cut and color hair. First on herself, then on her daughter and her daughter's friends, and then on other willing participants who had nothing to lose. Like Nicole, who used the occasion of losing her job at Needham's after twenty-five years to dye her hair purple. (Though Jane had refused to do her whole head because, as she said, "You'll look like an aging anime character. And not in a good way." One chic violet stripe in her brown hair was the compromise.)

Early in her career, Jane had been a chemist in the beauty business like her father and grandfather before her, mixing up skin care concoctions at a commercial lab that worked with all the big brands. But once she had Carson and her trust fund kicked in, thanks to the breakthrough collagen compound her grandfather had invented, she turned to teaching science at the French American school that her daughter attended. The closure of all the salons in town had forced her back into the laboratory to keep her shiny silver locks shiny and silver. There would be no yellowing for Jane Goodby.

Using the dog wash setup that Brianna had insisted they put in the mudroom as a base of operations, Jane mastered the science and art of coloring hair. The cutting was a little more hit or miss. She'd even contemplated going to beauty school to get her license, but it turned out beauty school was a lot of hours and mandatory apprenticeships. A big no for Jane. Instead, she watched a lot of YouTube videos, ordered the highest-grade products, and stuck with her pop-up salon for friends and family only.

The minute she pulled away from PDX earlier in the day, Nicole knew she wanted to make a change. New adventure, new hair color. "I want to start this sabbatical with something totally unexpected."

Tessa, who poured herself the last of the prosecco, started to chant, "Blonde! Blonde! Blonde! Blonde!" The others joined in.

Jane examined Nicole's precision cut chin-length bob, the style she'd adapted since becoming a mother, then decreed, "First, I applaud your instincts. It's time for the purple to go. So mid-pandemic. It's over. Unfortunately, I can't make you a blonde without bleaching, and that will look terrible. But I can make you blonder."

There was a group cheer.

"I'll take it."

"You promise to maintain your new color at a good salon in Santa Fe?"

"I promise."

"Then let's balayage."

Chapter 9

Portland
July 2001

"Nic? Are you okay?" Jason called through the bathroom door while Nicole tossed her mimosa and the rest of the contents of her stomach into their new low flush toilet. It was a Sunday morning and Jason had invited a few new publishing friends over for brunch. Nicole had worked late on Saturday night, doing a midsummer inventory check at the store. The last thing she had wanted to do was entertain this morning, but Jason loved to show off the house and had perfected his frittata, so brunch it was.

But the minute the mimosa hit her lips, she knew something was off. This last week, she'd been working doubles at Needham's, on the sales floor during the day and merchandising into the evening, coming home more exhausted than usual. She chalked it up to PMS, because it usually was. But by Friday, when her period still hadn't started, she pulled out her calendar and started counting. Thirty-five days! Now thirty-seven days. She was never late.

They'd taken an anniversary trip to Seattle in June, turning a work trip for her into a mini vacation and celebration. Jason was very good at planning those kinds of work/fun double dips, stretching every free hotel night into a romantic getaway. There had been late nights in local bars, leisurely mornings at their favorite hotel in Pike Place Market, and a shared sense of throwing caution to the wind on all fronts. She had forgotten to pack her birth control pills, but she could double up when she got home, she thought.

Now this, throwing up in her own bathroom while half a dozen art directors, illustrators, and writers helped themselves to food and drinks in their kitchen. "Give me a minute. I think it's stress. Work's been hard lately."

"Are you sure?" No one would accuse Jason of being finely attuned to the rhythm of Nicole's body, but he wasn't clueless either. He was the son of two doctors, after all. His imitation of his mother giving him the driest, most medically accurate birds and bees talk was in his repertoire of stories about his childhood. "Can you open the door, please?"

She did. And then she started to cry. "I think . . ."

". . . you're pregnant?" he finished.

"I'm so sorry. I'm so sorry, Jace." She wiped her face with a cold washcloth and leaned up against the vanity, hanging her head, too embarrassed to meet his eyes. How had she let this happen? This wasn't their plan. She was going to wait until she was thirty so she could fully establish her career at the highest level before stepping away on maternity leave. And Jason had started talking about buying out his boss and running Stumptown on his own in the next few years, like it was a real possibility. If they had a baby now, none of that could happen for either of them. She was only twenty-six. He was twenty-nine. This wasn't their plan.

He took her in his arms, wrapping her up. "Don't apologize. We don't know for sure, but if it turns out to be true, then we'll celebrate. This is what we're here for, Nic. You and me. And whatever life brings. I'm only sorry you feel bad." He lifted her head and looked right into her eyes. "Puking is bad, but this is good news. Let's get rid of these guests as soon as we can, okay?"

She nodded. It was going to be okay. They could take care of this baby. The two of them. It would be an adventure.

He smiled. And it felt like a bomb went off in his chest. How was he going to take care of them all?

To: Nicole
From: Jason

Arrived in Puerto Varas, Chile, after nearly twenty-four hours in the air. As expected, the town is a stunning combination of the blue waters of Lake Llanquihue, snowcapped volcanoes in the distance, and the charming Bavarian architecture favored by German settlers in the nineteenth century. It's like I've landed in the wrong country. Last night's dinner was bratwurst and empanadas. Spending the two weeks here working on my fitness, hiking and mountain biking, and trying to understand the strangely accented Spanish.

All is good. Jason

To: Jason
From: Nicole

Good to hear from you. I'm glad all your travel worked out. It took me longer to get to Santa Fe than it took you to get to Chile. I made stops in Boise on night one. Remember my coworker Kimberly from Needham's? She lives there now and when I asked for a hotel recommendation, she insisted I stay with her and her five kids. She's homeschooling and canning and I suspect her husband is stockpiling ammo. Reminded me of my mom's ex, Bud. I couldn't get out of there soon enough.

Then I had a ten-hour drive to Vegas. How have we never been to Vegas? We must be the only adults in America who've never been there because it appears that all the other adults are currently there right now. I had a day to kill before I could get into my rental in Santa Fe, so I spent hours walking in and out of all the retail on the Strip. (See, I talk like a local now.) Jane had some charity event gift bag coupon for two nights at the Mandarin Oriental that she gave to me, declaring that she could never support a city so oblivious to climate change. Classic Jane. Beautiful hotel.

Pulled out of Vegas in the early morning so I would get to Santa Fe to take advantage of the sunset as I drove in through the Sangre de Cristo Mountains. Wow. Maybe not Patagonia wow, but wow. And then the light on the adobe buildings as I pulled into Santa Fe was like a postcard. I thought all that orange-brown adobe might look gimmicky or only really be represented in a few blocks around the historic Plaza, but no. It's all adobe, all the time here and the result is both soothing and stunning.

Santa Fe is filled with shops, galleries, charming restaurants, churches, public art, and tourists. I know this isn't your area of interest, but the shopping is amazing here with stores selling everything from handloomed cashmere to Peruvian textiles to ceramics that break your heart. Don't worry, minding my budget. Window-shopping (mostly). Pacing myself on the Canyon Road art galleries because I have plenty of time to walk through them all over the next year.

My VRBO condo is small and dark and overlooks a parking lot, so finding better housing is top of my priority list after I start classes next week. I feel like a new high schooler, nervous and excited.

Love seeing the photos from the kids. They appear to be having the best time, each in their own way.

More in a week.

xo Nic

To: Nicole
From: Jason

As you know, motorcycle portion of the tour starts tomorrow. Itinerary begins with bike orientation and several hours of safety instructions followed by our first group dinner. The next day, we cross into Argentina to explore the lake district and start the 4,000-mile journey. Am trying to get used to talking in kilometers, but not having much luck. Am eager to hit the road, but this is a great spot for everything from rafting to running to eating German cake in the afternoon.

More in a week.

Jason

To: Jason
From: Nicole

Okay, I know I'm breaking the one-week rule but tomorrow is my first day of school and I'm so nervous, I had to tell someone. I miss you, Jace.

Oh, and I went to this ceremony last night called the Burning of Zozobra. It's an annual ritual to rid the town of doom and gloom. The whole city shows up to see this fifty-foot creepy marionette be torched to renew the goodness in the people. The Norwegians staying in the apartment next to me came all the way from Norway to see this thing burn, so I guess it's a big deal. They dragged me along. Google it when you have a chance. Very primal and thrilling. The weirdest part? It's put on by the Kiwanis Club.

More in a week.

xo

Nicole

Chapter 10

Santa Fe
September

"Let's get started. I'm Roger Kingman. I run the jewelry design department here at Santa Fe Community College," announced the professor, if that was the right term for a fortyish British man in ancient faded blue jeans, an impressive belt with a silver and turquoise buckle, and a perfectly shaggy haircut. "I'll be working in the studio with you on design and construction.

"Let me introduce Dr. Raven Cotter. She'll teach the history of design portion of the class, as she has a PhD in art history. She's also a fourth-generation Navajo jewelry maker and her own work is museum quality. Like the lovely piece she is wearing around her neck, which is about to be shipped to a lucky private collector. Right, Raven?"

The sturdy, athletic woman in jeans, boots, a white T-shirt, and a dramatic silver and turquoise necklace that somehow looked like falling leaves nodded her head. "Unless you make me a better offer, Roger."

The class laughed but Nicole caught her breath. Compared to Raven's and Roger's work, she was sure her first effort would be the college equivalent of those painted macaroni-on-a-string necklaces her kids gave her for Mother's Day when they were in preschool. She was in over her head.

"Today is an orientation day," Roger continued, giving the word *orientation* a few more syllables with his accent. "We'll take you through the curriculum, the calendar, and some studio safety training, which is mandatory. I hope you all appreciate this glorious studio. Let's not burn it down."

Nicole did appreciate the glorious studio. The pictures on the website were impressive, but the real thing was a stunner. She had gotten a chill walking through the doors of the classroom and into the large open space. Big bright windows faced out to the mountains in the distance. A dozen workstations were complete with everything a real silversmith would need: soldering boards, hand torches, hammers, pliers, and vises. Shaping and polishing tools of every variety. The array of tools made her small personal set in her backpack seem beyond inadequate. And best of all, along one wall behind a locked gate, there were sheets of silver, ready to be molded.

Roger let the impressive space sink in before continuing. "Today is the day we start to get to know each other. We're going to be spending a lot of time together over the next nine months so why don't we each introduce ourselves?"

The professor scanned the room to pick a victim. The dozen or so students were spread out in chairs grouped around high tables. Some were fresh out of high school, others looked to be a few years into Medicare coverage. There were all shapes, sizes, and colors.

In the few weeks that she'd been in Santa Fe, she'd come to recognize this diverse cohort as typically New Mexican, a collection of Native American, Mexican, Spanish, and Anglo people that created a cultural tableau that dated back centuries. Every restaurant, store, and hotel bar seemed to be made up of the same mélange, so different from her segmented world in Portland. As one of the docents at the Museum of Indian Arts and Culture said to her the other day, "Santa Fe has one story to tell . . . from many different narrators." So, apparently, did the silversmithing program at SFCC.

One woman in the back row looked as if she'd wandered into the wrong classroom, too beautiful for community college, with bright blue eyes, a long dark braid streaked with gray, and a white linen shirt perfectly styled with a popped collar and rolled sleeves. She looked vaguely familiar, as if Nicole might have seen her at Needham's, but that seemed improbable. Was she a famous writer? Maybe.

Of course, Professor Roger spotted Nicole, who seemed to straddle the line between the young, tattooed group and the "I'm here to keep busy in my retirement" crowd. She was closest to Roger's age, at least that's what she assumed, so maybe that's why he zeroed in on her. Eye contact. Damn. Icebreakers like these were her worst nightmare.

Even after twenty-five years of professional life, she hated kicking off self-introductions in any meeting, preferring to let somebody else set the standard for details and then she'd follow the established pattern. Say too little and you look like a scared kid. Talk too much and you sound like a middle-aged woman desperate for friends. Which she was, kind of.

During the last week, she'd spent hours preparing for her first day of school in decades, from planning her outfit to art directing her backpack, packing and then repacking her modest set of tools, even going so far as doing a practice run to the campus on the bus. Nicole was determined to use public transportation as much as possible during her time in Santa Fe, reclaiming her commitment to walking from her early Portland days. But from eyeballing the map instead of googling the route, she'd really miscalculated the distance to the attractive but distant campus. Santa Fe Community College was in the middle of nowhere—about ten miles, a transfer and twenty-six stops from the depot downtown. The bus ride was an hour each way on a good day. Today, she was so nervous she'd left midmorning for a midafternoon class. In the bright cafeteria surrounded by mostly younger students, she had plenty of time to work out some first-day jitters.

She'd even rehearsed a few answers to the question, "What brings you to Santa Fe?" because she'd been asked that almost every day since arriving by baristas and bus drivers and strangers at the table next to her at Opuntia, the café where she went every morning for coffee and avocado toast. (She was going to have to break the habit. Her bank account was disappearing at an alarming rate.) As tempted as she was to say "Midlife crisis that includes letting my husband sleep with other women and dyeing my hair blonder" or "Poseur white girl thinks she can make jewelry better than actual artists," she went with the less aggressively truthful answer of a career reset combined with her desire to get out of the rain. People nodded at the first part of that sentence and laughed at the second. She was ready, even if she lacked confidence.

The Brit pointed to Nicole, as she predicted. "Why don't you start?"

Without missing a beat, she stood up so everyone in the room could see her, a power move she learned at professional development classes provided by her previous employer. Make them see you and they will remember you, the executive coach had told her. "My name is Nicole. I've relocated here for this program from Portland, Oregon. I wanted to get out of the rain, but, wow, I underestimated how much I'd have to moisturize here." The women in the crowd laughed at that one. "I've spent my whole career in retail, more specifically, in visual merchandising for Needham's at their flagship store in Portland. Like a lot of people, the pandemic forced me to reexamine my work life and explore other creative avenues. I did a lot of beadwork over the last few years and wanted to go deeper into other forms of jewelry making. I've only dabbled in metalsmithing, but I've always appreciated great design and craftsmanship. I'm hoping to learn both. Grateful to be here."

Ugh, grateful to be here? That was a spontaneous addition and it felt so corny, so trite. She had been on a roll and then a bad wrap-up. A woman she met in the produce aisle at Kaune's Neighborhood Market informed her that Santa Fe was filled with seekers and had an extra helping of spirituality compared to most state capitals. Maybe the others wouldn't notice her cheesy sign-off.

"Gratitude is always welcome here at Intro to Silversmithing," Professor Roger said in a dry manner that revealed he was not really the gratitude type. He'd noticed her cheesy sign-off for sure.

Raven, on the other hand, chimed in with an enthusiastic fist pump. "Portland in the house. Love that town. Welcome, Nicole."

Others in the class nodded and smiled, which relaxed her. She had done well, set the tone. Her professional motto saved her again: a little prep goes a long way. Only the woman in the linen shirt seemed to linger on her for an extra minute, taking stock of Nicole as Nicole had taken stock of her. Nicole had chosen a casual short black dress, ankle boots, and a delicate pair of silver hoops she splurged on the other day when she was feeling homesick. She vowed to herself to not get sucked into the Southwest look that so many of the boutiques in town featured. On her, a tiered prairie dress was a costume, not clothes, and she was sure she'd look like she was trying too hard if she started layering statement earrings, wide leather belts, and a cowboy hat over her Northwest basics. She smiled back at the woman, still wondering why she looked so familiar.

As the introductions continued, Nicole's confidence eroded. It seemed like everyone in the class came with more credibility than she did. There was Gary, the seventyish studio musician with four Grammys and a scorching rock and roll sense of style. Brittany, a recent graduate of UC Santa Cruz with a degree in architecture who wanted to move into jewelry design. Other students mentioned awards won in juried art shows, years spent apprenticing for local creators. One guy who called himself Tato said he was a fifth-generation silversmith from the Taos Pueblo and his grandparents had encouraged him to get a formal education so he could make it beyond the New Mexico border. Fifth generation! Nicole had watched a bunch of YouTube videos and decided this program was for her. Tato was half her age and ten times more experienced.

Then Clancy, who Nicole suspected might have a similar story because she was wearing clogs and pants with a pull-on waistband, informed the class that she was a blacksmith who worked on a ranch in Arizona shoeing horses for a decade, but then her husband left her for a barmaid and she wanted to make inspirational charms to guide women through divorce. She ended her introduction with a small power salute and said, "Fuck the Patriarchy."

Nicole was officially blown away.

"Yes, well, couldn't agree more, Clancy." Finally, Roger gestured to the serene vision in the back of the room. "Cleo, I think you're next."

Cleo! Of course, it was Cleo Jones. No, Nicole didn't know her, but everybody knew of her. Actress, style icon, yoga pioneer, woman who slept with every man in Hollywood without regret or shame. Some were lovers, some were husbands; all were gorgeous and famous. Cleo Jones was the star of a half dozen iconic movies of the eighties. She had dropped out of sight in the nineties when the powers that be in the entertainment business decided that forty was too old to be sexy and opportunities dried up, despite her Academy Award nomination. Nicole's mother had loved Cleo Jones and they watched her movies again and again on the VCR.

But Cleo got the last laugh and made a zillion dollars when she was the first to market with her yoga tape. Filmed in the desert against gleaming white sand, Cleo taught American women who loved her in *The Last Dance* to downward dog in their living rooms. Nicole's mother was between husbands, so she insisted they do Cleo's tape every afternoon and the two of them reached and breathed along with the dark-haired goddess in the white catsuit on the screen. My God, Cleo Jones in her class! Nicole was stunned.

"Thanks, Roger and Raven. I, too, have gratitude for being here," Cleo said, nodding to Nicole without judgment, only warmth. "I've lived in Santa Fe since before many of you were born. Not you, of course, Gary, but many of the rest of you. I'm an arts advocate and supporter of all things Santa Fe. My latest project is forming a collective for our talented young jewelry designers and I thought I should understand more of how the sausage is made so I can better serve the artists. That's an old expression for you vegans. I want to learn about the process and Roger and Raven, both old friends, are letting me audit the course. I won't be doing all the hard work like the rest of you, but I'll be watching, observing. Wonderful to be with you all."

Namaste, Nicole wanted to shout, but she held back. Others in the class seemed unimpressed with Cleo, but Clancy caught Nicole's attention, her eyes wide, and mouthed the words, "Cleo Jones."

"I know!" Nicole mouthed back. And that's when her stomach finally unclenched.

It was a physical sensation, the unclenching of the stress she'd been carrying for almost a month, since she told Jason she didn't want to go to Patagonia. For weeks, while packing or driving or walking the relentlessly charming streets of her new hometown, she'd felt a gripping in her gut, all her self-doubt being squeezed into a rubber ball that bounced around in her belly. But suddenly, here in the studio classroom with strangers and Cleo Jones, Nicole was at ease. Cleo was a sign that she'd done the right thing by blowing up her life. All that reaching and breathing in her dreary Corvallis living room in the early nineties was not for nothing. That woman at the grocery store was right; Santa Fe was a spiritual haven. She knew she was in the right place now. The adventure could begin.

"Do you need a lift somewhere? I'm headed into town." Cleo Jones leaned out the window of her black Range Rover and called to Nicole, who waited at the bus stop out in front of the college. Nicole looked over her shoulder, assuming there must be somebody behind her more worthy of a lift, an unstudied comedy bit. But, no, there wasn't anyone else waiting for the number 21 to downtown Santa Fe. Cleo appeared to be talking to her.

"Sure. Thanks." She gathered her backpack and hopped in the front seat, noticing the car was so clean you could eat off the floor and the leather seats were nicer than her furniture at home. What a magical ride share! She turned to Cleo to explain, "I'm trying to reduce my carbon footprint. But the bus ride out here may break me. And it's been one day!"

"Good for you. In full support of your efforts. You and the people who refuse to use plastic are saving the planet. I have a meeting downtown at the theater. My friend Cheryl forced me to join the board. Again. Fundraiser coming up. Where can I drop you?"

Nicole thought a moment. The central part of Santa Fe, where her dreary rental was located, was small and compact; almost everything she needed was nearby. She'd learned it was easier to walk most places than to move her car less than a mile and search for parking. (It made her commitment to going carless easy and less altruistic than it seemed.) She wanted to pick a spot that wouldn't inconvenience Cleo. "How about Kaune's? Do you know that grocery store?"

"Know it? I think I've consumed more of their gazpacho than any person in town. And have you checked out Beadweaver next door? Great bead store. You said you did beadwork, right?"

Nicole was taken aback by the recall. "I do and I have. I admit, sitting in that class today, I think I should stick to beading and leave the silver to the real artists." The program that Roger and Raven outlined was rigorous and exacting. The students would need to finish ten specific projects over the course of the year, with a final project at the end. Each project related to a specific skill or technique they were expected to master, from creating a perfect circle to engraving to inlaying stones. Alongside all the studio work, there was history, art history, and design theory to learn. So many students were so far ahead of Nicole in terms of skills, she was in panic mode already.

"I'm sure you have gifts yet to be discovered. And, you had the best-looking safety goggles. You must tell me where you got those. Roger and Raven are amazing teachers. I've worked with both before in other settings. Did you know that Roger's wedding ring sets are the hottest thing in Hollywood now? They are gorgeous, set with beautiful precious stones. Very modern and yet *Game of Thrones*-y at the same time. And Raven is so good at bringing the history of jewelry to life. I've seen her lecture at various museums over the years. She knows her stuff. You're lucky to have them as teachers," Cleo said, pulling out of the campus entrance with ease.

Nicole had wanted to text her mother right then and there to tell her who she was with. Then she realized that maybe that broke some sort of covenant, that Cleo's appearance in her class was contingent upon her anonymity. She could only be a real person in the class if outsiders didn't reveal her existence in texts or Instagram posts. Nicole decided to keep her secret. "Do you live near Kaune's?" Cleo asked.

"Sort of. And temporarily. I'm in a short-term rental now, which is not my dream home. I'm looking for something on the Eastside, but those are hard to find and much more expensive than I thought. Moving to Santa Fe was a bit of a spur-of-the-moment decision and I guess my due diligence was more wishful thinking."

To that, Cleo laughed. "All the best decisions are made that way. If we really knew what we were getting into, would we ever leave the house? My advice is to tell everyone you meet you are looking, because Santa Fe is filled with empty houses and strange arrangements. People who will pay you to live in their place to water their plants while they go to an ashram in India for six months. Or older folks who want to see some signs of life in their guesthouse, so they let it for a song."

"I can't believe you said that because the other day I drove out to Pojoaque to answer an ad about a guesthouse that sounded perfect. The older man said he'd give it to me for free if I performed fellatio on him twice a month. That's exactly what he said. He was so charming and straightforward, it wasn't even that creepy. Still, I declined."

Cleo laughed. "Was his name Howard?"

"Yes!"

"That has been his deal for years. He's an equal opportunity landlord, by the way. Women, men, whatever. He gets takers! A lotta weird stuff goes on around here. Are you here alone?"

"I am. My husband is in South America for nine months, traveling and writing, and I'm here. A little . . . marriage sabbatical while we each do our own thing."

Open-mouthed, Cleo turned to Nicole. "Marriage sabbatical! That is brilliant. You should hold workshops on that topic! Who doesn't want in on that? I might still be married if we could have taken a little break from each other occasionally. Well, from Husband Two anyway. Husbands One and Three were short-term situations from the start."

"Who was Husband Two?" Nicole asked. She thought Cleo might be on Husband Four or Five.

"Michael Carmody, the film producer. So smart, so handsome, but got bored easily. Always running off to Morocco to scout locations or sleep with other women. But tons of fun when we were together," Cleo said, flipping the blinker for emphasis. She maneuvered that Range Rover like a rally driver, constantly changing lanes. "Three marriages were enough for me. I have Australian cattle dogs and that's my primary relationship. Plus, a cute neighbor and we'll leave it at that."

"When I know you better, I'm going to want details about the neighbor."

Cleo smoothly exited the highway and navigated the city streets with confidence. "Frankly, most people are surprised that I'm still alive. They know me from movies I made forty years ago. Or that damn yoga tape."

"You brought a lot of joy and calm to our house when I was a teenager. My mom was so into your yoga tape, she swore off men for a while and stopped getting married. It was a nice break for me."

"Thank you for saying that. I bought my house in Tesuque thanks to that tape," Cleo answered, dropping the name of the glamorous village ten minutes outside of Santa Fe that was home to a large pueblo, plus artists, actors, and others who wanted space, privacy, and views of the mountains. "Does she still practice?"

"Yoga? Yes, at the local YMCA now. Marriage, no. She's sticking to boyfriends only." In fact, when Nicole had asked her mother if she wanted to be her road trip buddy from Portland to New Mexico, she had declined, saying that she was headed off to Wyoming in an RV with Frank, her new boyfriend, a retired sheriff. Something about elk season.

"Smart woman. Do you still practice?"

"Isn't it the law that we all have to take yoga now?"

"It should be. I'll get to work on that," Cleo said, pulling into the parking lot of the grocery store. By now, Nicole was so enamored of her new friend, she believed Cleo could get mandatory yoga on the ballot in the state of New Mexico. That's when Cleo shut off the engine and turned to her with intent. "Listen, I wanted to ask you about your retailing experience. Twenty-five years at Needham's is impressive. One of my partners in this jewelry collective has a retail store in town featuring some of our artists. Her name is Billie Jo Swiftwater and she has a wonderful eye for talent. She's great at nurturing artists from all backgrounds. But her retailing skills aren't strong, particularly merchandising. I'm a silent partner in the business and I like to keep silent. But I would love to get your thoughts on what we could do to make the store really pop. It's not my place to tell Billie Jo what to do. But with your background, I think she'd take advice from you. Is that something you're interested in?"

Nicole's face flushed so quickly, she wasn't sure if it was genuine excitement or her first hot flash. Honestly, if Cleo had asked if she was interested in detailing her car or taking out her garbage cans every week, she would have said yes. But this was a dream ask. "I'd be happy to walk the store with Billie Jo and do some consulting. My honor really. Thank you."

"Great. I'll talk to Billie Jo and then connect with you next class. Good luck with the housing! Tell everybody. You never know!" And off she went, the star of the eighties, now in her seventies but still mesmerizing. She was keeping Cleo a secret, her secret.

Nicole made herself a cup of tea and opened her laptop, intending to start the reading that Raven had assigned for Thursday's class about jewelry in the ancient world, but instead she got distracted by the family's photo sharing site. She studied new photos of Jack at a baseball game in Tokyo and Chelsea underwater at the Great Barrier Reef and drinking beer afterward with new mates. Smiling at the images of her grown children, she noted that Jason was right. Their kids could take care of themselves. They included their parents in their lives, not every minute of every day, but enough to share their photos from halfway around the world. She felt a rush of satisfaction.

Just then a notification pinged, more photos that Jason posted. She clicked on them, shot after shot of lush green scenery and high mountain lakes, an uncanny blue. And then finally, after weeks of nothing but scenery, a photo of Jason himself with his fellow travelers. Nicole felt like the gesture was meant for her, an olive branch of sorts, inviting her into his trip even though she had refused to go. A shot of four people, three men covered in leather, dirt, and facial hair. And a tall, lean woman, holding her helmet under her arm, with spiky short blonde hair, a tanned youthful face, and a dynamic smile. Nicole studied the shot, searching for any signs of anything, really. Like an indication that the blonde was more than a riding partner. She breathed deeply. *This was my idea.*

Jason captioned the photo *Jason, Abigail, Rico & Jonesy: The Fearless Foursome,* and that ball of anxiety in her gut was back.

To: Tessa
From: Nicole

Hi. Sending you an email instead of a text because I don't want you to read this out loud to the Wolfpack for fun, then discover the contents are meant to be private. You know you do that sometimes, like the time you mistakenly announced your husband's small bonus to us after he got that brutal 360 review.

I'm freaking out about what I've done. Jason sent some photos today and there is this Amazonian blonde on the trip with him. Imagine a woman who is The Opposite of Me in human form.

I feel like I should get on a plane right now. What was I thinking?

Idiotically, Nicole

To: Nicole
From: Tessa

You were thinking that after twenty years of sleeping with the same person, let somebody else deal with him for a bit. Don't get on the plane. Get busy there in Santa Fe! Go out. Have some fun. Or not, but you can't spend the next nine months projecting.

You've inspired me. Maybe your solution is the solution for all of us. A Grown-Up Gap Year but with a much better understanding of what we want out of life than at eighteen. Especially our sex lives. Attached is a list of books, podcasts, and articles I've put together related to this topic. Start with *The Ethical Slut*.

Who knows? Maybe you'll find the Amazon kind of a turn-on. Have you used your gift yet?

xo Tessa

FYI, his bonus rebounded the next year.

Chapter 11

Esquel, Argentina
September

Like all the other riders, Jason had gotten into the habit of stripping off his leathers outside at the end of the day wherever they might be staying—from luxury ranchero to low-rent campsite—and giving them a good shake to avoid bringing the dirt inside his sleeping space. Last night, they'd all bunked together in a barn. Tonight, the accommodations were on the deluxe side. He couldn't wait to get into the shower, every muscle in his body aching. But first, he stripped down to his underwear. Jason looked around to make eye contact with his fellow travelers, wanting to bond in this moment of public undressing, as today had felt particularly epic. They had ridden hundreds of miles on dirt roads to get to Butch Cassidy's hideout in the town of Esquel. Butch Cassidy's hideout!

He and Charlie had watched that movie a dozen times in college, occasionally calling each other "Butch" and "Sundance" because that's what guys did. He had never missed Charlie more in the last three years than he had today when he stood outside that log cabin with a bunch of total strangers. Not one of them understood what it had meant to make it all that way and not have Charlie there. Not the group of rich Texans. Not the three loud Irishmen. Certainly not that humorless lawyer from Chicago—Ned and his poor wife, Connie, both of whom would have been better suited on a river cruise than a motorcycle trip.

For the first time in a month, as he stood outside his room thinking about the day and Charlie and the absurdity of being in his boxers and the Grateful Dead T-shirt from a 1992 Eugene show that Clare had given him the day of Charlie's funeral, he missed Nicole. She would have at least understood the significance of today.

He thought about texting her, but no bars. Plus, they had agreed to once-a-week emails. Maybe this week he'd make more of an effort in his emails. He'd been short, stingy in his updates, not wanting to let her into his experience because he was still mad about the whole Santa Fe thing. But at the end of every day, like right now, when he was stripping off layers of dirt, he knew she would have hated this whole experience. Last night's barn? She would have flipped. He wouldn't describe Nicole as high needs, but she wasn't no needs either. Sleeping on the floor of a barn for a premium price would have eaten away at her. She had a whole monologue about "proportional expectations" worked up when it came to spending money. She didn't need to splurge on accommodations, but when she did, she wanted her money's worth. He laughed to himself thinking about her reaction to the bedrolls in the hayloft for hundreds of dollars per night.

"Nice skivvies!" he heard the familiar voice say from down the hall. It was Abigail, the Australian and his one buddy on the ride today. The two of them had gotten into the habit of riding together during the day and dining together at night, along with two other Americans from San Diego, Rico and Jonesy, both ex-Navy guys. Jason had attempted to keep up with the Irish and the Texans at the bar on the first night and was so hungover the next day, he could barely make the easy hundred-mile ride. That's when he switched dinner partners from the heavy drinkers to the more moderate drinkers, who had a glass or two of Malbec and called it a night. It made riding the next day safer and more enjoyable.

Thanks to the detective work of Ned the lawyer, who appeared to have googled every person on the trip as a way of ingratiating himself, which had really backfired for the folks who wanted to stay anonymous, Abigail, or Abby as she told everyone to call her, was an Olympic medalist in the 200 and 400 fly and the free relay. After she was outed one night at cocktails by Ned, she admitted that she'd won her medals in Seoul 1988 and then retired from the sport, bouncing around from career to career for a decade before settling in hospitality. Not that Jason spent a long time on the math, but he figured she was in her late fifties or early sixties, still fit like an athlete, and completely capable in all aspects of outdoor adventuring, having run a guest lodge in Perth for the past twenty years. She'd lost her partner, Amelia, the previous spring, sold her interest in the lodge to Amelia's kids, and embarked on a solo trip around the world with the proceeds. "I was on the waitlist, but a last-minute spot opened up and I packed my bags," she told the group at dinner one night early in the trip.

Presumably, it was Nicole's spot, but Jason said nothing. Truth was that Abby was a better riding partner than Nicole, but he kept that to himself. And she'd been a font of information about where to go and what to do in Australia that he passed along to Chelsea, hungry for insider information. But there were other things he liked about Abby, too, like her broad shoulders and long legs. And her short hair that she spiked up for dinner, the only one in the group who did much grooming. She had a great neck. As he watched her approach in her own skivvies, Jason opened the door to his room. "I cannot wait to get in the shower. I need somebody to explain the physics of dirt to me. How does it get through the leather into my private parts?"

She stopped at the room across from his and inserted her own key in the lock. Turning back over her shoulder, she said, "Determination or desire, I guess."

And for a moment their eyes locked, and something shifted. Seismically.

After a pause, Jason said, "See you at dinner," and walked into his room, closing the door behind him.

———

What the hell was that, Jason thought as the warm water of the shower rushed over his body. He did not expect to feel that surge of electricity from his riding buddy. By Abby's description of her relationship with her late partner, he assumed she was only into women. But maybe not. And that was kind of hot. It certainly felt like something sexual in the hallway. Was that a good thing or a bad? Maybe Abigail was exactly what he needed.

He hadn't cashed in on the Five Hundred Mile Rule yet, even though he'd had opportunities in Puerto Varas, where he stayed for the first few weeks before heading off on the bike. But those opportunities had come from professionals, women who approached him in bars or out in front of his hotel with vivid offers and limited English. Instead, he gave the women a small amount of cash so they would stop bothering him, which appeared to confuse them. Or maybe it was his Spanish that was the issue. They were so young and all he could hear was the voice of his college-age daughter in his head, discussing the plight of sex workers around the world after seeing a Netflix documentary at school. Granted, as a marine biologist focused on saving endangered species, she'd never given much thought to sex work in the past. But now after one doc, she was all in on being against it. It reminded him of all the conversations he'd had with women in college about the anti-porn documentary *Not a Love Story*, which seemed to be mandatory viewing at liberal arts colleges for a time and made him feel guilty for the years he spent reading *Penthouse*.

Truth was, he wasn't comfortable paying for sex and, frankly, it seemed to be contrary to the spirit of the Five Hundred Mile Rule. Plus, the possibility of a sexually transmitted disease was a no-go for both him and Nic.

As he soaped up his body and let his mind wander, he thought about the possibility of Abby. Almost six feet, sculpted, with a wicked sense of humor and raucous laugh. She wasn't beautiful, but she was vibrant. She exuded energy and enthusiasm, but she came by it authentically, not like she was putting on an act. Maybe some of that vibrancy would rub off on him; he'd felt so deflated since Charlie's death. She was older than him by six or seven years and he assumed that meant she couldn't get pregnant, another one of Nicole's stipulations. But, really, what did he know about menopause? When the women around him mentioned the word, he tuned out. He'd have to look that up online, but he was pretty sure the Aussie's baby-making days were over.

She certainly didn't act like her life was over. She had a huge sense of fun, another thing that had been missing in his life lately. She was present, always in tune with what was right in front of her. That moment in the hallway meant something, he was sure of it.

As he thought about the possibility of himself with her, he felt himself get aroused. The water rushed over his body and his mind wandered even further. This must mean something, too, he thought.

Chapter 12

Santa Fe
September

Nicole perched at the end of the bar at the Dragon Room, inside the famed Pink Adobe restaurant, a Santa Fe staple since the forties. The room was packed, as an unseasonal monsoon had blown through an hour ago, clearing the patio and sending regulars and tourists inside to the colorful bar area. Nicole counted snagging bar seats as one of her solid gold skills. She studied the situation and sensed when one was about to open up. She stood nearby, waiting to poach it from others eyeing the bar. Her method was soft but firm as she willed the current occupant to leave. Jason often joked it was why he married her—because she could find a seat at any hot place in Portland.

But Nicole knew the real secret: she was short. She had to rely on being wily, not imposing, to catch the bartender's attention. A seat at the bar was the best way to get service. She nursed a five-dollar happy hour margarita and waited for her stew to arrive, a bowl of steaming chicken, tomatoes, and green chiles served with blue corn piñon bread, also discounted. She had to get out of her apartment and out of her head and the place had come highly recommended by the barista at the coffee shop she tried this morning. (Every time she interacted with a local, she came away with new places to eat or things to do. Today, it was Green Dragon for happy hour and Jackalope for rugs and pottery. She added both to the growing list on her phone.)

She also thought about Tessa's directive to go out and have some fun, which was such an easy task for an extrovert like Tessa. But Nicole knew that her friend was partially right. Dwelling on what might be happening in Patagonia was no way to spend her new-found freedom. Plus, the Norwegians next door were going at it like newlyweds, or maybe just like Norwegians, and the condo walls were very thin. So, she applied some lipstick, misted her hair with spray that allegedly created a beachy texture, and walked over to the bar for a cheap dinner out and maybe some company. Not company, as in taking someone back to her place, but she needed to test out a few social skills that had lain dormant for years. She had the fleeting thought of What Would Jen Do, her neighbor who would have parlayed this entire year as a Five Hundred Mile Rule marathon, racking up conquest after conquest in bars exactly like this one. But then blocked the image from her mind. She and Jen were nothing alike. This was Nicole's year. Hers.

The bar seemed filled with couples and groups, no singles who might want to share a conversation, a little flirtation test-drive. Lipstick wasted.

When her stew arrived, she took in the rich aroma, blew on it like a child, and took a small bite, challenging her ability to withstand the Santa Fe heat in every dish. While she ate, she studied the couple next to her, an attractive woman and an average-looking man in their forties whose bodies were making contact in so many places she couldn't figure out how they were staying on their respective stools. They had no time or inclination to acknowledge Nicole because they were too busy staring into each other's eyes and rubbing each other's thighs. She wondered how long it had been since she and Jason had indulged in that sort of oblivious PDA at a bar. Maybe never? For sure it had been at least twenty years. She could recollect one night about six months after Jack was born that got a little out of hand at Alexis, that classic Greek taverna in Old Town where shots of ouzo always seemed like a good idea. That was probably the night they conceived Chelsea, some sort of cosmic payback for her desire, she supposed.

Just then, the hostess came to take the couple to their table, freeing up the seat next to hers. A man about her age grabbed the spot, giving her a look up and down. He was in a suit and had a briefcase with him, a sign that even in a town filled with artists, somebody had to do the work of making the government run. Santa Fe was a state capital after all. He was handsome enough, if a little worn down from a long day at work. She sat up a bit taller and gave him a smile, as if some muscle memory from twenty-five years ago had kicked in. *This is what Jen would do*, she thought. And she decided to make Tessa proud and toss out the first verbal volley, "Long day at work?"

Not a good line, she chided herself. That's what you say to your spouse, not a stranger.

He grunted in response, a noise that sounded like agreement. Then he immediately turned away, ordered a draft beer and a plate of nachos, and watched the door for a familiar face. He had zero interest in Nicole. None. It felt like she wore the invisibility cloak of middle age. This guy would rather stare out into space than exchange a few words with her. The bartender delivered his beer with flare, flipping the coaster before he put down the glass in a polished routine. Nicole was about to comment on the gesture when the man's head swiveled around to watch a beautiful thirtyish woman in a navy-blue suit walk in the door. As he waved his hand, Nicole caught sight of his expensive watch. And wedding ring. Of course this woman, at least fifteen years his junior, was his wife.

"Hey, babe," she cooed as she slid onto the stool next to him, rubbing her hand across his shoulders as she greeted him.

"Hey, yourself. How was your day?" They kissed. And then kissed again. What was in the air at this bar?

Nicole stared at her dinner because she wanted to stop staring at them. When she and Jason interacted, were they this affectionate? Did she really kiss him at the end of the day? Could she ever call him "babe" and not sound like an idiot? She figured the answer to all these questions was no.

Then she called for a to-go box and the check. She'd walk home, take a shower, and scroll through real estate listings.

She texted Tessa: *I went out. Had zero fun.*

Chapter 13

Portland
March 2003

"What do you think? Do I look bespoke?" Jason puffed up as he said the word *bespoke* because he'd only learned the definition a few hours earlier when he was buying the Ermenegildo Zegna jacket at Marios, the high-end men's store in downtown Portland. The navy blue with teal windowpane fabric looked amazing with his eyes; the cut made him look taller and leaner. He was packing for his first major business trip abroad, a week at the London Book Fair. It was a huge step forward in his career and Nicole knew she should be at her most supportive.

Seeing him there in their bedroom with his fresh haircut and new jacket took her back to the day they remet at Needham's. She loved reliving that day in her mind, like a movie scene, again and again. But this time, he had shopped at another store without her guidance and without the family discount. And seemed thrilled at his extravagance. She tried not to let her touch of bitterness show. This trip was a big deal for him.

"Very, very bespoke. The London ladies and gents will swoon," she said in a terrible British accent.

See, she could be happy for him, even if he was leaving her with a one-year-old and another on the way. Somehow, she'd manage her never-ending morning sickness, her action-oriented baby boy, Jack, her part-time job at Needham's, and the shy college student who watched Jack two nights a week so she could work. Her friend Angela was staying for the week while they fumigated her apartment so there would be adult conversation and movies after Jack went down. Plus, she was going to try that moms' group meet-up again. It would all be fine, as Jason always said.

Except now this expensive Italian jacket arrived in their bedroom, a reminder that she and Jason were on very different career paths. Different paths, period. And there was that resentment that bubbled up every so often.

When Jack arrived, healthy and hearty at full-term, Nicole knew immediately she couldn't pull off full-time work. There were no options to job share or take a leave, even unpaid, longer than six weeks, so she had to drop out of the industry-standard training program that would have taken her to Needham's stores up and down the West Coast, conferences on the weekends, and marketing meetings with the best in the business in New York and Seattle. Plus, her actual work hours at the store every week. It was impossible to figure out how she would manage the childcare she needed on her salary. They couldn't afford to lose money now so that she could have a better job in the future.

She and Jason decided that for a few years, his career would be the priority and he'd be the primary breadwinner. It seemed to make sense as she was the one who had to do the breastfeeding and, as Jason argued, it would be easier for her to jump back onto a corporate train in a few years than for him to return to the small publishing shop he was at. "You have a real HR department that will work with you. I'm lucky I have health insurance."

We're both lucky you have health insurance, she thought.

She'd ask to move to twenty hours a week to "keep her hand in," as her mother-in-law suggested, warning, "If you drop out completely, you'll never get back in!" It was the only time her mother-in-law had seemed invested in her life, so Nicole did as she was told.

Her own mother was horrified at her plan to have more than one child at all, never mind the timing. "I thought your body bounced back great after Jack. Why risk it?"

The Mommy Wars was front-page news and Nicole soaked in every word via talk radio, her only adult companionship in the early days of motherhood. She knew being home with Jack as much as she could made the most sense for her and her baby, but she was determined to get back to work full-time as soon as she could. There was no way she was relying on only Jason's income. She was not going to be one of those women who didn't have their own money, their own way to support themselves if life threw a curveball. Her mother didn't have too many life lessons to share because she spent most of her adult life trying to regain her youth, but she always got up and went to work and that sunk in. Putting all her eggs in the Jason basket was not an option.

What if something happened to him? It could on this very trip with the terror alert being so high in London.

Still, she had to admit that at this very moment the thought of flying off to England to schmooze with colleagues at lively hotel bars and fancy restaurants sounded heavenly. She'd pay a million dollars to be the one headed to the UK instead of her husband. Forget the travel, even. She'd enjoy waltzing into a store like Marios and buying an expensive designer item that wasn't even on sale. The freedom! The independence! She wanted to feel that again.

She wasn't proud of her jealousy. She knew Jason was under tremendous pressure, so she tried to stay positive. They were a team, weren't they?

"Are you nervous?" Nicole asked.

"Yes! No! I mean, I'm excited," he said, taking off the jacket and carefully draping it over the chair in their bedroom before getting to work on packing the rest of his small bag. "Thank God for *Ten Ways the World Will End* and that Neil is afraid to fly."

Neil Goldman was the owner of Stumptown Press. He didn't much like to leave Portland as it was, but when the attacks on the World Trade Center and the Pentagon rocked the world, Neil swore off all unnecessary travel—which, in his mind, included trips to the DMV to renew his license or a short drive across the bridge to Vancouver, Washington, to bury his mother. London was an absolute no-go. Essentially, he'd become a shut-in, a victim of his own anxiety, and so Jason jumped on it to be the public face of the company.

While Jason was very good at developing big ideas and editing books, he was masterful at selling books. Neil recognized and rewarded him for his skills. Together, the two of them had produced an unlikely *New York Times* bestseller in the wake of 9/11 called *Ten Ways the World Will End,* written by a history professor and futurist at the University of Washington named Dr. Karl Berk. When Dr. Berk pitched the book, Neil saw it as a cheeky way to address serious topics like climate change, plagues and pandemics, gun violence, chemical warfare, and terrorist attacks. A quickie primer for the academic cocktail party set who wanted an introduction to disaster but written in peppy prose and explained in nifty diagrams. The book was going to be a hit for Father's Day, Neil predicted.

But on September 12, Jason realized they had something special in their hands, an unpublished manuscript that correctly predicted the attacks in terms of their nature and origin and went into depth on the threat of chemical weapons, a timely topic now. He convinced Neil and Dr. Berk to rethink the marketing strategy and take the book from upbeat to newsworthy. In the next month, they scraped the book of anything remotely cheeky, reworked the diagrams and illustrations to be less humorous and more ominous, redesigned the cover, and pushed that book out onto the market. A glowing review in the *Times* and a robust public radio appearance schedule drove their little doomsday tome to number one on the bestseller list. And there it stayed for forty-seven weeks and counting. Jason's reward was a raise plus a bonus and a trip to London to sell the foreign language rights to both the first book and the sequel, *Ten Ways the World Will Rebound.*

Jason was ready for this career leap. He was thirty, and he'd done his time in the trenches learning the business from the ground up. More important, he could sense that it was the right time and place to be in Portland. The city was a small market where he had access to world-class creatives. He was in the mix with everyone who mattered. Big fish, small pond was totally his style. He wanted to bring that confidence to London.

But he felt guilty that he felt no guilt over leaving pregnant Nicole and baby Jack for a week. He loved being a father and a husband, but sometimes he needed a break. He knew a successful conference meant that they could take a trip to Hawaii next summer and then afford full-time childcare in the fall when the new baby arrived. It might even lead to Jason buying out Neil, who'd made it clear that he wanted to be less involved with the company now that it was successful—exactly the kind of instinct that had ensured Stumptown's meager bottom line for years. Jason had his eyes on the prize: buying Stumptown and expanding its offerings.

In the middle of the grind of the last few years, Nic had gotten it in her head that it would be easier to have kids back-to-back instead of spacing them out three or four years apart, like Jason and his siblings were. Or, really, the kids of any other sane working couple they knew. She had argued that the sooner they had baby number two, the sooner they could be empty nesters, which—although true—still seemed like an awfully long way off to get some relief. But Nic was adamant, and Jason was riding the *Ten Ways* high, so he agreed.

All it took was a rare night with a babysitter and a couple of shots of ouzo and Nicole was pregnant again.

There was a sound from the baby's room, enough of a wail to alert the parents, but not enough to rush to Jack's aid. Nicole sprung off the bed, poised to report for duty if the crying continued. "Please go back to sleep, please go back to sleep," Nicole whispered.

"Yes, please," Jason agreed, nuzzling up behind his pregnant wife as she stood in the doorway of their bedroom. He rubbed his hand across her belly as he kissed her neck and waited. Silence. "He's definitely back asleep."

"I'm sleepy, too," Nicole announced with a theatrical yawn, stepping away from the door and taking Jason's hand. "I need to go to bed immediately." She removed her oversize DKNY V-neck sweater that had gotten her through nine months of the first pregnancy and was still working for her this time around, too. Jason watched as she revealed a white tank top stretched to its max. His preferred lingerie.

"Wow. Your boobs," said Jason, the wordsmith.

"Yes, they have arrived. Thank you." She could tell he was fully invested now and that sent a charge through her body. "Now, can you do me a favor? Can you take everything off except your new jacket, so I can feel that fine Italian silk-linen blend for myself?"

"I love that you love menswear. Let me go get bespoke. I'll be right back."

See, we are a team, Nicole thought as she lit a candle, turned off the lights, and positioned herself on the bed and waited for her husband to reappear. Everything would be fine.

To: Jason
From: Nicole

Great news! I scored a great house for the remainder of my stay here. I am so relieved. It's a two-bedroom, two-bath casita in a historic neighborhood. House is new but looks like the other 1920s adobe places on the street. It's a long story but belongs to a friend of a friend and needs some cleaning out and TLC before it will be my Barbie dream house. Doing at this place what I did to get our house in Portland ready for the renters.

But it will be worth it. More details later, but know that I am in a good, safe neighborhood with access to coffee, enchiladas, and world-class art. So excited.

Speaking of renters, the Galvez-Riley family loves Portland and has nothing but nice things to say about the house, the street, and the neighbors Jen & Rich!!!!! There was an issue with the dishwasher, which I took care of, and they confessed to breaking the garage door opener and will replace it themselves. I didn't tell them it breaks all the time. Is that bad?

xo

Nic

To: Nicole
From: Jason

Glad you secured a decent living situation. This week, we've been in some of the most remote territory we'll cover, hundreds of miles from any towns or cell service. We see the occasional building that serves as the store, post office, doctor's office, and bar. Our accommodations included a log cabin, a lodge with no running water, and a bunkhouse on a working estancia. At least on the estancia we ate roasted lamb for dinner. The scenery and the lamb were amazing. The bunkhouse, not so much. But it's all part of the experience.

Tonight, we're in a legit lodge with phone service and showers! Feels like the Four Seasons in comparison. Dinnertime. Gotta run.

Take care, J.

Chapter 14

Santa Fe
October

It had been six weeks and, finally, Nicole felt acclimated to Santa Fe. Acclimated to the seven-thousand-foot elevation, which had drained her stamina on her runs when she first arrived. Acclimated to being back in school, an arena where she had never excelled in the past but now found some peace and purpose in the studio. Acclimated to the dryness that sucked every last drop of moisture out of her dewy Portland skin and required application of face oil every few hours. Acclimated to making small talk at stores, coffee shops, and art galleries she visited to stay connected to other human beings and maybe pick up an acquaintance or two. Acclimated to red chile or green chile—or the combination the locals called "Christmas"—being piled on everything from eggs to cheeseburgers.

Most of all, she had acclimated to being alone, adjusting to the unrelenting stillness of the house in the evening, the long stretches of time without conversation during the day, and the many hours of "me time" that were not nearly as relaxing or entertaining as she had imagined. In Portland, especially over the last few years, she felt like she was never alone in her home and found herself wishing her family would all disappear for a few hours every afternoon so she could soak in the quiet. But here, the quiet provided no solace. In fact, she was having trouble sleeping without a body, Jason's body, in bed next to her. She missed the sounds of the kids' footsteps at night in the kitchen, keeping hours much later than her own. But she was adjusting, planning at least two activities each day to stay in exploration mode, discovering new corners of the city and being forced to adapt on a daily basis. And listening to podcasts at night to fall asleep.

Yes, she was acclimating.

She walked slowly, cooling down after her daily four miles. In her first few weeks, it felt like she counted every step of her run, acutely aware of the distance she had left to cover, missing the Wolfpack and their nonstop questions, comments, and gossip. But lately, as she grew more comfortable with her surroundings and her new route on a trail alongside a creek shaded by aspen trees, her mind wandered as it should. To the beauty of her surroundings. To worrying about her children in foreign countries. To where to go for lunch or happy hour that day, her way of trying all the local cuisine without paying dinner prices. And yes, to Jason and what he might be up to.

Today, as she walked up to her little casita on the Eastside, a short distance to the famed Canyon Road with its art galleries and shops, she knew that at least she'd won the housing lottery. She had done as Cleo suggested and told everyone within earshot about her housing needs. Of course, Gary, the old rock drummer, had offered a room in his house right off the bat. "Private entrance in the back. Behind the studio so it can get a bit loud on nights when we jam. And occasionally, you'll have to share it with my ex, who likes to come out a few times a year and have her chakras realigned. But it's yours if you want it. Do you cook? I could use a cook."

Nicole thanked him and politely declined. "I'm taking the year off cooking." And jamming. And dealing with exes.

It was her teacher Roger who had flagged her down as she was leaving class with the winning proposition. As it happened, he had a friend, a ceramicist, who'd been offered a full-time gig at a prep school in Vermont at the last minute. Would she be interested in house-sitting?

"There's a caveat, though," Roger had said with lifted brows.

"Fellatio? Cooking?"

Roger was taken aback. "Oh dear, nothing that drastic. Holly has just lost her mum and is a bit of a mess. And the house is also a bit of a mess. And her mother's dog ran away the other day and even though Holly wasn't a big fan, it made her feel worse. I'm afraid she'll let this opportunity slip by because it's all too overwhelming. I told her you might be able to help her with organizing it all and, you know, getting her out the door and to Vermont. She really needs this job. But she has to be there in ten days and left to her own devices . . ."

"Let me guess, she's an old girlfriend?"

"Yes." Roger nodded.

So much for not dealing with exes. "Sticky."

"Especially with my new wife."

"Stickier." Ironically, this jewelry maker to the stars didn't wear a wedding ring. Of course, he'd moved on, with his thick gray hair and handsome tanned face. Nicole didn't need to know this Holly to guess that she probably hadn't moved on from dreamy Roger.

In the few weeks she'd been in Santa Fe, he was the only candidate she'd identified to put the Five Hundred Mile Rule to the test. She knew it was the most obvious form of sexual attraction, zeroing in on your handsome professor with the British accent. How basic, her daughter would say. When she texted Tessa a photo of him, her friend had replied with a torrent of vaguely obscene emojis in response that had made her laugh. But now that she knew he was married, she'd put her crush aside. In her twisted rule book for the Five Hundred Mile Rule, she'd determined that two married people was not allowed. That was an affair, not an opportunity. He was off the table.

Roger continued, "Amicable split a few years ago, but I still feel responsible for her. When you and I talked the other night at the class barbecue at Raven's and you told me about packing up your own house to move here, it seemed you might be a good fit. I know I don't know you well, but you seem very responsible, organized, and hardworking."

Nicole clung to every syllable of his praise because her self-confidence in terms of her metalwork was zero. Even though the object of her fantasies was implying that she seemed like the class mom, as opposed to a creative and talented designer, she was pleased. "Holly could never rent the house out as it is now. But, if you're willing to put in a little time on the front end—packing and sorting and, frankly, tossing a lot of stuff out—I think you could negotiate a good deal on the rent for the school year."

"So obviously, you've told her about me." Nicole imagined him tossing out her name as some sort of salvo to get her off the phone so he could get back to wifey. "Be straight. Is this a hoarding situation? I'm not a mental health professional."

"Oh, no. More along the lines of too much stuff to deal with and too much going on. Both Holly and her mom downsized into this smaller house at the same time. A temporary plan, but they never had a chance to get things sorted before her mother's health declined rapidly. She broke her hip while unloading boxes from her car on the day of the move. Never recovered. Died of an infection after surgery."

"That is awful," Nicole said, imagining a stubborn older woman who wouldn't let anyone help her unpack her stupid car. She'd seen the type at Needham's, the octogenarians who spent hours in the dressing room because they wouldn't let the saleswoman help with a zipper. One time, an elderly man insisted on reaching to the top of a perfume tower to choose a bottle, even though Nicole had offered him a pre-wrapped box of the same product. Of course, he brought the whole display down and with it, two dozen bottles of L'Air du Temps. What a mess and the stench! The glorification of independence in old age was a mystery to Nicole, but she put that thought aside because she wanted this house. "How terrible for Holly. Where's the house?"

Roger was ready to move on from Holly's family drama as well. "The place is charming, at least it could be, and in a great location on the Eastside."

That was the magic word: *Eastside*. It was her dream neighborhood. The historic streets featured a mix of authentic one-story adobe houses, sleek modern haciendas, and even a few Arts and Crafts–inspired houses hidden behind thick walls and brilliant flowering vines. And all that real estate glory was close to everything that Santa Fe had come to symbolize to her: art, beauty, food, nature, coffee, and a bit of magic in the form of light, color, and clouds. She had walked the curved, narrow streets almost every day looking for elusive For Rent signs. "Give me her number. I can go over there this afternoon if she'll see me."

"Oh, she'll see you."

And by the end of the week, Nicole had a place to live. Granted, she had spent the first few days psyching Holly up for the move. Holly, in her late thirties with big earthy girl energy, was a pile of grief and indecision, and although Nicole had never lost a parent, she had known the feeling of being on her own since she was eighteen. She couldn't let Holly get paralyzed by the task at hand and didn't. They sorted, strategized, and created a solid action plan.

According to Cleo, who had become her regular ride home when she had time to show up to the class she was merely auditing, Holly's mother, Mimi Arledge, was once the private secretary for a wealthy globe-trotting couple who had houses all over the world, including Santa Fe. "She was a wonderful woman. I've served with her on multiple boards over the years, like the opera. She loved the opera. I do not. But her real work was with health care for women and children on the reservations. She was instrumental in setting up a half dozen clinics at various pueblos with great commitment and inclusiveness. Really admirable. Plus, she was very fashionable. Exquisite taste and knew how to wear clothes."

Over the years, thanks to the largesse of her employer, her own travels, and many trips to Bergdorf's, Mimi had amassed quite a collection of vintage fashion items and a good eye for antiques and housewares. Carefully packed boxes of treasures filled the entire garage and second bedroom. After Nicole sorted through a few boxes, spotting labels from Pucci, Oleg Cassini, and Geoffrey Beene, she asked Holly, "Are you sure you don't want to keep any of these?"

Holly shook her head. "I'm eight inches taller and fifty pounds heavier than my mother. Those look like doll's dresses to me." Holly's style was more Southwestern Boho than New York in the Seventies, anyway.

"Well, these aren't Goodwill items. Let me sort these out. I've done online vintage resale before," Nicole said with authority, even though her Poshmark experience consisted of the sale of a handful of jackets with shoulder pads and her entire collection of Nicole Miller dresses circa 1997. "And I'm sure I can find a dealer here for the furniture and artwork you don't want." Her plan was to go straight to Cleo for recommendations.

"That's so nice of you," said naïve, tall, curvy Holly.

"Holly, to be clear, I'm going to take a cut. Twenty percent of whatever I can sell or consign. Cool?"

"Oh, of course. Cool."

Within a week, progress had been made and more deals had been struck. At first, Nicole was tempted to offer a generous rent along with the decluttering work because she wanted this house. But after assessing the amount of schlepping and hustle it would take to reorganize the house and sell the vintage items, she lowballed the rent. She could hear Jason's voice in her head when he counseled her on how to price the freelance merchandising work she had picked up after her layoff: "Value your time. You are good at what you do. Double your hourly."

Plus, Holly was in no position to play hardball.

Holly agreed to rent the house for a flat fee of five thousand dollars for the next eight months and Nicole agreed to empty the guest room and garage, maybe even paint the interior. The rent was a steal, but the sweat equity was real. Crunching the numbers, Nicole figured she could save enough on the rent and make enough on the resale items to cover most of her costs. Maybe she wouldn't need another job after all.

In exchange, Holly could get in her Range Rover, drive to Vermont, and expect her boxes of warm weather clothes and other assorted items to be waiting for her when she arrived. And when she returned at the end of May, the house would be clean and clutter-free, suitable for living, renting, or selling.

The only unsettled question was the miniature poodle named Bardot. Holly was sure she'd been dognapped. "She was a looker. And they are so trendy. Everyone wants a doodle now and you need a poodle for that. Bardot is what aficionados call an apricot minipoo, not one of the big guys or a tiny toy. Shorter nose, cute face, so soft. Puppy mills would want her for her size. I'm sure it's a black-market situation."

Nicole didn't know, because paying a lot of money for a dog seemed like the most privileged act in the universe. When people in Portland had started to go on about their designer dogs, she tuned out. That sort of conversation served as a reminder to her that even though her life now looked like an art-directed magazine spread, she came from more humble, less curated beginnings. She understood spending money on clothes or cars or furniture, but not on puppies, not when the pound was full of them. They'd gotten their beloved Lab mix free on Big Dog Adoption Day and he was the greatest dog ever. "Maybe she'll turn up. I guess I can ship the dog, too."

"Please don't," Holly said. "We didn't really get along. We had a lot of control issues over my mother. Bardot was very possessive and didn't appreciate my presence. Adored my mother, tolerated me."

Nicole let it drop, convinced that if Bardot was still alive, she'd been taken in by some adoring gay couple with a sunken living room and a fluffy dog bed who probably also called her Bardot.

Three weeks after Holly's departure and nonstop work, the house felt like her home. Now, the place was clean and simple, and most of the boxes were out of the house and stored in the garage, a major victory. She was using the second bedroom as a staging area for her Poshmark business, which she was calling Sincerely, Mimi after finding several letters in a desk drawer signed that way. She'd created a mini studio and workroom for shooting and shipping the items. For now, she was aiming to sell three or four pieces a week, studying the market to get the pricing right, and the response was enthusiastic. It broke her heart to sell off the 1970s vintage Pauline Trigère black silk chiffon and satin halter bow-tiered dress because it fit her to a tee. But at a purchase price of twelve hundred dollars, she knew it had to go. Maybe she'd keep a few things if the sales continued at this pace, paying Holly the fair resale price.

With Clancy's help, she'd even slapped on a new coat of snowy white paint in the cozy living room and kitchen area. Clancy, her classmate who was used to blacksmithing on a working ranch twelve hours a day, loved manual labor. When she wasn't in class, on a horse, or bartending at the classic restaurant El Farol right down the street from the casita, she was up for whatever task Nicole needed. Mainly, it was moving heavy things around and hanging artwork, thanks to her stud finder and level.

Nicole discovered some great pieces of furniture hidden underneath all the mess. Some antique rugs were buried in the garage, along with a handful of beautiful lamps. She salvaged a few pieces of art for the walls, leaving the good stuff to be sold. Or to pass on to Holly when she was ready to deal with her mother's possessions. Looking around, she had a tremendous sense of pride in what she'd created. The casita was a sanctuary. Now, it felt like the real estate deal of the century.

She imagined what it would be like to share it with Jason, fire burning, candles lit, and shadows dancing against the wall. Yes, she missed his presence, his scent, the feel of his chest. She was surprised how her body ached for him, a physical longing. She pulled out that gift vibrator more than once, imagining him there.

Flushed at the memory, she opened the front door and walked inside to get water, because she was always thirsty in this climate, but especially after a run. Standing at the sink filling her water bottle, she heard barking, a hearty greeting. She looked up and there was the distinct sophisticated face of the apricot mini poodle from the lost dog poster that Holly had created out of guilt. The dog—scruffy, dirty, and with a smirk on her face like she'd been on the best bender of her life for the last month—made a beeline for Nicole. The minipoo couldn't have been more pleased to find it was Nicole, not Holly, standing at the sink. After allowing a few belly rubs, she scooted into the back of the house with nonchalance. Bardot was back.

She wasn't alone anymore.

Chapter 15

"Who's this?" Billie Jo said in a welcoming voice as Nicole stepped inside the Zia Collective, a jewelry and textile shop a few blocks off the Plaza in downtown Santa Fe. From the minute that Cleo had introduced the two women, there had been a connection. Billie Jo, the proprietress, was in her late thirties. She had been educated at the University of New Mexico and had a degree in anthropology with a master's in public administration. She was a single mother by choice, a member of the Tesuque Pueblo, and seemed to be related to half the population of the state, judging by the number of times she said "That's my uncle . . ." or "My cousin owns that place" during conversation. She had spent a decade as an administrator at the Institute of American Indian Arts in Santa Fe, doing everything from development to producing events to creating private/public partnerships for the school and student body. Her roots ran so deep in so many aspects of Santa Fe life that Nicole called her the Mayor.

But one thing Billie Jo didn't really know how to do was run a retail store. When Nicole walked through the door, eager to help but respectful of Billie Jo's reputation, it proved to be the perfect partnership. They were spending several afternoons together a week, learning from each other. Nicole shared her retail knowledge and Billie Jo schooled her on the history of Native arts in Santa Fe.

It was part business school, part cultural exchange and it worked for both of them.

Which is why Nicole didn't think she'd mind the dog. "The famous Bardot has returned, and she is a delight," Nicole announced.

It was true. Upon her return to the casita, Bardot took one loop around the inside to check out the new vibe (and to make sure Holly was gone) and settled right into Nicole's life. Nicole took her to the groomer, whose card she had found in the junk drawer, for a spa day with instructions to leave her fluffy. She hauled the chic dog bed out of the garage, bought new food and water dishes, and replaced her missing collar with a tasteful beaded one from a local artist that she'd seen on Canyon Road. Bardot was pleased with all of it.

The dog was the model of calm, exhibiting none of the behaviors Holly described. Used to big dogs, Nicole thought of miniature poodles as fussy, but Bardot was a gung-ho gal. She joined Nicole on runs, the rare trips in the car, and all her walks. At night, the two of them enjoyed watching TV in bed. At first, Nicole was hesitant to contact Holly because she didn't want her to force Nicole to bring the dog to the pound. No way could she face the shame of an "Owner Surrender." Now she didn't want to let Holly know Bardot was back because she was afraid Holly would want to reclaim her in a fit of grief over her mother. (Holly was clearly working through her mother's death. Every time Nicole texted to inform her of a clothing sale, Holly responded with the crying face emoji and a black heart.) Bardot would be another secret Nicole kept, at least for a while.

"I hope you don't mind. She's more human than canine. And she has very good taste. She loved the Laura Ashley dresses I posted this week. Classics."

"I have no idea what a Laura Ashley dress is, but I'll believe you that it's a classic." Bardot allowed Billie Jo to pet her and then found a cozy corner to occupy. Billie Jo pointed to the poodle and said, "This is the bougie vibe we need here at Zia. Where did you get that collar? We should carry those!"

Nicole gave Billie Jo a look. "What have we talked about?"

"Product discipline," she replied dutifully. "I need to curate the merchandise to target our consumer."

"Yes. Ask yourself, do seventy-five-dollar dog collars belong in my store? The answer may be yes because they do count as jewelry for dogs. But ask the question before you start stocking them," Nicole said, scanning the store to see how it looked today.

For the last three Friday afternoons, if the store was quiet, Nicole and Billie Jo had met to go over some retail marketing basics. As Cleo promised, her protégé had an eye for modern Native American jewelry and textiles, but no clue how to merchandise a retail space to show off those wares. And Billie Jo had a hard time saying no to anyone who wanted to hang up a poster for their event or consign cheap baubles to fund the Little League team. The small shop was cluttered, unfocused, even slightly dusty.

It was clear to Nicole after spending a few hours with Billie Jo that while she had a fantastic business plan for marketing the two dozen hand-chosen artists under the banner of the Zia Collective, a strong plan for in-person trunk shows around the country, and a website and catalogue to extend their brand reach, she had zero interest in running a brick-and-mortar store. Zia had potential, but it needed polish.

According to Billie Jo, the space had fallen into her lap. "My dad and uncle own this building. Family lore says my great-grandmother Fatima won it in a poker game a hundred years ago. Thanks to the pandemic, the building was a little light on tenants and my dad wanted something in here for optics, so I opened the store a year ago. I had no idea how time-consuming running a shop could be. Someone has to be here to sell the stuff."

In exchange, she listened as Billie Jo told her the history of Native American jewelry in New Mexico, a tradition dating back to the 1800s and explored by area tribes. For a good chunk of the last hundred years, the silver and turquoise creations were geared to the tourist trade, but that direction was changing. Artists were now encouraged to think beyond traditional designs and take their work wherever their imagination and skill led them. At the annual Santa Fe Indian Market, an event that attracted thousands of artists and collectors every August, the best in Native American arts would be on display and the jewelry competition would be fierce and highly regarded in the jewelry world. It was that sense of excitement that Billie Jo wanted to capture with the Zia Collective and take on the road.

When she described her desire to expand the Santa Fe look, quality, and spiritual nature of these designs to appreciative consumers in New York and Los Angeles, Nicole could see it in her mind's eye and could feel her passion. "We need to capture your dream in this store. This is a testing ground for your ideas that you'll take to those trunk shows Cleo is setting up. Your vision isn't clear in this store. Focus."

Nicole suggested weaving the narratives of the artists into the displays with photos and information cards. The store itself had to tell a story, but first, they had to focus on basic retailing dos and don'ts. Nicole explained about adding height and areas of focus to draw in buyers. Random posters came down, cases were dusted, windows and mirrors polished. Textile pieces were grouped on one wall and a small collection of oil paintings on the opposite wall. More affordable bracelets and necklaces were displayed near the front of the store to lure in shoppers. Fresh flowers and a few scented candles added warmth. All the random items that Billie Jo had stocked—from spice mixes to sunscreen ("White people need sunscreen like all the time here," Billie Jo had argued)—were gathered in a basket, marked clearance, and put out front. They sold in a day.

"I'm sorry to say, no one wants to see your lunch," Nicole said. Food was banished to the small back storage room, out of view of the customers. Even Billie Jo's omnipresent iced coffee was re-cupped, from the single use plastic she favored to a beautiful tall ceramic vessel.

Up next was painting a mural on the wall that faced the door. Billie Jo picked the name the Zia Collective to reflect the New Mexican roots of all the artists represented. The stylized sun graphic, the Zia, was the well-recognized symbol of New Mexico. It originated with the Zia Pueblo in ancient times and remained a powerful visual. Nicole had suggested that Billie Jo commission an artist from that pueblo to create a mural in the shop that would draw people into the store. The painting was set to begin in days. It was Billie Jo's idea to have the artist paint it during business hours, so people could watch, both in the store and on socials.

In less than a month, the look of Zia had transformed into a bright, welcoming space where the art was the star, but Billie Jo herself was the heart of the operation. Nicole made sure to remind her of that truth. "I love these," Nicole said, pointing to the photos of the three featured artists of the week, rich black-and-white portraits. "And the story cards about the artists are great. How do people respond?"

"They ask me questions all day long. It's like you said, if they get invested in the artist, they invest in the art. Honestly, it's easier for me to sell the artist than the jewelry. I think I'm a terrible salesperson."

"You're not. I've seen you in action and you draw people in. My old boss at Needham's used to say that nothing sells itself except lemonade on a hot day. You let people walk away. We're going to work on you closing the sale."

"I think, do they really need that bracelet?"

"People do. They need a one-of-a-kind piece of art to remind them of their time in Santa Fe. Never feel bad about selling a memory," Nicole said. Billie Jo nodded.

Nicole continued, "But I do think you need to hire some help because some days you're distracted by the other tasks you need to do for Zia. You barely look up from the computer. It's understandable because you're working on the website and social media and setting up the trunk shows with Cleo, but you make it easy for customers to walk in, look around, and leave without ever connecting with them. Six days a week working on the floor is burnout territory, even in a small shop like this. Do you have anyone who could work a shift or two for you?"

"I'd love a Sunday off," Billie Jo agreed. "To get one more day along with my regular Monday off would really make a difference. My daughter has started to call me by my first name because she says I'm more like a roommate than a mom."

Nicole's Mom Guilt returned in an instant, flooding her brain with memories of similar conversations with her daughter when she had to work weekends or holidays or any day that Chelsea needed a ride to the mall and Nicole couldn't give her one. There was an entire decade, from Jack's sixth birthday to his sixteenth, when she felt like she put on her running shoes in the morning and sprinted to the end of the day, fourteen hours later. When Jack got his license and could drive the two of them around, it was the happiest day of her life. But the years before that magical day, it seemed like she had guilt being administered by a slow drip, always in her bloodstream at some barely manageable level. A late pickup at soccer practice. A no-show at a midday school event. A half-assed effort helping the kids study for a test because of exhaustion and disinterest. Drip, drip, drip. The period of time with a job on the weekends and young teens at home was the worst, right where Billie Jo was trapped. At least she had Jason to pick up the slack. Billie Jo was a single parent. "I get that. Why do we even have children? Nobody tosses a guilt bomb like your own flesh and blood."

Billie Jo's face lit up. "Could you work on Sunday? You're not in school on the weekends, right?"

Nicole's face registered surprise. She figured that Billie Jo would want someone younger, trendier, and Native American to run the shop. She didn't quite know what to say. Did she want to take on more work on top of smithing, the vintage shop, and Bardot?

"I'd pay you, of course," Billie Jo offered, assuming her silence was some sort of passive-aggressive negotiating tactic.

"It's not that. We'll work out a fee or maybe payment in kind," Nicole said, pointing to a case of delicate necklaces. "But I'm thinking that there should be a better representative for your vision behind the counter than a middle-aged white lady from Oregon."

"You're probably right. But I don't know how I'm going to get through the holidays by myself. And I don't have time to find and train someone right now. How about Sundays through January? We could have so much fun planning events around Christmas. It looks so beautiful here at that time of year, with all the trees lit up in the Plaza. Wait till you see the farolitos on every building. The Chamber of Commerce markets an art and shopping event every weekend from now through the end of the year and they each have a theme. And I've been wanting to do something with the other tenants in the building . . ."

Nicole interrupted. "And you say you're not a saleswoman. You're selling this hard!"

Just then, the door chimed and a guy with a wine bottle strolled in. "Hey! Want to try the new sparkling rosé? Ready to be uncorked!"

"Marcos! Yes to bubbles! How was the harvest? I saw all your posts about the picking parties. It looked like you had a ton of helping hands. And then the food your mother cooked for everybody! It looked amazing." Billie Jo hugged this handsome newcomer like an old friend and took the wine from his hands. "I can't wait to give this a try. Thank you."

"It's always more work than it looks like in the pictures," Marcos said, turning his attention to Nicole. But Nicole had already turned her attention to him. Late thirties, maybe forty. Dark-haired, trim beard, deep tan, light green eyes. Not tall but athletic. He had a suede jacket on over a black T-shirt. Nicole had always thought suede was an undervalued material, losing out to leather in popularity. This Marcos had style. And wine. And something else that stirred her.

Bardot, usually content to stay close to Nicole and keep quiet, padded over to the newcomer with unbridled enthusiasm, tail wagging. "Hey, Bardot. My little buddy. You're back! What brings you here?" He looked up and locked eyes with Nicole.

Billie Jo chimed in. "This is Nicole. She's house-sitting for Holly. You know Holly, right?"

"Sure, we went to school together. I'm Marcos Cabrera. I work over at the O Rosal Tasting Room. It's nice to meet you." He stretched out his hand and she shook it. It was rough, like he'd been picking grapes for sure, but the rest of him—his clothes, manners, voice—was refined. "You must be the angel that pulled Holly together. And found Bardot! Holly sent out frantic texts to all her friends to be on the lookout. I didn't know she'd been found."

"It was recent," Nicole said, knowing now she would have to inform Holly before the word got back to her. "I'm waiting to tell her once she's more settled."

"I'm sorry I missed her goodbye party at El Farol. As you heard, we had the harvest at the vineyard, so it was an all-hands situation. Too much going on to come back to town. How's she doing?"

"She seems very glad to be in Vermont. Like it was a good move."

"And you? Are you happy?"

Either Marcos knew more about her situation than he let on or he guessed the exact phrase she needed to hear at this moment. In any case, she smiled and answered, "Yes, I am happy. I love living here." And the second she said it, she knew it was true.

"Nicole's a friend of Cleo's and she's been helping me with the store," Billie Jo said, waving around her hand like she was a showcase model. "Doesn't it look great?"

"I love the changes. It's less chaotic," Marcos said.

"Don't say I told you so," Billie Jo warned Nicole with a smile.

"It was always in you. But we had to clear the clutter in your busy mind," Nicole said.

"Perfect answer!" Marcos turned back to Nicole. "Are you a regular at El Farol on Sunday nights? You can walk to it from Holly's place, right?"

"Yes. I've been a couple of times, including the going-away party. Does that make me a regular?" Nicole managed, sounding more like an awkward teenager than a grown woman, not sure she fit in with the cool crowd yet.

The classic old Santa Fe bar was a hangout for locals on Sunday nights. While most of the town rolled up sidewalks early at the end of the weekend, El Farol kept the bar open until ten to serve drinks and their signature paella to fellow restaurant workers, gallery owners, hotel staff, and the like after they got off shift. The vibe was warm and convivial, an easy opportunity to meet people without too much pretense.

When Holly had her going-away party there, Nicole discovered that her classmate Clancy had worked there since her arrival two years before. To stave off the Sunday night blues without her family, the last few weeks Nicole had walked down on her own and planted herself at the end of the bar, talking to Clancy and whoever else might be nearby. She was surprised how quickly she got to know the other patrons, who welcomed her once they found out she was a resident and not a tourist. She surmised that in a town like this, with residents coming and going for chunks of time throughout the year and seasonal workers filling in, there was more of an openness to new faces. Often, she'd see these acquaintances throughout the week, working at restaurants or galleries or boutiques, and be greeted with smiles of recognition. Just yesterday, Mary at the spice shop had greeted her like an old friend, making Nicole feel like a real local in front of the tourists. Maybe she was a regular.

"My friend Clancy is the bartender. And Holly was a regular before she moved. I feel like I'm keeping her seat at the bar warm. Do you stop in on Sunday nights?"

"When I'm in Santa Fe and not out at the vineyard, I do. Most Sunday nights, especially in the winter. And then I dream about that paella the rest of the week."

"It's delicious paella," she said, wishing she could have come up with something more poetic. The word *paella* brought back the memory of the gloppy mess that Jen had served in her backyard in Portland two months ago. That felt like two years ago to Nicole. *Look at that pan*, Jason had exclaimed. She was tempted to try and explain the absurdity of the moment to Billie Jo and Marcos, but she knew there was no point. She had to move on. Be in this moment and not that previous moment. This was her life now. But she couldn't think straight with Marcos standing so close. What was happening to her?

Marcos didn't seem to notice. He wandered around the small shop, taking in the changes. "So, you know Cleo, Clancy, Holly, and Billie Jo? You've made all the right friends if you're new here. As I said, I went to school with Holly. Cleo and my mom play mahjong together and Billie Jo and I go way back. And Clancy beat out a handful of other barbacks to get that Sunday night bartending spot. Between those four, you'll know all our secrets. That's why Santa Fe is more like a big high school than a small city."

"High school with money," Billie Jo added and then held up the wine bottle. "Let's try this stuff!"

She put two glasses and the bottle on a glass table in the front of the store. Then she flipped the Open sign to Closed. It was almost five, but not quite. Nicole liked to be very disciplined about opening and closing times, respecting the people who dashed in with five minutes to go for a perfect anniversary gift or birthday present. But she wasn't going to lecture Billie Jo now on that topic. Yes, a glass of wine on a Friday at 4:45 p.m. was acceptable.

"Let me go get another glass then we can open this. It's the latest vintage of our signature sparkling wine," Marcos said, moving toward the doorway. "We have to have a toast to Santa Fe's newest resident."

When the door closed, Billie Jo turned to Nicole immediately. "He likes you!"

"Please. He's being friendly because I'm your friend. And you sound like you're thirteen."

Billie Jo shook her head. "That's not all! When we have more time, I'll tell you his whole life story. Known him forever. He's been through the wringer lately. But here's the short version: he's divorced, no steady girlfriend, no kids. And, his family owns the vineyard, so when he says he's 'at' the tasting room, what he means is that he's the marketing manager for O Rosal, which is doing very well thanks to his work. Their sparkling wine business has exploded thanks to the rebranding and PR efforts. And of course, now everybody drinks rosé all day. He also consults with other restaurants in town on their wine lists, so he knows everybody. He likes to come over at the end of the day and share whatever wine he has left. He's a doll."

Billie Jo finished her personal Wikipedia page recital as Marcos returned brandishing another wineglass. He opened the bottle expertly while asking Nicole about what she was doing in town, "besides bailing out Holly." She filled him in on the basic details as he listened like an experienced barkeep, with one ear on the customer and one eye on the pour. He moved with finesse. He passed the half-filled glasses and then lifted his. "To Nicole. Welcome to the City Different."

They clinked glasses and took a sip of the dry pink sparkling wine. It was delicious and Marcos nodded with a certain pride when Nicole told him so. "My family has been in the wine business for many generations. I think we got this one right."

She wanted to know more about his story, but Billie Jo piped up, "Help me, Marcos. I am begging Nicole to take Sundays for me here at the store. You should see her, Marcos. She's a retail genius. You should hire her to look at the new retail space you're adding at the vineyard."

"I'll spare Nicole the drama of going out to the new store at the vineyard," he said, addressing Billie Jo and then turning his attention to Nicole to explain further. "My ex-wife is running the store and I can tell you from personal experience that she is always right. At least, that's what she thinks. I'm not sure she'd be open to new ideas."

"Your ex-wife works at your family vineyard?" Nicole asked, too curious not to inquire. First the suede, then the wine, and now an ex-wife who won't leave. Messy family stories intrigued her; they made her feel better about her own life.

"Well, she's engaged to my cousin now. So, yes. She's still there and that's why I live in town. If you take the Sunday shift, I can give you the full story, if Billie Jo didn't fill you in during the twelve seconds I was getting the extra glass."

"I didn't say a word," Billie Jo lied without hesitation.

"Do I believe you?" Marcos asked, adding another splash to her glass. He focused in on Nicole. "I work Sundays and I like knowing that somebody else is in the same boat. We could go to El Farol's together, too. I really want to try the flamenco lessons, but I need a partner."

Nicole couldn't believe this man had said those words. Early in the evening, on Sundays, there was a free community flamenco lesson taught by professionals. Nicole loved watching the dancers and listening to the rhythmic stomping and the clang of castanets. She hadn't taken a dance class in years, but she was tempted to join in. The teachers, an older couple, were so elegant, so sexy.

She'd been mesmerized by the short performance of the professionals before the students took the floor and started stomping around and waving their arms to the strong beat of the guitar strumming. It looked intense, alive. She almost joined in last week, but lost her nerve. There were some good dancers on the floor, and she was self-conscious of her sneakers and joggers next to the full skirts and proper shoes of the other women.

Marcos's interest seemed like a sign, a nod of approval. She knew that technically you didn't need a partner to join in the community dance class, because she'd already asked the instructor last week, but she didn't want to let him know that.

Or that the shirt he was wearing made the most of his green eyes.

She turned to Billie Jo. "I'll work Sundays, at least through the holidays or until you find a permanent employee who can grow with you. I'm happy to train somebody, but they must be someone who can represent the Zia Collective and your story, okay?" She turned to Marcos and said, "And I'll try the flamenco with you if you promise not to laugh. I haven't taken a dance class since we learned the 'Thriller' combination at work for a flash mob when flash mobs were a thing. But I'm intrigued by flamenco. Deal?"

"Deal," Billie Jo said, lifting her glass.

"Yes, deal," Marcos confirmed quietly.

Nicole felt her face flush and her chest constrict. Had she just made a date?

To: Holly Arledge
From: Nicole Elswick

Hi Holly. Hope you are doing well. A couple of updates:

Sincerely, Mimi is off to a brisk start! Your mother had lovely taste and her items are in wonderful condition. I've sold a few already, including the Bill Blass orange lizard print sequined suit. It went for $1,500! A costume designer from LA picked it up almost as soon as I listed it. She's interested in a bunch of the other items as well. I need to catalogue and price them, but it looks like she'll be a good customer. The rest of the sales are documented in the spreadsheet.

Also, Bardot returned! She made her way back to the casita and onto the new couch. No sign of where she'd been, but she looked like she had a swell time. She has adjusted very well to my presence, and I love taking care of her. I am more than happy to keep her until you decide what you'd like to do. She's a fave in the neighborhood. Attached is a photo.

To: Nicole Elswick
From: Holly Arledge

OMG, you do spreadsheets, too! Honestly, don't know what I'd do without you, Nicole. You should be a LIFE COACH!

The Sincerely, Mimi thing is blowing my mind. I would have totally donated those to the Goodwill without even opening a box. Now, I feel a little guilty, so I'll make a monetary donation to a charity instead. If there is anything you'd like to keep for yourself, please do. My gift to you.

As for Bardot. I need more time. I wish we had bonded but we didn't. She needs somebody who loves her like my mom did. Can you keep her for a bit more? I can't make that decision right now. Life here is so hectic and I'm so out of my league creating a curriculum for teenagers. HELP.

But fall in Vermont = Perfection!

Peace out, Holly

Chapter 16

Marcos was a flamenco ringer. Nicole had expected that he'd be stomping around in the back row with her, sharing a good laugh over their mutual lack of coordination. But from the moment they arrived together at El Farol for the free lesson, it was clear that he had street cred in the dance community. He was greeted with waves by a handful of the others.

Ava the teacher made her way over and embraced him immediately. "Marcos, thank you for coming. We need a few more gentlemen on the floor. And I see you brought a new dancer?" Her voice was hopeful, but her look was doubtful that the woman in the running shoes and yoga pants was going to light the floor on fire.

"This is Nicole. She's an artist. And she tells me she used to do musical theater in high school. Nicole, this is Ava Vargas, a true flamenco legend here in New Mexico and my first dance teacher. And that's her husband, Brian," he said, pointing to a tall, slim man who might be the whitest-looking guy she'd seen in Santa Fe. "They danced professionally all over the world but retired a few years ago. Now, they spread their love of the dance locally. We're in good hands." Ava was in her seventies, tall and regal, wearing a black ruffled skirt, red blouse, and black lace shawl. Her hair was up in a bun secured with a silver clip, and her olive skin was lined with years of passion and life, no doubt. She had on full makeup, her lips dark red.

Even if she devoted the rest of her life to flamenco, Nicole knew she could never move with the grace and soul of this woman. "It's lovely to meet you. I'm not sure a back row position in my high school production of *Pippin* qualifies me as a dancer. And *artist* is a strong word for my efforts in silversmithing."

Ava dramatically patted her hand on her heart. "Nonsense. I believe we are all dancers in here. Open yourself up to the movement and you will find the heart of flamenco. Same with art." Then Ava rested her hand on Nicole's chest. "You'll feel it here. Let yourself go."

Nicole was mesmerized by her touch. She could swear she felt an opening in her sternum, but was snapped back to reality when Ava added, "Marcos, can you warm her up and start with something very basic? I don't think she's ready for the twelve count we are working on. Start with the eight count. See how she does with that." And off Ava went to join her husband and run the real dancers through their warm-up.

"You duped me," Nicole accused Marcos with a dramatic flair. "Is this a trick? Did Billie Jo put you up to this?"

"No. I haven't danced in years, not since I discovered basketball in middle school. Which, at my height, you can see was a waste of effort." Marcos was stripped down to a black T-shirt, jeans, and real dance shoes that he'd pulled out of a bag. "It's my grandfather who really had the flamenco chops. He came here from Andalusia in Spain to work in the wine business. But, in here"—Marcos touched his heart with a smirk—"he was a *bailaor*, a flamenco dancer. My father didn't follow in his footsteps in terms of dancing, but once my mother caught wind of the Cabrera flamenco lineage, she forced my sisters and me to learn. Mind you, my mother is from Wisconsin. But she embraced all things New Mexican. And New Mexico is the flamenco capital of North America."

Nicole listened while stretching out her stiff joints. She looked around the room at the range of dancers in terms of age, size, shape, and coordination level. She put herself squarely in the middle in a couple of categories and that was enough for her. "Let's get to it. I'm going to show Miss Ava over there that I can master the eight count, whatever that is."

Marcos started slowly, clapping for eight and moving his hips four counts to the right and four counts to the left. It should have been easy, but the rhythm of the count had its own rhyme. It wasn't straightforward. There were nuances to the emphasis—Marcos looked smooth and commanding while demonstrating, but Nicole could barely coordinate her feet with her hands. She was humiliated. *Somehow, I'm worse at this than I am at silversmithing*, she thought.

"May I?" Marcos asked, standing behind her, his hands poised at her hips.

"Yes."

"Let's work on your steps first." He put his hands on her waist and moved his body closer to hers. He began to count slowly and softly as he pressed his hands into her hips to indicate what foot should move. "Right, two, three, four, left, six, seven, eight. Right, two, three, four, left, six, seven, eight." Nicole could feel his breath on her neck, and her hips loosened up with the gentle push and pull of his hands. Back and forth they went in sync until she could feel the rhythm and then something else entirely: desire.

"Now add your arms. May I?" he asked again before touching her shoulders.

Nicole was thinking that there was a lot to be said for this whole consent thing the younger generations practiced. The anticipation of his touch on her shoulders was tantalizing. "Yes."

"Keep moving your hips, three, four, add the arms, seven eight." He put light pressure on her arms to indicate which beats had emphasis. She was trying to stay focused on counting but was losing the battle. His presence was too much.

She stepped away and turned to him. "Let me try this on my own. I think I've got it."

"I think you do, too." His meaning was clear.

They both stood still, barely breathing, until Ava interrupted them. "Well done, Nicole. I think you are ready to join the group. You must start learning the dance for the show."

"The show?"

"Yes, didn't Marcos tell you? We are going to put on a flamenco show in December. We needed more bodies and here you are! You have much to learn!" Ava took Nicole's arm and led her toward the group. But not before she had a chance to look at Marcos, shake her head, and mouth, "Duped."

To: Jason
From: Nicole

Hi!

I loved your photos from this week. The color of the water at those glaciers. Does it sound too materialistic to say I'd like a pashmina in that color?

A couple of updates from Santa Fe. First of all, I love this dog. Second, I am back to working retail. Stop laughing, I can hear you from here. I've missed being on the floor of a store, even though this small, lovely jewelry and gift store is very different than Needham's. It's a collective that features pieces by Native American artisans. Officially, I'm working one day a week, but I'm there more often to help with special events, which happen every other day here. Two weeks ago, it was Octoberfiesta—hilarious, right?—and it's another excuse to have a citywide sidewalk art sale and margaritas. Next week, all the holiday-related promotional events start. It feels like I'm right back where I was pre-pandemic.

And finally, I'm taking flamenco. Watch out is all I'm saying. This could be my next career.

xo Nic

To: Nicole
From: Jason

Is this a dance-off challenge? Do I need to take tango lessons? I'll look into that.

Yes, the week at Parque Nacional los Glaciares was spectacular, worth the detour. I paired it with a reread of Jon Krakauer's *Into Thin Air*, which made the Irishmen superstitious and the Texans howl. We spent several nights at a sheep estancia and I can tell you, shepherding is not in my future.

We're off tomorrow for another long day. Will write in a week.

J.

Chapter 17

Puerto Guadal, Chile
November

The first time Jason slept with Abigail, it came as a surprise to him. A few weeks after The Look, as Jason had come to think of their charged exchange in the hotel hallway, the Australian showed up at his cabin door one afternoon on a rest day. They had ridden more than four hundred miles in the previous two days and now had a day off on the shores of Carrera Lake, a high mountain wonder with snowcapped mountain views. Some had opted to go fishing or boating, but Jason had opted to do nothing. He spent the morning on the cabin deck drinking coffee and reading a collection of Hemingway short stories he'd swiped from the last decent guest lodge they'd stayed in. He had plans for a nap to rest his battered body when he heard a knock on the door. It was Abigail and she asked, "Can I come in?" He said yes and that was that.

She was new and unfamiliar but not intimidating. He felt confident.

He had been dreading the guilt after she went back to her own cabin to prepare for dinner—the expectation of it so strong, he delayed his own urges for her for weeks—but there was none. By now in his journey in Patagonia, he felt so far disconnected from his family, his job, the normal activities of his life over the last decades, that sleeping with Abby was compartmentalized into this moment and this place. He guessed this was how men in war felt, tapping into his Inner Ernest, but he knew that he didn't deserve that kind of comparison. Motorcycling through the mountains on a luxury guided tour was hardly warfare. But it was an experience so removed from his previous life and so demanding physically and mentally that the release with Abby made sense.

And he was enjoying himself. My God, he was enjoying himself.

Abby proved to be the perfect partner for the Five Hundred Mile Rule, also living in the moment, not looking toward the future, only looking to devour this once-in-a-lifetime trip to the fullest. It wasn't every night, not even every night when they were in a decent guesthouse with real beds. But occasionally, after a satisfying day, they engaged in a satisfying night. She always came to his room and she always left afterward. In bed, she was open, generous, funny. Sometimes incredibly fast and, at other times, very deliberate. The next day, she could hop on her bike without a sideways glance at Jason and be one of the boys.

This seemed to be the elusive friends with benefits relationship that his millennial coworkers spoke about, but which his generation missed out on. Gen Xers usually took the drunken one-night stand with tortured interactions afterward route. The concept of mutually agreed upon sex followed by unembarrassed relations had never occurred to them. Indeed, he liked Abby as a friend and that came with some legit benefits. The arrangement suited them both and didn't seem to disturb the balance of the rest of the group.

Jason suspected a few of them guessed what was going on, like Ned the lawyer's wife, Connie, who sat herself down at their dinner table and started to ask a lot of questions about Jason's wife and children. No doubt she and Ned had been researching Jason online and digging up articles about him in *Publishers Weekly* and *The New York Times*. Certainly, there were photos of Nicole and him at various book events or charity dinners. It seemed that Connie had a mission. Her inquiry was pointed, as if to inform Abby that the person she suspected she was sleeping with had a family. But Jason didn't lose a beat filling Connie in on his family. Why should he? Abby was his wife's idea, after all.

Still, later that night, after they had had sex, Abby asked a few questions. "It's not my responsibility to care more about your marriage than you do, but what is the deal? Because you certainly sounded like a happily married man at dinner tonight."

"Wait, are you jealous?" Jason joked, because there was zero indication that anything that had happened between them was romantic. It was purely a matter of proximity and companionship.

"Of course not. I have no desire to be shackled to a man or the institution of marriage," she said, half-kidding, half-strident. "But I am curious."

"Okay, here goes. You're the only person I've told this to, but Nicole and I made a deal for this year and this year only," Jason said. He explained the sabbatical, the dinner with the neighbors, Nicole's decision, and eventually her suggestion that they take a break from all of it for the year, even their marriage vows. "It's like a hall pass with an expiration date."

"And then you go back to Portland and monogamy."

"That's the plan." He hadn't really thought about it in such stark terms, but she was right.

"Risky. I'm shocked," Abby said after he'd spilled all the details. "You seem a little too straitlaced for this sort of grand sexual experiment."

"Ouch, that hurts," Jason said, paranoid that this was a commentary on his sexual prowess. "I'll have you know that I was honored with a Visionary Award by Portland City Council."

"Impressive. But what I see is a successful publishing exec with a pretty wife, two kids, a historic home in Portland. Not exactly the profile of a risk-taker," she said, turning over on her side to look at him.

"How do you know what Nic looks like?"

"Look at you," Abby responded, reaching out to touch his face. "You're gorgeous, so of course she's pretty. I'm surprised you're here with me. Every night, there have been much younger, much lovelier women serving us dinner or hanging out at the bar who I'm sure would love to keep you company. Why me?"

"Well, you made the first move," he said with flair. "And we have some rules: no pregnancies and no diseases."

"And I look clean and barren?"

"Yes." They both laughed. "You still got it going on and you know that. Plus, I must say, the bisexual thing is kind of a turn-on." Abby had explained that she was into people, not labels. Her relationship with Amelia had been long and strong, fifteen years of love and support, but not formalized in marriage. Amelia's family was not supportive of her relationship with Abby—concerned about the damage to the children, as if her alcoholic ex-husband had been a dream parent—so there was some shame and pretending over the years.

For Abby, there had been others along the way, men and women, like there had always been. She described herself as an athlete and a physical person. Her family was proud of her medals but not of all her life choices and preferred to look the other way as well. Jason was fascinated by the fluidity.

"You straight white guys are pretty predictable in that area."

"Again with the dismissive comments," he said, disappointed in himself to be so predictable. "I have a tattoo, you know."

"So do I," she said, pointing out the Olympic rings on her left shoulder. *Touché.*

Jason changed his tone. "What did you think before tonight? That I was some shitty guy cheating on his wife?"

"I didn't care that much. I was only interested in having sex," she replied, getting up from the bed to put her joggers and camisole back on. "I suppose I imagined you were separated from your wife and this trip was your midlife crisis. Look around, isn't everyone in the group on some quest to recapture something? I know I am. But this sabbatical idea is quite brilliant. High stakes but low consequences. I'm honored now to be your first. I should be asking you what it feels like to be with somebody else not your wife."

"Exciting," Jason responded truthfully, watching her slip a fleece hoodie over her head and shake out her short hair. He didn't mention that it also made him think of Nicole more, not less. It made him wonder if she was with somebody else in the separate world she had created in Santa Fe. And that didn't make him jealous, it made him aroused. "It's new, after twenty-three years, this is all new. And that's stimulating."

"And then you'll return to the familiar. And that will feel new for a while, won't it?"

Again, he hadn't considered what sensations repatriation might bring. But Abby had. "I guess it will."

The conversation was over, as far as Abby was concerned. "What do you think we're having for breakfast?" she asked as she stood at the door, ready to go.

"Sushi." The answer had become their inside joke. In the land of lamb, beef, and potatoes, they had been served lamb, beef, and potatoes at every meal. They both craved something different.

"Good. I love sushi."

Chapter 18

Portland
March 2006

"Wow. You look amazing."

That was the reaction Nicole had been hoping for when she asked Katie in the better ready-to-wear department to help her find an outfit for the Stumptown Press party. With her expert eye and strong sense of accessories, Katie had talked her into a Ralph Lauren getup that was part wool, part suede, a touch of faux fur, and a statement belt that Nicole had been assured would be a classic one day, justifying the price, which even with the employee discount was too much. But having Jason acknowledge her made the expense seem worth it. "Thank you. Here's your suit," she said, hanging up the long black bag in his new office.

"I appreciate you getting it at the dry cleaner's. I lost track of time today. This party, the official move in on Monday . . . so many details." He stood up from his desk and crossed toward her, surprising her with a kiss, deep and lingering. Jason wasn't usually demonstrative in public, especially at work. They'd been at dozens of events together, from book signings to awards dinners, where his most intimate gesture was usually a quick squeeze of her hand. She hoped the handful of young women working for him took notice of how he greeted his wife. She'd waved to them all on the way in as they stood around and waited for the guests to arrive. *Are they watching now?* This kiss was new and old at the same time. Like he used to greet her, before marriage, kids, endless to-do list items that needed to be checked off every day. *He must be excited*, Nicole thought. *Like, really excited.*

Tonight was his night. The purchase of Stumptown Press was complete. The little publishing company that could was all his, after a decade of grinding away, creating a decent back catalogue of bestsellers in cooking, food, lifestyle, and nonfiction that celebrated the Pacific Northwest, Portland, and lifestyle trends that stretched beyond those borders. Jason had secured the bank financing to buy the company from Neil before some other, much bigger publishing entity swooped in and bought it out from under him. It was only after the deal was complete that Neil confessed that he'd floated the business in the early days with gobs of family money before Jason came along and pushed them into the bright lights. Neil thought this was a hilarious reveal, his secret fortune; Jason wanted to choke him, thinking of the years he'd worked night and day on a crappy salary in a crappy office with crappy resources to keep Stumptown afloat.

He was almost mad enough to tell Neil that he'd lowballed him and if he'd spent ten minutes doing any due diligence, he'd know that. But no need. Portland was small. The publishing world was smaller. Jason smiled, signed the contract, and shook Neil's hand. But he was damn glad that his former boss wasn't coming to the party tonight, too anxious to mix with strangers. Jason was in charge now.

His first order of business was to sign a new lease in a renovated building in the Pearl District, right around the corner from the loft apartment where he had lived a decade earlier when the area was beginning redevelopment from blocks of abandoned warehouses to a new district of luxury housing and sleek eating establishments. Jason called himself a Pearl pioneer, an early adapter. These days, the entire neighborhood was awash in creative energy and Jason wanted Stumptown to be a part of it.

The company had ten full-time employees, a full floor of open office space. It was light and bright with high ceilings, walls of glass, and exposed brick. Book posters for their cheeky line of city guides, *Don't Move to Portland: It's Terrible Here* and *Don't Move to Seattle: You'll Hate the Rain*, decorated the conference room. The community kitchen featured concrete countertops, stainless-steel appliances, craft beer in the fridge, and a professional-grade espresso machine gleaming on the counter. But it was the entrance that best defined Stumptown Press: a warm space built out to look and feel like a library with bookshelves, cozy chairs, and a fireplace projected on the wall. (Apparently, a real one was a fire hazard.) There was also another, smaller espresso maker because, after all, it was Portland.

Tonight, the office would be filled with the people who had gotten him here: friends, family, employees, his stable of talented freelance writers, designers, photographers, and illustrators. The chefs whose cookbooks garnered James Beard nominations. The memoirists who bared their souls and inspired others to do the same. Plus, luminaries in the Portland creative community who had encouraged him to act locally but think globally in terms of business.

And, of course, Nicole. Always Nicole. The one who plugged the holes at home while he spent his hours at Stumptown. The one who believed in him when his parents and family barely acknowledged his work. He studied her in her new outfit, one that made her look more like the wife of a successful man than a shopgirl who would sell to a successful man's wife. He liked that look on her because he finally felt successful on his own terms. Success was a full-body sensation.

"I'm gonna get changed. Look, I'm the boss. I have my own en suite bathroom. Do you want to . . . tie my tie?" he asked, using a goofy euphemism for sex as was his habit.

"Not in an office with glass walls." She liked the fact that he wrapped her in his arms again, a hand drifting down her backside, rubbing against the grain of the suede.

"How about later? After everyone's gone home." He pulled her tighter. He was excited.

So was she. "What's gotten into you?" She rubbed the back of his neck, arching her back a little more than she needed to.

"Success." He kissed her again, then stepped away. "It's going to be a great night."

"I believe a city is only as vibrant as its creative life. And we have a deep bench here in Portland. I look forward to decades of good work out of Stumptown and generations of creators to come in Portland. Thank you for being here. Cheers." Jason stood at the front of the room on a stage that had been brought in for the event, along with a sound system and a deejay. He was wrapping up his speech in which he'd thanked practically everyone in the room. His parents. His college friends. All his employees, past and present, by name. The barista at the Coffee People near his old office and the barista at the Coffee People near his new office. All the creatives who had worked with him on various projects, even future collaborators who might be in the room.

But he hadn't thanked Nicole.

She stood like an idiot, she would later think, expecting her husband to double back after the cheers and devote a minute or two to her, the support she'd given him over the years. But he didn't. He'd already stepped off the riser and into the waiting crowd, being greeted with backslaps, hugs, high fives. His eyes were shining from the adoration and the booze. The deejay fired up "Gold Digger," the ubiquitous hit of the year, which made the slight feel more intentional to her. The lights dimmed and the crowd was ready to party now that the business of the evening was over. They started to groove collectively, getting down as the refrain instructed. And still Nicole stood there, waiting for acknowledgment.

Suddenly, she felt eyes on her and turned to see a small circle of assistants looking her way. The same women that she hoped had seen her make-out session with Jason earlier were now witnessing her humiliation. She wasn't the only one to notice his omission.

She had to get out of here.

"Nic, where are you going?"

It was Jason, calling out the front door of the office to stop her. His tone was somewhere between concerned and annoyed. He walked toward her, more unsteady on his feet than she would have thought after his polished speech. "Are you okay?"

Nicole knew she had to make a quick decision: she could ignite a scene here, on the street, and ruin Jason's night while getting none of her own satisfaction. Or she could make an excuse for her sudden departure, then confront him tomorrow after her run when she was less angry and he was more sober. There was no doubt that earlier in their marriage she would have chosen the former, unable to stop herself from venting. Or worse, foretelling the issue by saying in a prim manner, "We can talk about it at home. I don't want to talk about it here." Punctuated by her storming off, of course.

But this time, she chose to wait and hold her fire for the morning. The highest of roads in a marital spat. She heard the voices of her friends Tessa and Jane in her ears. Tessa was a one-woman watchdog group against passive-aggressiveness, particularly in women. And Jane had a sister-in-law who ruined almost every family holiday with her faux indecision about where to go and what she wanted for dinner only to complain after the fact that she never wanted to go skiing or eat at the Thai restaurant. As the two of them extolled their grievances about this behavior on their runs, Nicole could see a lot of herself in their examples. She wasn't forthcoming about her preferences or desires. She pretended to be enjoying herself, only to whine about it later and hold Jason accountable for her misery. Her friendship with Tessa and Jane, both older, wiser, and way more confident than she could ever hope to be, opened her eyes to the more immature parts of her personality. She was actively trying to change her ways, or be more "aggressive-aggressive," as Jane put it.

But tonight, she went with "passive-passive." She knew if she told him now that he hadn't thanked her from the stage, he'd insist on going back inside, shutting down the music, and making an over-the-top declaration of love and support into the microphone, which would be both embarrassing to her and obvious to everyone else that he'd forgotten her in the first place. And they were both in their thirties, way too old to make a scene on the street. No, she'd feign illness and talk to him in the morning.

"I have one of my migraines. I took a pill, but I'd like to walk for a little bit. Then I'll call a cab," she said, having no intention of calling a cab. She wanted to pound out her frustration on the pavement as she walked toward home via Glisan Street, a straight shot from the Pearl District to her leafy northwest neighborhood. It was only nine, not too late to be on her own in that part of town. She felt safe in this neighborhood now. Then, she lied again. "I looked for you but the music and the lights were too much."

"Are you sure? I can drive you . . ." he said with zero enthusiasm.

"You shouldn't drive. I'll be fine. The fresh air feels good and the rain has stopped." Because there was no way she'd walk home in this suede skirt if it was raining. But a few miles in the cool evening to argue with herself and get her head straight was what she needed. "I'll talk to you in the morning. Promise me you'll take a cab."

He nodded. "I'll take a cab. Love you, Nic."

"Love you," she replied, turning her back on him and heading up the street, one step at a time.

Chapter 19

Santa Fe
November

"There's a lot of improvement here," Professor Roger said, standing over Nicole's shoulder in the studio and watching her wield the soldering torch on the inlaid bracelet that had bedeviled her for days. *What a relief*, thought Nicole, trying to take in the kind words and not screw up the task at hand. "Starting to see your intent."

After ten weeks of class, she finally felt like she was making some progress with skills. She was nowhere near the rest of her classmates in terms of craft. Tato, the son of a son of a son of a Zuni silversmith, was making pieces that were practically museum quality. Clancy had turned out three silver belt buckles with provocative feminist engravings that Gary, the rock drummer, bought and immediately resold to his friends, The Chicks. Even Brittany, the architecture student who'd never created a single piece of jewelry except on paper before showing up to class, had surpassed her in terms of assignments and competence. She was already making molds out of native plants and pressing beautiful rings that looked like tiny piñon leaves and cones. They were so detailed and charming that Raven had gushed, "Make as many of these as you can before the student show. You'll sell them all." Roger agreed.

But for Nicole, this was truly the first unsolicited positive comment from her teacher if she didn't count the nice email that she received from him for helping out his ex-girlfriend Holly. "You're working with a lot more confidence. Can you feel that?"

"I guess. Yes," Nicole replied, laying down the personal blowtorch she called Mr. Duplicity, after the cad immortalized in Alanis Morissette's "You Oughta Know," a song that she'd rediscovered since moving to Santa Fe after hearing the supermarket version in the frozen food aisle one day. It inspired her to buy a player and a box of used CDs at Big Star Books & Music. She'd spent a lot of quiet nights in her casita rolling through her pile of Angry Women of the Nineties albums from Alanis to Liz Phair to En Vogue, while updating her Poshmark site, two activities that made her incredibly satisfied. She guessed it was romanticizing her twenties combined with her current level of sexual frustration that made her nostalgic for the music of that decade.

She wished she felt that same level of satisfaction in the studio, like she was in the right place at the right time doing what she loved. There were fleeting moments when she was one with the process, in the zone, and other days when she felt like she wandered into the fantasy life. "Some days, I feel confident. Today is one of those days." She looked at the simple silver bangle with inlaid coral, denim and dark blue lapis, turquoise, and spiny oyster shell. She loved creating the mosaic of stones in a cobblestone pattern, choosing the colors and textures to work together. But it was the silversmithing part that led to hours of frustration. "Roger, I feel like I'm not very good at this. I'm not, am I?"

She spoke quietly so her classmates working on their own designs couldn't hear how discouraged she was. They were always so supportive in their critiques, but she could hear the pity in their voices, like they were talking to a third grader attempting tenth grade–level English, as if she were reading Dickens out loud without understanding most of the words. She wondered why she was doing this at all. Had she just wanted to avoid the trip to Patagonia and grasped at jewelry design as an excuse to step away from Jason and her responsibilities?

Her big idea, her new product line that looked fresh in Portland, was so underwhelming now that she had seen what good silverwork looked like in Santa Fe. On any day of the week, the work of the vendors who laid out their creations on blankets on the ground in front of the Palace of the Governors surpassed her concept by a mile. Seriously, hammered cuffs? Groundbreaking, as Miranda Priestly would scoff.

"I think you have a very good eye. You understand what you want to make, which is where some students wobble. This is a beautiful design with a complicated pattern and colors that really pop. But the inlay work is sloppy; it needs refinement," Roger said, pointing to her bracelet. "But you'll get there."

"Will I?"

Roger studied her a bit before answering, like he was taking stock of her mental fortitude. "Let's talk after class. Do you have time? I hear you're working multiple jobs these days. Like a real local. No one here has one job."

It was true. Between selling vintage clothes, working at the Zia Collective, and class, she had very few free days on her calendar. Cleo also asked her to consult on a few more nonprofit projects she steered, from website design to event planning, some for a modest fee, others volunteer. But she always kept her Tuesday nights free. The only obligations on her calendar were a walk for Bardot and dinner at home. "I have time. I'd appreciate your perspective."

Once the others in class had left—including Cleo, who had stopped by for the last hour to check in and comment on everybody else's work as she rarely did her own pieces—Roger indicated to Nicole to pull up a stool at his workspace. "What's on your mind?"

Nicole dove in, the gift of age. She never would have talked to her college professors in this way. "I'm contemplating not returning for the second semester. I'm not sure it's worth the money."

Roger looked surprised and slightly offended. "Ouch. I'm sorry you feel that way."

"Oh, no, you're not the issue. Or Raven. I'm the issue. I'm not sure I'm worth the money."

"I see. What about Raven's class? Has that been more satisfying?"

"Yes, because I'm good at that material. Raven's class is like the lunchtime brown-bag sessions we had at Needham's, learning about a specific product line. Except in this case, instead of Michael Kors or Betsey Johnson, it's the Egyptians, the Etruscans, and those Druids, whose work I love. I'm good at studying merchandise and then repeating back what I've learned. I don't want to miss next term's focus on Native American jewelry. After being here for a few months, I realize I'm pitifully undereducated about that piece of history. But your class is so much harder than I thought. I can't seem to relax into the work. I dread the hours in the studio and I don't see my own work headed toward a professional level. I don't know why I thought I'd be good at this."

Roger nodded. "I get it. I do. I thought I could paint and took two years off to explore abstract landscapes. I was terrible, like art-class-at-the-senior-center bad. I spent a fortune on oils and canvases. I exploited all my friendships here in town to try to get a gallery to show my work. People were kind but firm. I had no talent for painting. It was a dismal failure. And that's how I ended up teaching here! Steady salary and health insurance made up for my folly."

"So, you think I should drop the program?" Nicole asked, a little hurt that Roger had responded with his own story of failure instead of a rousing pep talk about her untapped potential. Even though she didn't grow up in the generation of participation trophies, she was hoping for a little more esteem-boosting from her teacher.

"I'm not sure what you think of as a professional level. Some people make a few earrings or simple bracelets and sell them at craft fairs and enjoy that experience. That's one definition of professional. If you envision yourself creating a line and then selling to Ortega's on the Plaza, I think you're a long way off. It could be years before your work is polished enough for that level of success. If ever. That's an honest assessment."

It was hard to take the truth from someone so handsome. Even in a posh British accent, it hurt. But she knew he was right. She hid her pain. "Are you saying that because you don't want the competition?"

He laughed. "That's it. Your skills scare me. I'm telling you this because you've asked. And you're a grown-up who should hear the truth. But from what I understand from Cleo, you've done amazing work with the Zia Collective. She said you've transformed the store. To quote her, 'The sales reflect the new energy.' I hear you've consulted on the website and been a huge help moving Billie Jo forward in retail. It seems like you are good at that. Don't undervalue how important the work you do is to the artists who create the jewelry. You can always commission artists to do the work you envision, you know. And Holly told me you've made her more money from what she called 'Mom's old crap' than she ever imagined. Those are some skills . . . in retail, if not silversmithing."

"I hadn't thought about it like that." She thought about her work at Zia as paying it forward, even though Cleo and Billie Jo had been effusive in their praise. And selling on Sincerely, Mimi had seemed more like a real estate play than retail. But then she thought about the other night at the casita, working with the music cranked, snapping photos, and writing cheeky copy for each item. That was a thousand times more fun than four hours in the studio trying to hammer her bangle into submission or achieve a symmetrical circle. "If I decided to drop the program, could I still take Raven's class second semester?"

Roger clutched his chest in mock horror. "I'm hurt again. But yes, you can take it as a nonmatriculating student. If that's the way you decide to go, then I understand. That said, with your experience, I'd be happy to work you into our curriculum somehow. We have a professional practices class for all students in the arts here and your retail and merchandising skills could be useful to advanced students trying to sell their work. You could guest lecture. Would you be interested in that?"

An exit ramp, a face-saving exit ramp. Maybe this was the payback for shipping his ex to Vermont without too much drama. "Can I think about it?"

"Of course."

It was dark outside the classroom, the November days getting shorter and colder, a liability to her walking lifestyle. She wouldn't mind the quiet time on the bus tonight, the dark enshrouding her as she listened to a podcast and turned off her brain for an hour. As she put on her hat and gloves to trudge to the bus stop, she thought about what was in her fridge for dinner. Eggs, onions, zucchini, frozen spinach, and wine. Enough for one. But first, poor little Bardot would need a walk after a longer stretch than usual inside.

Then a Range Rover pulled up next to her. It was Cleo. "Need a ride?"

"You waited?" Nicole was stunned. She'd been in with Roger for at least a half hour, but her friend had stuck around in solidarity. In the few months she'd known Cleo, Nicole had come to appreciate her powers of observation, how in tune she was to the vibe of any situation. Maybe that's why she'd been such a good actor and why she was now well respected in a community that was home to so many different points of view. Her emotional intelligence was inspiring.

"I had email to respond to," Cleo said. "Always email. Plus, that looked like a heavy conversation. Hop in."

"Thank you."

Cleo's car was warm and clean inside, as usual. For some reason, it smelled familiar, too. Nicole was transported back to the Needham's beauty counter of her youth. "Are you wearing Opium?"

"Yes! I'm trying to bring it back. I mean, professionally. I've been asked to do an ad campaign for them. 'Nostalgia meets now,' the agency said. I'd be paired with the 'Cleo Jones of Today,' according to the twenty-five-year-old who pitched me over Zoom. She didn't mention the name, but I'm intrigued. What do you think?"

"A chance to introduce yourself to the Sephora crowd. I love it."

"Do they sell it there?" Cleo said, wincing a bit as she swung the vehicle onto the highway, hitting the gas pedal.

"I'm afraid so. But power to the people, right? Opium for all! You can shape the hearts and minds of Gen Z. I say, go for it." The conversation took Nicole's mind off her dilemma, but Cleo wasn't having it. She hadn't waited in a cold, dark parking lot for nothing.

"So, what was that about?" she said, not overexplaining. They both knew what she meant. "If you want to talk about it."

"It was about me coming to terms with my creative limitations. And ego. And complete lack of skill in metalwork. You know, the usual." Nicole filled Cleo in on the details of the conversation, including Roger's brutal honesty about her professional chances. "At least he gave me credit for being a grown-up. If one of my kids had told me one of their professors had assessed them like this, I'd tell them to march back in that office and stand up for themselves. Don't be a quitter, I'd lecture. But, in my case, I think he's right. Why am I putting myself through this? This was supposed to be the year of me. I dread going to class."

"Is this about your husband?"

"No, I don't think so. Is it?"

"I don't know him. But I know I was competitive with my spouses. All of them! I didn't want to get behind them in terms of accomplishments. Are you trying to prove something to him?"

"I thought I was trying to prove something to myself. But maybe this is about Jason." Nicole thought about her husband, her partner who was off conquering the wilds of Patagonia, writing his novel, living out his fantasy life without a single complaint about the conditions in his emails. She wanted to be able to reunite with him in six months with her own story of triumph. Had she always been competitive with him? She didn't think so. She had put her career on hold, soldiered through many more parenting crises than he had, let him take the lead on so many occasions. But she felt like she held her own career-wise, after her time off to birth two children. She knew her kids were better off emotionally because of her, at least that's what she assumed simply because she was always at home when Jason was so often away. And even though Jason seemed to know everyone in Portland, her friendships were deeper, longer.

Oops, there it was. Death by comparison.

Nicole changed tack with an admission. "It never occurred to me that I might be mediocre at this."

"Anyone with a healthy self-image fails to realize their limitations on occasion. Not to diminish your creative talents, but jewelry making is an art form, not a craft. But it doesn't mean you can't learn from the process, even if the outcome isn't what you expected. Plus, look at what else you've done. The casita, the online store, Zia. This town is filled with midlife single women looking to reinvent themselves. They always spend the first year doing hot yoga and buying crystals before they get their act together. You've already accomplished something."

"Thank you," Nicole said, appreciative of Cleo's cheerleading, though the yoga-and-crystals route sounded appealing to her at this moment. She wished she had the self-care gene. "Roger said the same thing."

Cleo turned onto Nicole's street. Their relationship had progressed from parking lot drop-offs to front door delivery. The crunch of gravel under the tires sounded like home to Nicole now. In Santa

Fe, the better the address, the more likely the street would be un-paved. Cleo pulled into the driveway and put the Range Rover in park. "You don't have to decide anything right now. This isn't a test of your character. You have my permission to do what you want, including doing nothing at all. But I don't think that's how you're built. And please don't quit Zia before Christmas! We need you."

"I won't. I promise. I love working there. We have the big Holiday Open House this week! Thank you for the ride. And for listening." Nicole had the urge to reach over and hug Cleo, but she didn't. Cleo wasn't a hugger; she maintained a physical barrier even while being emotionally open. Still, Nicole was grateful for any attention Cleo gave her. She wasn't quite like the mother she never had, because Nicole suspected that Cleo's adult son was every bit as messed up about her three marriages as Nicole was about her mother's many men. But at least Cleo had gained wisdom; her own mother had only gained a second mortgage bailing her boyfriends out of debt. So instead of a hug, Nicole simply said, "See you Thursday."

Bardot greeted her like a conquering hero, then went and sat next to her dish, demanding dinner. Nicole complied. At least the dog thought she was doing a professional job at feeding and walking.

As she spooned out the dog's sweet potato and salmon "stew" into the handmade ceramic bowl she'd bought at the Saturday farmers market, Nicole thought about what Cleo had said. Was she competitive with Jason? Did she want to win the sabbatical? She knew the answer was no. And it was no because for their first few years together, she never thought she was in the same league as Jason. How could she compete with someone so much more polished than she was?

She'd been intimidated by his intelligence and education. She'd been insecure about her upbringing compared to his. She felt in-debted to him for choosing her when he could have had so many other women. It wasn't like he had rescued her in some Disney princess way, but being with him had opened her world. Still, she knew what she brought to the relationship: love and warmth and tenderness. That was new to him. He hadn't grown up in that kind of household. Jason's family seemed to keep a running scorecard on every family member. Wins and losses. Accomplishments and failures. But Nicole never graded his life choices. She was his biggest fan. Once he'd experienced that in an authentic manner, he was hers. As much as she was his.

"C'mon, noodle," she said to the dog after she finished dinner. "Let's go for a walk."

"I wish you would. But you never do." He tossed the noodles with butter and grabbed some salad greens from the fridge. She watched him work. It had been a long two years for him, too. After the high of buying Stumptown, the lows of having to lay off half his staff took it out of him. As bookstore after bookstore closed in the meltdown, small presses like Jason's struggled to hold on. He'd had a few titles keep him afloat, including a memoir about assisted suicide by a daughter who assisted her mother. It managed to be both emotionally gutting and uplifting. It somehow captured the mood of the nation and the attention of Oprah Winfrey. Jason hired back a few employees, foregoing any kind of bonus for himself. With Nicole back at work full-time and then some, they were making ends meet, no room for extravagance. "Lounging in bed is a free activity. We can cover that."

"Serta Island! Another exotic vacation!" Nicole said, adding to a running joke they'd had over the last two years, as they cut back on everything from childcare to meat consumption to summer camps to travel. They'd take everyday activities and turn them into vacations: Mt. Laundry; Getting Gas & Spa; Côte de Starbucks.

"We'll turn the heat up and I'll make you a mai tai. It will be just like Hawaii."

She wished. She was bone-tired. "Should I summon the kids?" On cue, they came running into the kitchen.

"Mom's home! Mom's home!" Jack chanted, jumping up on the couch. It was on its last legs, having served the family well through the toddler and early elementary years. Any day now, the springs would bust through and the last of the decorative buttons would pop off and they'd be forced to retire Couch-y, as they called the blue-and-white-striped behemoth. But right now, even with her discount, they couldn't afford a new one. "Dad said we can play charades after dinner. I get to go first." Going first was Jack's only life goal, no matter what the activity. Playing charades, taking a bath, picking a show to watch. As long as he was first, he was happy. And Chelsea was a complete pushover. She'd take second any day of the week.

Chapter 20

"You're home," Jason announced, as if he had delivered her from work himself, instead of holding down the fort on New Year's Day. She'd worked twelve hours while he entertained kids, packed away the Christmas decorations, dragged the tree out to the curb for recycling, and made a Crock-Pot stew that might not win any culinary awards, but smelled delicious. He was in the kitchen draining egg noodles and listening to St. Vincent. The children were nowhere to be seen. "Shhh. Keep your voice down. You'll alert the monsters to your presence."

It was a cold, dark, rainy night in Portland, typical weather for this time of year, and Nicole was grateful to be home and facing three days off in a row. It had been a grueling holiday season, but better than the previous two in the middle of the global financial crisis. Sales were up but staffing remained at the bare minimum, so the employees on the job were doing long shifts and multiple tasks. She'd worked her share of overtime and had the paychecks and the tired legs to show for it.

"How was work?" he asked, handing her a glass of red wine, giving her a peck and a quick back rub. "You look tired."

"I am. A lot of schlepping today. I also took down the holiday decor and packed it away for next year. Tomorrow, I'm staying in bed and doing nothing."

"What did you guys do today?" Nicole asked, hoping for the short version so she could go change out of her work clothes into fleece anything.

"Dad let us watch movies all day. Have you ever seen *Beverly Hills Chihuahua*? It is so funny," Jack insisted in a volume five times louder than it had to be. Chelsea proceeded to give a recap of the movie that might have been longer than the movie itself. The entire time, Jason kept shaking his head saying that it wasn't all day long. They had walked the dog before the rain started.

And then for no reason, Jack punched Chelsea in the arm because, according to the Wolfpack, he was nearly ten and that's when the hitting, tackling, and endless physicality of boy puberty started. Sarah, whose kids were a few years ahead of the others, summed up the middle school years by saying, "Girls cry and boys beat the shit out of each other. For, like, three years straight."

Chelsea hit back, or at least attempted to. She was no match for her brother, who wanted a brawl with an easy target. Chelsea grabbed Nicole and hid behind her while Jack tried to reach around and land a blow.

Nicole was about to lose it. Just once she'd like to walk in from work and not have to referee her children. But before she could verbalize anything, Jason stepped in. "Okay, okay, okay. Jack, there was no need to hit your sister. I'm going to get you a punching bag and hang it up in the basement downstairs. And you can hit that all day long. Should we do that tomorrow?" Jack nodded. "Now say you're sorry to Chelsea. Chelsea, let go of your mother. She's going to go change out of her work clothes and she'll be back when she's ready. Do not touch your mother as she walks out of the room. No touching. Let her leave. Who wants to set the table? Chelsea? Jack, you'll clear the dishes."

Nicole held her glass of wine steady and mouthed a thank-you to Jason. She needed ten minutes to herself, maybe twenty. Long day, long week. Jason always joked, "Reentry is hard."

———

By nine, the kitchen was clean, the charades were finished, and Nicole had put the kids to bed. Well, she had put them in their bedrooms, anyway. Jack would stay up and read; Chelsea would play with her dolls quietly until she went to sleep. If there was a parenting prize for Best at Establishing a Bedtime Routine, Nicole and Jason would be in line to win. The two embraced a set regimen when Jack was a baby and rarely allowed exceptions. Nicole and Jason were too tired at the end of the day for exceptions. And they needed at least one hour of adult time. What they had come to discover was that Jack and Chelsea needed their own space, too. The hour had changed over the years, but not the routine. For the weekends, it was in bed at nine and lights out by ten. But Nicole imagined that Jack's hours would be changing soon, based on the energy he displayed tonight. She was not looking forward to middle school.

Jason had moved into the living room, where the couch had all its buttons and the fire was lit. He was resting his head on the back of the couch, minutes, maybe seconds from sleep, when Nicole came into the room, nearly empty wine bottle in hand. "Do you want a splash more?"

"No. You finish it."

She poured the rest in her glass and curled up next to her husband. The wind had picked up and she could hear the rain against the windows. She reached for the blanket on the arm of the couch and wrapped it around them. "Thank you for dinner."

"My pleasure. I should cook more, shouldn't I?"

"Feel free."

"Huge Saturday night. Will we make it to ten?"

"You know there are people our age who still go out to party on Saturday nights. Half the makeup department is older than thirty-five and they were using all the free samples to get glammed up for a night on the town. And they went out on New Year's Eve. Two nights in a row."

"We could go dancing if we wanted. Right now. I know we could rally. Like it's 1994, baby. The point is that we choose not to go dancing. This is the hottest spot in Portland," he said, squeezing her tighter and kissing the top of her head. "No place I'd rather be."

"Me either." And she closed her eyes.

Chapter 21

The doorbell set off Bardot's bark. Nicole had gotten more visitors here in a few months in Santa Fe than she'd had in years in Portland. There seemed to be some sort of drop-in culture here, as if residents had no idea that texting first was common in other parts of the country. Clancy would drop by with extra firewood she had chopped. Cleo would drop by with books or other reading material she thought Nicole might be interested in, never coming in but standing on the porch for a good half hour talking. Her neighbors, Albert and Peter, determined to expand her palate and crank up her heat tolerance, stopped by before dinner with individual portions of chipotle marinade, red chile croutons, or poblano crema for her to add to a chicken breast or salad. But an evening drop-by was unusual, so she called through the door, "Who is it?"

"Marcos."

Her face flushed. She blew out a deep breath and opened the door. Bardot and Marcos had formed a bond, thanks to Sundays at the shop. The dog stopped her barking and started wagging her tail, greeting Marcos as if it had been years, not days.

"Somebody's happy to see me. Is this a bad time? I'm sorry, I should have called. I was in the neighborhood dropping off a couple of cases of white for a good client and had these in my truck. I thought you might want them." Marcos held out a black silk bag. Nicole opened the gift and pulled out a pair of dance shoes, made from soft black leather with a buckled strap in what looked to be about her size. They weren't new, but they were barely used, and they were gorgeous.

"Please don't tell me these were your ex-wife's. That would be too creepy." After a few weeks of dance lessons coupled with beers and paella after class, Nicole and Marcos had reached the point where they knew enough about each other to make jokes. She knew, for instance, that Marcos had spent his twenties and early thirties traveling the world working in wineries, restaurants, and hotels, including a long stint at his family's ancestral home in O Rosal, Spain. When he returned home to New Mexico, he married Missy, a transplant from San Diego who'd done her own world tour working in entertainment on cruise ships. Five years later, she was pregnant with his cousin's baby. Yes, his cousin Mateo, who was the winemaker at the family vineyard and married with two of his own children, had taken up with Marcos's wife.

The scandal was shocking and messy, but mostly humiliating. He'd spent nine months thinking he was going to be a father only to find out after the baby's birth that he was only a second cousin. Or a cousin once removed. Whatever the term was for the child of your cousin. Marcos didn't bother to google it after the two of them admitted to their affair and the subsequent blood test proved that he couldn't be the father. Whatever he was to the baby, he wasn't Daddy.

He moved out of the cottage on his family compound in Dixon, forty-five miles north of Santa Fe, and set up house in town to get as far away from the happy couple as he could manage and still do the marketing for the winery. Mateo left his wife and kids and shacked up (at least that's what his tia Clemencia called it) with Missy and the baby, Harmony. ("Harmony! She named the baby Harmony!" howled his tia when the truth came out.) Initially, interaction among the three adults was excruciating, but increasingly Marcos began to believe he'd dodged a bullet. Nothing was too good for Harmony, and by extension, her mother, Missy. (Even his own mother, not a fan of his ex-wife but taking the high road for the sake of the family name, had said, "Mama Missy is really a piece of work. It's a baby, not the next Queen of England.") Marcos wouldn't want to be in Mateo's shoes. But that didn't mean he still didn't want to smack him sometimes.

Marcos told all this to Nicole with punch lines and a well-rehearsed lightness, but it was clear that the betrayal still hurt. "No, the shoes belong to a neighbor of mine. She bought them, took one class, and decided pickleball was more her speed. She's donating them to a good cause."

"Me? I'm the cause? What did you tell her?" Nicole said, moving around her tidy kitchen, pouring Marcos a beer and putting out some roasted nuts for him. She'd been warming them to toss on her salad, a rare act of effort on the part of her dinner for one. She was nervous having him in her home like this, but she hoped it didn't show.

Marcos took a sip of beer and a handful of nuts. "I told her you had potential but not in those Nikes. I took a chance on the size. They looked about right."

This thought flashed across her mind: *Would Jason know my shoe size?*

"Thank you. These are the real deal, much better than the ones I was going to order from Discount Dance," she said, finding the 7.5 printed on the inside of the shoes. "The size is close enough. Can I pay her for these? I believe in resale."

"Nini's family owns a gold mine. Literally. She's in the condo because her four-million-dollar house on Museum Hill is being re-modeled for the next year. We went to high school together, so I know a pair of shoes won't break the bank."

"It seems like you went to high school with half the city." Marcos had already explained that he and Holly, owner of the casita, had gone to the rarest of institutions: a public boarding school called New Mexico Prep, meant to attract students from all over the state, especially rural areas and reservations. It was in Santa Fe and shared facilities with St. John's University, a school where students studied the Great Books and only the Great Books. Prep was small, quirky, and ended up being more like a refuge for wealthy parents to park their teenagers while they traveled, like Holly's mom. Marcos, of modest means and agrarian roots, was the exception, not the rule. His mother, who had grown up on a dairy farm in Wisconsin, had wanted him to experience a life away from morning and afternoon chores. He loved the experience; it was challenging and eye-opening for a kid from a farm. Plus, the four years had led to deep, loyal friendships that had lasted decades.

"Nini changes passions, as she calls her hobbies, about every three months. Next, she'll be off pickleball and on to infrared saunas. She was happy to pass these on to relieve her white privilege. At least that's what she told me." He took another swig from the beer, taking in the casita for the first time.

Nicole had gotten home from class late. No Cleo in class today, and the bus ride lasted forever. She spent the time thinking about the expensive salmon and single baked potato she had at home. After two months of eating leftovers or cottage cheese and salsa, she recommitted to a hot meal at the end of the day. She'd even signed up for a few cooking classes at Santa Fe Cooking School so she could get her chiles straight. Tonight, though, she was going full Pac Northwest in her menu choices. She popped the potato in the oven as soon as she got home, the fish a few minutes ago.

After walking the dog, she changed into the black fleece jumpsuit she'd lived in since the weather turned colder. Her contacts were out and her glasses were on. She'd swiped colored lip balm on, because there was never enough moisture in the air here. She lit a fire and some candles—the light bounced off the textured walls and made her home look like a shelter magazine cover shot. She poured herself a glass of red and another glass of water, her hydration secret. A music mix she made called Sad Girls, Bad Boys was streaming from her speakers, a Townes Van Zandt song playing. The house looked warm and smelled delicious. The whole scene looked like something sexier and more complicated might happen later.

Marcos turned to her as a light dawned. "Oh. You must be expecting someone. I'm sorry, I didn't mean to intrude."

"Oh, no worries. Believe me, there's no one coming. The house is so beautiful at night. Even if it's only me, I light the fire. And I can't let these plastered walls go to waste. I'm burning candles at a furious rate. Please stay," she said as she reached out and put her hand on his arm. There was a spark of something. She'd felt the same heat last Sunday when they touched briefly during their flamenco lesson. It had unnerved her then and now.

She recovered enough to say, "Have you had dinner? I have salmon and a baked potato in the oven. I can make a salad. If, you know, that qualifies as dinner to you." She opened the fridge and started taking out vegetables to prove to him that she had enough food. Barely, but she could squeeze something out of cucumbers, radishes, and a bunch of celery.

"Are you sure? I'm sure there's an end seat at a bar where I can get dinner. I like to call it the Divorced Guy Special," he said, taking a seat at the kitchen island.

"I bet you have every server in town twisted around your little finger."

"I do okay on the free appetizers." He leaned in to watch her wash the celery like it was the most erotic thing he had witnessed in a while. Maybe it was. Though she had a hard time imagining him having trouble finding a date. Still, it was the closest they'd come to flirting since that first night on the dance floor. Marcos must have sensed it. He pulled back a bit. "I would love to stay for dinner. But first, what's the deal with your husband?"

There it was. The question she'd been dreading now out in the open with no hesitation. She had to admire this younger generation's no bullshit tolerance.

She wrapped the wet celery in a paper towel. "He's in Patagonia."

"I know that. You've told me. Billie Jo's told me. Clancy reminded me of that fact at the bar last week. It sounds like a fake place to me, even though I know it's real. Like it's code for something. Maybe he's in rehab or special forces. I guess what I really mean is, why are you in Santa Fe when he is in Patagonia?"

She put up her finger to indicate she needed a moment. She pulled the fish out of the oven; this conversation would take a while. Deep breath. "We have an arrangement," she said, hoping that sounded both sophisticated and humble, if that was a possible combination. And she proceeded to tell him the terms of the deal, at least most of the terms. She left out the caveat about falling in love. It seemed too juvenile to mention. The Five Hundred Mile Rule was about physical needs, not emotional ones. "It's a sabbatical, not a separation."

"That's very European of you both," he said, which made her laugh. "Well, northern European, like the kind of arrangement the German or the Swedes would work out. Uncomplicated, efficient with an end date. And I say that as someone who has spent a third of his life in Europe. My people are too passionate to be so pragmatic."

"Thank you?" she said, starting to chop the vegetables, wanting the conversation to end. It was one thing to tell Tessa or Cleo, women who would understand the pressures of being someone's wife and partner every damn day, about her need to let go of that definition of herself for a year. They were women who had their own arrangements. They could commiserate without consequences. But with Marcos, the truth could be an invitation. Was she ready for that?

"And how is it working out?" This was very intimate territory and Marcos spoke softly, his tone curious, his eyes mischievous.

Nicole hesitated, then answered honestly, because there was no reason not to. A line had been crossed between the two of them and she didn't want to go back. She was ready, after all. The life she had created here seemed to be all her own. She got to make the rules. "I haven't tested it out yet. I don't know if I will."

"Why not?"

"I'm scared."

"Of what?"

She stopped chopping and put down the knife. She took in Marcos, sitting at the quartz island in her warm kitchen in a blue jean shirt with a wool scarf casually hung around his neck; his down jacket hung over the back of the chair. The beer, the roasted nuts, his smile. He unnerved her. Made her ache. "I'm scared of enjoying it too much. Now, I have a question for you."

"Okay . . . ?" he said, not sure where this was leading.

"How old are you?"

He burst out laughing. "I thought it was going to be a lot more complex than that! I'm thirty-eight. Is that old enough for you?"

"Yes." Nine years' difference was nothing, hardly cradle-robbing. She moved toward him as he stood and reached for her. It was spontaneous and mutual. There was a slight hesitation before their lips met, so she could stroke his beard and breathe him in. He ran his hand through her hair and said, "Are you sure?"

And she responded, "Are you sure?"

Then there was no hesitation. A bolt ran through Nicole. It had been a long time since a kiss made her feel like this, like a fire was spreading through her body. Marcos ran his hands across her shoulders, down her arms, and rested them on her hips. She found the back of his neck with her hands and pulled him closer. His mouth felt amazing. He seemed to feel the same way about her mouth, increasing the pressure, moving his hands down her body. There was no letup until Marcos pulled away. He brushed the hair out of her eyes and smiled at her.

"Are we stopping?" she asked.

"I think we should," he said.

"It's not too high school to stop at a make-out session?"

"It may be the height of maturity. This may be the most responsible thing I've ever done," he answered. They stood facing each other, somehow holding hands. There was no awkwardness between the two. Just the vestiges of heat.

My God, he is handsome, Nicole thought. "Marcos, I want you to understand that I'm not available to you except in a physical sense. I know you've been through a lot recently in terms of infidelity and betrayal. I don't want to lead you on. I may not be the best option for you right now."

"To be clear, we're talking about the fact that you're only open to sleeping with me, but not being with me."

"Yes."

"You understand that is the situation that most men dream of." They both laughed.

"I can see why. It feels pretty powerful to lay down the parameters like that," Nicole answered with a bit of a swagger. Age and experience had some benefits.

"Do you want to think about it?"

"You tell me. You're single. You're a man. I haven't been in this position in twenty-five years. Should I think about it? I feel like the whole point of the Five Hundred Mile Rule was to not think about it."

"Normally, I would say no. But you seem like a very thoughtful person. So yes, think about it. But understand that I volunteer as tribute if you decide to go for it."

She was grateful for the reprieve. She did need to think about it. "Thank you. I need some time. But I have registered your offer." She pulled the baked potato out of the oven, grateful for the distraction of dinner prep. "Do you still want to stay? For dinner, I mean?"

"I think I better find a seat at the end of a bar somewhere. Because, while I respect your desire to think about it, I have very different desires right now." He kissed her one more time. She almost changed her mind. "See you Sunday."

Chapter 22

Tierra del Fuego
December

"Salud!" The cry went up and the intrepid bikers of Team TDF, as they had come to call themselves over the ten-week trip, raised their glasses and drank. Some riders had come and gone, some staying only a few weeks by choice, others, like the lawyer from Chicago and his wife, calling it quits because of weather or wind or, as Tommy the Irishman said, "an overwhelming case of wuss." Tommy's Irish counterpart, Danny, was airlifted from an estancia in Argentina because of an overwhelming case of gout, but Mick, Danny's brother, ensured no jokes were made about his departure or the booze and beef that had probably caused the attack. A few rolled off before the Tierra del Fuego portion began, headed back to their lives as bankers or contractors. The small tribe that had remained for the entirety of the sixty-seven days was now a tight group—the Texans, Tommy, Mick, Rico, Jonesy, Abigail, and Jason. And the celebration for their last night together was well underway in what constituted a luxury hotel in this part of the world—the end of it: a seventy-two-dollar-a-night lodge with a small bar where they held their dinner.

Guillermo, the guide who had been with them for the entire trip, was leading the charge on the drinking front, finally able to cut loose because his work was done. But the others weren't far behind. Jason was pacing himself, taking in the moment and thinking about tomorrow. Most of the conversation had turned to logistics, who was flying where and when. Some were headed home; others, like Abby, were on an extended world tour. She was slowly making her way to Tortola in the British Virgin Islands by the first of January. Her plan was to work at a resort managed by an Australian friend for the winter season, maybe longer. She was in no hurry to return to Perth, with Amelia gone and the lodge sold. "I'm not really sure where home is anymore," she explained to Jason the other day as they soaked in a hot tub looking out over the Chilean fjords.

The next few weeks, before he headed to Nicaragua, was the part of the trip that Jason had wanted to play by ear, improvise on the spot. But a month ago, he started making his plans. He had a book idea—not a novel, but a combination wine, cooking, and travel book about Argentina. He hadn't drunk his weight in Malbec without thinking about how to capture the spirit of the place. But first, he needed to spend time in the Uco Valley, the so-called "Napa Valley of Argentina." He booked himself into a guesthouse in the heart of the wine-producing region, hoping to find inspiration. But before that, he needed solitude.

Unlike the rest of Team TDF, he wasn't flying out of Puerto Natales to Santiago and then points north tomorrow. He was headed to Weskar Lodge, an isolated hotel about twenty miles away. His room had a bed, a desk, and a view of the sea. Maybe he'd venture out to the caves nearby, but more likely, he'd sit on the porch, have a beer, and stare at the water. He needed to rest, decompress from the physicality of the trip, and process.

So much to process: the accomplishment of the ride, the loss of his friend Charlie, the fucking awesomeness of the natural world, his inability to write a single word of fiction the entire trip, the state of his marriage, the state of his career, and Abby. He needed to process Abby.

She had been the companion he needed on this journey, even though he hated to admit it. Nicole never would have made it and they would have ended up sniping at each other and eventually abandoning the tour like the Chicago lawyer and his wife. He missed Nic but was grateful she had bailed. He had to make that clear to her when he saw her. She needed to know that her absence was a gift to him.

But what did he need to tell Abby before she left in the morning? That she was easy, in all the right ways. That she had a sense of adventure, stamina, and the same attitude toward sex that he had, using it like she would use a sleeping pill or a massage, to wind down after a long day. Should he tell her that he appreciated that she could be as selfish as he could in the bedroom, focused on her own needs first, and that was such a turn-on? But then she could engage with playfulness and generosity to service him, which also turned him on. Jesus, he would miss her. He knew he had to say goodbye to her, because the longer their after-hours relationship went on, the harder it would be to stay neutral about her.

"Hey, Book Guy, you're up," Abby called from across the bar, knocking him back to the present moment. It was his turn to toast and Jason being Jason wasn't going to let it go by with a simple raised glass. He'd prepared notes. "Thank you, my fellow riders. Thank you, Guillermo and Paco. We owe you everything and I'm guessing that's what you're expecting in these envelopes you slipped under our doors this afternoon." Jason flashed the envelope as a prop while cheers went up. "More than four thousand miles and almost as many bathroom breaks for Jonesy! What an adventure. We experienced joy and danger and mud and so much dirt. We endured wind and rain and wind and wind and wind. Rota 7! Rota 40! The Straits of Magellan! We've seen mountains, volcanoes, rivers, rainforests, glaciers, penguins, and, God damn if we didn't see the moonrise over the fjords. Oh, wait, that was Tommy's ass when he was taking a dip." The crowd roared. "We laughed, the Irishmen cried, we drank a shit ton, and got on our bikes the next day like we were the champions of drinking. Abby took us for all the pennies in poker. The Texans sang more Garth Brooks than we wanted. And let's all be thankful that Rico is a medic or most of us would have died of that flesh-eating bacteria thanks to the blisters, burns, and cuts. But look at us! We made it to the end of the earth. To the end of the earth. To quote Shackleton: *Fortitudine vincimus.* By endurance we conquer. Salud!"

"Salud!" The glasses went up and the drink went down and to Jason's surprise, he found himself more emotional than he imagined because he had done it. He had made it to the end of the earth. Alone.

Just then, the opening organ strains of "Where the Streets Have No Name" rose above the chatter. By the time the signature guitar arpeggio kicked in, everyone in the room was riveted to the screen, where Mick the Irishman had put together a slide show with some shockingly decent photos of the trip. Who knew he could shoot like that? And edit? The U2 music choice was a little obvious to Jason, but he forgave him because everything he had mentioned in his toast was on the screen—the road, the scenery, the characters, the camaraderie, the penguins, the dirt. And then a shot popped up of Abby and him, leaning up against their BMW bikes at the end of a day, helmets off, sweaty and dirty, heads thrown back in laughter. It looked like they'd been together forever.

He smiled at her across the room. She smiled back. Yes, he had to say goodbye to her.

Abby hadn't come to Jason's room last night. They were both a little drunk at the end of the celebration, so it was for the best. And typical of her to exit without ceremony. He was about to drag himself out of bed for a shower and coffee so he could say goodbye to her in the lobby when his phone pinged. It was a text from her: *I'm off.* Followed by another text with her mailing address in Perth, with the note: *In case you ever find yourself in Australia. Cheers, A*

And that was it.

He stared at his phone for a long time, then replied: *Safe travels*.

His mind wandered to her broad shoulders, her long legs, the way she moved her hips, the way she caressed his earlobes. He looked back at the contact information she had sent and deleted the thread.

Then he deleted her number.

Chapter 23

Santa Fe
December

Marcos popped his head in the store. "You ready? We don't want to be late. Showtime!" Tonight was the winter performance, the culmination of eight weeks of Sunday night flamenco lessons and countless hours taking Zoom classes to catch up to the more experienced dancers. Or at least trying to get a handle on the choreography so she didn't look like a fool. Marcos, on the other hand, rated a solo and a featured spot in several other numbers, thanks to his childhood dance experience. But whatever her role, Nicole couldn't believe she was performing in public for the first time since an East Corvallis High production of *Pippin*.

She looked at her watch. It was a few minutes before five. After a day of brisk sales, she'd been so busy restocking the beaded dog collars, a store bestseller, that she hadn't noticed the time. The shop had been quiet for the last hour, most tourists headed home by now on a dark winter Sunday, so she justified closing a bit early. "Can you give me a few minutes? I have to reconcile the books."

"Want me to take Bardot around the block?" The dog and the man had formed a fast bond. It was like Bardot knew that her reward for walking the mile and a half to Zia in the morning and being a good girl in the shop was a walk with her favorite wine guy at the end of the day. He also carried smoked salmon dog treats that made Bardot his friend for life, but seemed like cheating to Nicole.

The ultimate capper for Bardot came when she got to ride home in Marcos's truck. She leaped into the front seat like she had worked on a ranch in another life. Bardot didn't get in on the flamenco and paella later in the evening, but she didn't seem to mind. Marcos grabbed the leash and a bag from behind the counter. "We'll be back."

Nicole watched the pair stroll out the door. She locked it behind them. For a second, she thought of what her life would be like if this were her life. Her real life, not the pretend one she'd been playing at since September. In her mind, she and Marcos created this Sunday routine that they would keep for years: working, dancing, dining, desire. Her casita would become their casita. His work would coexist with her work. Their mutual friends would become their couple friends. In this make-believe life, Chelsea and Jack would become visitors. The Wolfpack would be relegated to occasional texts and annual holiday cards. And there was certainly no spot for Jason.

This was the easy part right now, a tight, seamless circle of Marcos and Nicole and Bardot, rotating around one another with care and anticipation. But would Marcos be so thoughtful after twenty-something years of marriage? Would she still find herself getting flushed imagining his touch? Would they be taking flamenco lessons and exchanging glances? Or would the two of them hit the same wall of indifference that she and Jason had crashed into and end up in the same place, thousands of miles apart?

She had to focus. Her attraction to Marcos had crept into her thoughts more than she wished during the two weeks since their kiss at the casita. She was ashamed to have fallen into the cliché of feeling like a teenager with her first crush again. (If her first crush had been a smoking hot winemaker in the perfect jeans and a Pendleton jacket.) It was the stuff of tell-all essays in the down-market women's magazines she read at the nail salon. She wished she could be cool and distant, brushing off the kiss with a sophisticated shrug. But, instead, she was like a sophomore doodling his initials on her notebook in class. She knew it was foolish, her infatuation, but she hadn't been foolish in decades and it felt electric.

She felt like she needed a clear head to get through tonight, their last flamenco and paella of the year. With the holidays bearing down on Santa Fe and the tourist count mounting every day until Christmas arrived, the locals ceded their haunts to the folks with bigger wallets and bigger tips for the sake of the common good. Every place in town needed a lucrative December to make it through the cold and quiet of January and February. El Farol would be hosting the professionals and their dinner show most nights for the next month, charging a hefty prix fixe dinner price with a ticket fee on top. As they should. It meant the professionals took over and the amateurs took a break.

Tonight would be the last chance for Nicole and Marcos to be together on the floor for a while. They'd been rehearsing the group choreography for the last three weeks with the intensity of an approaching Broadway opening instead of an amateur talent show in front of a bunch of buzzed waiters, shopkeepers, and artists. When she wasn't thinking of Marcos, she was running through the choreography in her head. Or watching the video their teacher Ava had posted so she could rehearse in her living room. She was ready.

She went over the day's tally one more time, marveling over how much easier keeping the register was nowadays with software to do all the work versus the time-consuming counting and shuffling of cash and receipts in her early years of retail. The East Corvallis Mall Era, as she thought of it. She'd come a long way and yet, she was as nervous about tonight as about any high school theater performance. Maybe it wasn't only the dancing she was nervous about. Maybe the nerves had more to do with what might happen afterward.

There was a tap on the door. Marcos and Bardot had returned. She unlocked the door to let them in. "Let me get my bag. Guard the door! No more customers! We had an unbelievable day today. My personal best."

"This calls for some dancing. Are you ready to baile, my baila-ora?" Marcos said, using the proper flamenco terms.

"Sí, sí! Vamaños! Let us discover the heart of flamenco!"

They only had a few minutes to change at the casita before they had to leave for the restaurant to warm up. Ava had told them to wear black or red or some combination of the two so their ragtag band of dancers had a cohesive look. Knowing the timing would be tight, Nicole had laid out her outfit before work in the morning. She quickly slipped into the competition dress she had found on Etsy for a steal—a fitted black number with a deep V in the back, bohemian bell sleeves with white ruffles, and white roses embroidered around the neckline and down the back. The skirt fanned out in layers of ruffles, as it should to emphasize the movement. Her dancing didn't deserve a dress like this, but she bought it anyway. She checked herself in the mirror and wondered why she hadn't taken up flamenco years ago? The cut of the dress made the most of what her mother-in-law would call "her figure." Between the walking, the standing in the studio and shop, and the dancing, she sloughed off the sourdough ten she'd gained during the pandemic. She felt like a million bucks.

She slicked her hair back, pinned a white rose clip behind her ear (another Etsy score), and did a quick makeup job finishing with the same Chanel Rouge Allure lipstick she'd been buying since 1994. She spritzed on some Opium, her homage to Cleo, from a vintage bottle she'd found at a resale store in town. ("If properly stored, perfume doesn't spoil or fade. Old perfume was created to last. I buy some classic scents at garage sales that scream Grandma. Nothing beats the old bottles," Bette in the perfume department at Needham's once told her.) One more mirror check. One foot in her twenties and one foot in her forties.

For one flash, she wished Jason could see her now. It had been a long time since she'd been pushed to a physical and mental edge and this flamenco dancing had done it. She felt alive. Now she understood his email, about how he had felt making it to Tierra del Fuego, crossing into a territory so few had ventured. He had that accomplishment, but she had this. Less death-defying but every bit as thrilling to her.

She stepped into the living room and met Marcos's eyes. He was in all black, no frills. It suited him. He was staring at her in a way that made his desires clear. She started speaking to cut the tension, using a phrase she felt was the stupidest in the English language: "You clean up well."

"You look . . . amazing. That dress . . ."

"I'm hoping it distracts the audience from my missteps," she said, aware of his gaze. "And wait until you see my glorious fan. It can hide my entire face if I'm dying of embarrassment."

He continued to admire her. She thought back to when Jason had given her a look like that. Maybe the office opening? Was that the last time? There must have been one more recently, like a vacation or a fundraiser when she'd shed her work uniform for something softer. But her mind couldn't come up with anything. Then she willed herself to move forward. "I have my shoes," she said, holding up the silk bag. "But I'm going to wear my boots to walk the three blocks! And a puffer coat."

She needed help with her zipper, the last few inches out of her reach. But asking Marcos for assistance would be asking for trouble. She'd ask fellow dancer Sharon for help at El Farol, much safer.

Nicole gathered her things, including a bouquet intended for Ava at the end of the show and envelopes of cash for both teachers and the guitarist, the class gift she had organized. She patted Bardot and slipped out the door after Marcos. She noticed he'd left a bag of gear in the casita. He'd have to come back in after the show. Well, well, well.

———

The crowd stood on their feet and roared. It was a joyous sound. The dozen dancers, led by teachers Ava and Brian and guitarist Philippe, took their curtain call and accepted the applause. Nicole felt like her chest would explode with pride. She was thrilled that it was over and relieved that she hadn't made any major mistakes, but even more than that, she was satisfied with her performance. In October, she could barely follow along to the simplest twelve-count sequence; now she had performed with professionals without incident. Maybe not *with* professionals, but *alongside* them. She stood next to Marcos in the line of dancers holding hands. They raised them to the sky before taking a bow while soaking in the good-natured whoops and cheers of family and friends.

Billie Jo and her daughter, Georgie, were in the front row, using their own castanets to applaud. Unbeknownst to Nicole, Clancy had informed the entire silversmithing class of the performance and there was decent representation from the community college crew. Raven, Gary, Tato, and Brittany stood together near the back, chanting her name. Even Cleo had slipped in as the show started and was now standing on her feet, stomping in appreciation.

Nicole took a moment to appreciate this community of people she had accumulated in a few months in this new city with so many traditions that were new to her. When she left Portland, she couldn't have imagined herself here, in a ruffled dress, onstage with half a dozen of her classmates and her new friend and colleague Billie Jo supporting her. The dancing, the silversmithing, the independence. Embracing a new city and having it embrace her back. And Marcos holding her hand. How had this all happened?

This was why I came here, she thought. *This isn't a midlife crisis; this is a midlife triumph.*

———

After many pitchers of sangria and servings of paella, the crew at El Farol was starting to thin out. Raven, ever the professor, reminded her students that final papers were due next week as she covered her portion of the bill and left the table. Gary, Brittany, and Tato exited together, commiserating about finishing all the projects due in silversmithing and telling Nicole they'd see her in the studio on Tuesday. She gave them all hugs and thanked them again for being there. Billie Jo and Georgie left next with more hugs and well wishes.

Nicole was exhausted and wanted to get out of the dress and into her bed. She was glad when Cleo stood up to leave, surprised that she had stayed as long as she had, chatting with almost everyone there. Maybe she was lonely in the big house in Tesuque? She signaled to Nicole that she wanted a word before heading home. "My car is here. I don't like to drive at night anymore, especially when sangria is involved. Can you walk me out?"

"Of course," Nicole answered, even though making her way through the restaurant in a flamenco dress was harder than she imagined. "It was so nice of you to come, Cleo."

"You've done so much for me in the past few months. Your work at Zia has really made a difference," she said with genuine appreciation in her voice. "And you should never take this dress off. It looks incredible on you."

"I was thinking the same thing. Too much for our final critiques this week?"

"Better to be overdressed than underdressed. And Roger would totally fall for the oldest grade inflation trick in the book. You'd get an A-plus on all your embossing! You're staying in the class next semester, aren't you? You should."

"I'm still deciding."

"You have a bright spirit. You should continue to expand your worldview. Any new learning does that. Selfishly, I would miss our car rides together." Cleo checked the ride share app on her phone as they stood on the classic front porch of the restaurant, where patrons used to tie up their horses but now waited for Ubers. "Why does it do that? It said the car was here and now it says five minutes." She looked straight at Nicole. "I play mahjong with Marcos's mother."

"I heard."

"He's had a rough year. But he looks happy tonight."

"He's the teacher's pet. Ava adores him."

"I think there's another reason he's looking so . . . vital," Cleo said, with the arched brow and the delivery of an Academy Award nominee. There was no mistaking her meaning.

Nicole shook her head. "We are just friends."

"Friends make the best lovers." Again, with the pitch-perfect delivery. "Ciao."

"Before you go, can you unzip me?" Nicole asked Marcos once they made it back to the casita.

For sure, Marcos had used the bag he'd left in her kitchen as an excuse to come inside with her. He mentioned it several times on the walk home, too many for it not to be a deliberate tactic. She pretended it wasn't.

"Is this an invitation?" The lights in the casita were low. She had lit her gas fireplace as soon as she came in. Outside the weather was windy with plummeting temperatures, but, inside, it was getting warmer.

"The truth is I'm trapped in this dress," Nicole said. "But yes, it's also an invitation."

"Are you sure?"

"I appreciate the question, but you don't need to ask me that anymore. I'm sure."

"Good because I don't want this night to end."

"I don't want this night to end either." She turned her back to him, using one hand to brush the hair up off her neck so he could see the zipper clearly. He pulled the zipper down slowly and it was excruciating. She wanted to be overwhelmed so she didn't overthink what was about to happen. But Marcos had other ideas, about pace and intentionality and building to something.

Like his dancing, she thought.

The zipper was all the way down, exposing a sliver of her back. He kissed her neck. She knew it would be salty and warm on his lips. He ran a finger down her spine then back up again. Another kiss against the skin of her neck and then he turned her around.

"We stay friends, right?" she asked.

"Yes, we stay friends. Otherwise, I'd lose Bardot and that would hurt me," he answered.

He kissed her, gently at first and then deeper. It worked. This was what she wanted. She turned her brain off and responded with her whole body.

Nicole woke the next morning around six. The bed was crowded and warm, two sensations she had missed, sleeping alone the past months. Marcos and Bardot slept side by side, both dead to the world. Again, she had the thought about what if this were her real life. Then, she started to think about Jason, about how she loved getting into bed with him at night, even if they barely touched, feeling the heft of his body, the heat that came off him on a cold, rainy Portland night.

Yes, she preferred sleeping with someone rather than no one.

The thought made her aware, but not ashamed, that the other person in her bed was not her husband, and she slid out of bed. She'd take a shower in the other bathroom, so as not to disturb man or dog, and then make coffee. That would wash the night away and start the new day off right.

———

"Hey," Marcos said as he emerged from the bedroom an hour later, in boxers and a T-shirt, searching for the jeans he discarded in the middle of the living room the night before.

Nicole sat at the kitchen island, showered and dressed, pretending to read the paper on her tablet while drinking her second cup of coffee. She didn't want to engage him while he pulled on the jeans and organized himself. That seemed too couple-y. She didn't want to think about the series of actions that had led to him disrobing in the middle of her living room. Or the way she'd taken her dress off slowly and deliberately, sliding it over her hips and down to her feet. It was too much to think about. Instead, she responded with a brief greeting, then asked if he wanted coffee.

"Please. Smells delicious," he said. "Look at you, brewing up piñon coffee. Like a local!" It was true. Piñon coffee was an acquired taste that some tourists never stuck around long enough to acquire. The Santa Fe specialty was created by blending roasted Arabica beans with subtle Southwestern flavors. She'd grown to like it, as the distinct smell permeated every place that served coffee, from breakfast joints to art galleries that might be brewing up a pot in the back. It was the preferred blend over at the Santa Fe Community College coffee cart. She started every class with a fresh cup. Eventually, she'd started brewing her own in the mornings. She liked that he'd noticed.

"Milk? Sugar?"

"Milk. No sugar." Just like Jason.

She placed the cup in front of him. He took a sip.

"This isn't weird," she declared.

"No, not weird at all."

And it wasn't.

To: Tessa, Sarah, Jane
From: Nicole

Attached is the final itinerary for the Wolfpack Goes to Santa Fe Weekend. And by final, I mean, I'm not making any more plans on behalf of individuals or the group. I don't know how travel agents do it. If there is something specific you want to do that is not on the itin, you should make the plans yourself. Did I say that with love and affection?

A few notes before you read the attachment:

- Jane: You are at the Inn of Five Graces. I personally checked out your room and it's fabulous. Yes, the pillows are down alternative, the coffee is out in the lobby by 6 a.m., and your massage is with a male masseuse.
- Sarah: I know you had your heart set on the full O'Keeffe Experience, but it was hard to schedule a full day at Ghost Ranch and another half day at the museum in town with everything else the others wanted to do, which was not as art centric. Museum is set, though. We will stop by the Santa Fe Cooking School for spice mixes. And you do have your own room at the casita because of hot flashes and insomnia. It has its own thermostat so you can adjust as needed.
- Tessa: Yes, I will have plenty of wine. And, as requested, we'll have brunch at Café Pasqual's on Sunday.

Can't wait to see you at the airport! I'll be the one with the apricot minipoo and the long blonde tresses. Safe travels.

xo Nicole

Chapter 24

Santa Fe
December

Nicole and Bardot waited in arrivals at Albuquerque International Airport. Why was she so nervous to see her dear friends? Tessa, Jane, and Sarah represented twenty years of support, laughter, and advice. And so many miles running the trails of Forest Park. Yet all week, she felt that pit in her stomach again, from her early days in Santa Fe, like these women were invading, not visiting. She worried that her life in Santa Fe wouldn't live up to their expectations, even though she had no idea what those expectations might be.

They had Zoom calls and texts and that one giant fucking email chain about the visit, and the list of what they wanted to do, to buy, to eat, and to see was endless. She had started to think of all their requests as a list of demands. It was like each one of them wanted an individualized itinerary, created and executed by Nicole. Let's shop! (Tessa) Let's spa! (Jane) Let's see only sacred sights associated with Georgia O'Keeffe's work that I learned about last week in a guidebook I bought! (That was Sarah, who had recently discovered art as an activity now that her children had escaped the nest.) Nicole had planned four days that combined all the activities, plus a few that she'd been saving for their visit, including a road trip to the sacred site of Chamayo, an hour north of Santa Fe that even locals described as very mystical. And downtime, plenty of downtime.

Still, she suspected the entire operation would implode by day two when the afternoon options were either the folk art museum or Ten Thousand Waves thermal springs. Who wanted to make that choice? But she was hoping for a miracle.

She worried about her old friends mixing with her new friends, so she kept their interactions to a minimum. She was concerned the beds in the house weren't comfortable enough for Sarah's bad back, so she had asked Clancy to help her slide a piece of plywood in between the mattress and the box spring. Jane had insisted on staying at a hotel, because she needed her space and there was no way she was going to sleep on the pull-out couch or share a bed, so Nicole had called in a favor to make sure Jane got a choice room at the Inn of Five Graces, one of the most beautiful boutique hotels on the planet, never mind in Santa Fe. (Tina, whom she had gotten to know at her morning coffee stop, was a concierge there. In exchange, Nicole had arranged a 20 percent off coupon at the Zia Collective for hotel guests. That was how things worked in Santa Fe.) She'd even given Bardot a bath, so she'd look her best to greet the group at the airport. Still, Nicole was nervous she wouldn't pass muster.

But the minute they came into view at the airport in Albuquerque, she felt the love. Her friends were here to see her, not judge her. There were hugs all around and cries of how gorgeous and relaxed she looked. *You're so skinny! You look ten years younger. Okay, that's a stretch, five years younger. Did you make all your jewelry? It's gorgeous!* The talking was nonstop and overlapping. There was no lag time in their relationship—they picked up right where they left off months ago. Nicole let out a deep breath.

And Bardot was a huge hit, much to Bardot's pleasure.

"Where are we going first?" Sarah asked, pulling her luggage off the carousel, the only one out of the three to check a bag, leading to a few eye rolls from Tessa. Sarah never noticed slights like that. "That chocolate shop I texted you about? The one with the drinking chocolate?"

Another eye roll from Tessa.

Nicole looked at her watch, even though she knew it was 3:15 and had timed the plans down to the minute. But she wanted Sarah to be happy, not hangry. "It will take us about an hour to get to Santa Fe from here. We can check Jane into her hotel so she can freshen up, as my mother-in-law would say. Tessa and Sarah, we'll go to my casita so you can unpack, change if you need to. But before we head to my place, the three of us can swing by Kakawa for what they call an elixir but is essentially a hot chocolate pick-me-up. Jane, I'm sure your fancy hotel has elixirs running out of the faucet. Then we'll meet back at the hotel for a walk around the Plaza and dinner at a Santa Fe classic, the Coyote Cantina. Our dinner reservations are at seven. It's an early city. Sound good?"

"That's our girl. The planner. We've missed you telling us where to go and when to be there," Jane said, as if her own list of personal needs didn't make her the highest maintenance visitor of all. She had requested a certain brand of seltzer for the car ride from the airport to the hotel. Nicole had gone to three stores to find the blood orange flavor that Jane preferred. It was so much easier to comply than to complain.

"We've been wandering around Portland, lost and disorganized, without you," Tessa added. They all knew that was a lie, but Nicole liked that they acknowledged her absence in their lives in some way.

"By the way, I'm proud of the hair maintenance. Don't think I didn't notice," Jane said, touching Nicole's hair without consent.

"Oh, I knew you'd notice. My friend Cleo gave me the name of her hairdresser and I really can't afford her, but I did it for you, Jane."

"Will we meet this mysterious Cleo?" Tessa asked. "We're a little jealous that you have a new friend. You've mentioned her in a few communiqués."

"Maybe," Nicole answered, knowing it was highly unlikely. She hadn't wanted to share Cleo with the Wolfpack, but she wasn't sure exactly why. Would they embarrass her somehow in front of her new friend? Her new friend who thought she was capable and daring, even adventurous? Her Portland friends knew a different Nicole, more subdued, comfortable in the back of the room, not the front. Nicole wanted to keep that version of herself far away from her Santa Fe life. "We have so much planned, I'm not sure we have time for any more activities."

"Vamos!" Sarah, the group's directionally challenged member, pointed off in the wrong direction. They all laughed and turned her around.

And Nicole was filled with happiness.

The hotel drop-off went as well as could be expected, Jane making only a single comment about the use of too much sandalwood in the hotel's signature scent, a musky, woody whiff that hit you as soon as you walked into the lobby. She wasn't wrong. Jane the chemist had a nose for such things. But Nicole wished she'd occasionally keep an opinion to herself. She tried to imagine Jane greeting some of her SFCC classmates, whose enthusiasm for tattoos was surpassed only by their love of ripped denim. She was glad she aborted the plan to drive the three of them by the college on the way home from the airport. A community college wasn't Jane's speed. Nor were others in the Wolfpack interested, so Nicole just pointed off in a vague direction when they passed the campus on the highway.

The casita received high marks from Tessa and Sarah, who squealed with delight when she saw the art and antiques and the entire closet devoted to puzzles. "This place is so cozy. Maybe we should stay in tonight and do puzzles! That sounds fun."

Tessa made a sound like a game show buzzer, nixing the suggestion. "We did not come to Santa Fe to do puzzles. That's something you do on a rainy weekend at the coast with your family, which this is not."

"I wasn't serious, Tessa. I was trying to communicate how charming and cozy Nicole's house is, that's all," Sarah snapped back in her prim voice. The last thing Nicole wanted was to start the weekend with Sarah spiraling into her Poor Pitiful Me persona.

"Let me show you your rooms," Nicole said with so much enthusiasm her face hurt. "I put together some Santa Fe gift bags for each of you. I can't stress enough how much hydration and moisturization your skin is going to need. Use all the products! Sarah, you get the second bedroom. You'll have to share it with my Poshmark studio, but you should have enough room. And Tessa, you're in with me."

"So? What's happening? Tell me everything." Tessa wasted zero time getting down to business. "Any Five Hundred Mile Rule conquests? I feel like there must be. You look great. And you've been suspiciously absent on the group text when the issue of men or sex comes up."

Nicole wasn't ready to tell Tessa anything. She regretted having confided in her in the first place: even though Tessa had sworn she was a vault, a few drinks could pop it wide open.

Since the night of the dance performance, she'd seen Marcos two more times. A drink and burger after work that turned into much more. And a midweek encounter that was a straight-up booty call. She was finishing her paper for her History of Jewelry class on the symbolism of Celtic design and he texted her: *You Up?* It made her laugh out loud. The whole scenario felt like she was in college again, except this time with better technology. She texted back: *Finishing paper. Come in an hour. Bring wine.*

And he did.

But she didn't want to let Tessa in on any of this. The thought of rehashing what happened was too much for Nicole. She wanted to keep the details to herself, mainly because she felt as if she were a different woman with him. A woman with the confidence of a twentysomething but without the hang-ups, and the wisdom of a fortysomething without the insecurity about aging. It was like she was playing a role, Fancy Free Nicole, a little bit reckless and with the added pleasure of absorbing every sensation. And she didn't know whether she should feel guilty or grateful for the opportunity. The only way the Five Hundred Mile Rule was going to work was if she didn't overthink it, didn't question any of it. And dissecting the relationship with Marcos would fall into the category of questioning.

But she felt like she had to throw Tessa a bone. "I have nothing to report. But there is one possible person of interest. He works at a tasting room near Zia. We may see him on Saturday." Nicole had planned their entire schedule for the long weekend to make sure they "ran into" Marcos, but she hoped she played it off lightly.

"He's a bartender? Perfect," Tessa said, flashing her New England reverence for social hierarchy. "Low stakes."

Nicole was about to correct her but decided it would be better to do when she introduced Marcos to the Wolfpack. "I'm going to let you unpack. Can I get you a glass of bubbly?"

Sarah stuck her head in the master suite. "A drink before we go out for a drink? At this altitude? At least we're not driving. We're not driving, right?"

"No, we're not driving. We're walking. It's a mile to the restaurant and a mile back. I told you to pack sturdy shoes. And drink plenty of water. And wear a hat, like I instructed in my welcome email. It's cold but clear. There are mini flashlights for you both in your welcome basket!"

"Wow, Santa Fe Nicole is bossy," Tessa said. "I like it."

By Saturday afternoon, the Wolfpack was wiped out. There was eating, drinking, shopping, running, walking, sightseeing, art buying, museum going, and haggling over prices at an art walk where Tessa insisted on bargaining down the sweet student selling burning sage sticks, much to Nicole's horror. Jane skipped the Museum of International Folk Art to get a massage at her hotel. ("Too hokey!" she said, even though it was the finest collection in the world and not the slightest bit hokey.) But then she struck out on her own and bought a painting on Canyon Road, much to Sarah's dismay. ("I wanted to see someone buy art!") Tessa had way too many margaritas on the first night, overshared about her husband's lack of sex drive, and was too hungover to run the next day. And Sarah called her husband at least three times a day to tell him that she missed him and wished he were there with her. *Right in front of everyone else.*

For her part, Nicole was on the edge of exhaustion from playing tour guide, concierge, and dependable friend. But she rallied with a coffee at Collected Works Bookstore & Coffeehouse, one of her favorite spots in town, where they browsed and bought books and lattes before heading over to their next activity on Johnson Street.

The Saturday afternoon itinerary was a trip to the Georgia O'Keeffe Museum, followed by a stop at Zia and the O Rosal tasting room. Dinner was at Nicole's house, a pork adobo stew she had learned to make at the Santa Fe Cooking School for the occasion. She needed a break from being the one to split the check and do a special calculation for Sarah, who insisted she wasn't paying for Tessa's alcohol consumption when she usually had sparkling water. Nicole agreed that was fair, but she wished Sarah would do the math herself.

She was looking forward to a relaxed dinner at home and giving her friends the silver key fobs she had made for each of them, an outline of the state of New Mexico embossed with the logo of Santa Fe and inlaid turquoise stones. The fobs were her best work by far, well designed and well executed without looking cheesy. It was for her final project for class, and Roger had given her an A. It was the seal of approval she'd been waiting for all term. She hoped the Wolfpack appreciated the effort, or at least pretended to.

As they walked over to the museum, Sarah gave them a lecture on the life and art of Georgia O'Keeffe, all of which she'd learned from a Wikipedia page; the 2009 movie about the artist starring Joan Allen as Georgia and Jeremy Irons as her husband, photographer Alfred Stieglitz; and several podcasts on O'Keeffe's life. Sarah was in the zone, speaking to them as if she'd discovered Georgia O'Keeffe and was letting them in on a huge secret.

By the time they arrived at the small, tidy museum—a first for Nicole, who had purposely been saving her trip here until her friends came—Jane, Tessa, and Nicole popped in earbuds and followed along with the museum guide to shut Sarah up. It didn't work, as she continued to talk to them, attempting to drown out the audio being pumped into their ears with her own tour.

Fortunately, it was so crowded, it was easy to hide from her, which is exactly what Nicole did. She let herself be absorbed into the colors and shapes of O'Keeffe's work. She was glad she had waited to visit. She understood the vibe now in a way she never would have in September. O'Keeffe had fallen in love with New Mexico on first sight. It had taken Nicole longer, but she was there now.

"Well, that was a bit of a disappointment. I thought there would be more, so much more. But I guess her best work is in other museums or in private collections," Jane, newly self-appointed art critic, declared as they exited the gift shop. It was after five. The bright day had turned to a dark, cold night, but the glittering holiday lights around town propelled them forward for one more stop before dinner.

"But the gift shop is great!" Tessa said. "Look, Christmas gifts for my entire bridge club and tennis team!" She held up a dozen refrigerator magnets featuring quotes from the artist, but she was overshadowed by Sarah leaving the bookstore in the iconic Georgia

O'Keeffe wool gaucho hat. She looked ridiculous but so pleased with herself that even Tessa didn't roll her eyes.

"That is perfect for you," Nicole said. "You can wear it tomorrow when we head out of town to Chimayo to see the sanctuary and visit the galleries and textile studios."

"That was amazing! Thank you for taking us there. Did you know that Alfred Stieglitz never visited her here in Santa Fe? They were together for thirty years, and she spent months here at a time for decades, but he never wanted to leave New York. He never came. It's like you and Jason, Nicole! You're a modern-day Georgia and Alfred!" said Sarah.

Nicole didn't respond right away because she thought she'd give the whole situation away. She never wanted Jason to come here. It would throw off the entire balance of everything she had created. There was no room for him in her life in Santa Fe. She didn't even want Sarah, Tessa, and Jane here for one minute longer than they planned. "Maybe the point isn't that Stieglitz didn't come. Maybe the point is that O'Keeffe never invited him."

"Lemme guess. You went to the O'Keeffe Museum," Billie Jo said, pointing at Sarah's hat. "But please don't let me hear you go on and on about 'O'Keeffe Territory.' Because there were a lot of Native people living and creating there before that white girl from New York showed up."

"I got the memo. I understand the term is no longer acceptable and I'm in agreement with that sentiment," Sarah countered in good humor. The term had been applied by art collectors and curators to the area of New Mexico around O'Keeffe's Ghost Ranch for the better part of a hundred years. Until the Native population pointed out that they'd been there for thousands of years before the painter. "Is the hat too much?"

"That hat's on your people, not mine."

Nicole made introductions all around. There was small talk about what they'd done so far, where they'd been, and, of course, where they'd eaten. Billie Jo made a joke about them having to leave soon so that Nicole could get back to work. And then launched into a sincere monologue about how Nicole had influenced the store and her personally. Her friends chimed in by saying all sorts of lovely things about Nicole, how she always came to the rescue at their lowest moments.

The whole conversation made Nicole feel awful about any negative thoughts she'd had in the previous few days. "Thank you all very much. Let's do some shopping before Billie Jo has to head home. And don't worry. I'll work overtime next week."

"Did you see Cleo at the museum? She was there doing some photo shoot."

Fortunately not, thought Nicole. "No, we didn't."

"What can you tell us about the mysterious Cleo? Who is she?" Tessa asked Billie Jo.

"Cleo Jones. The movie star. She's a partner in this place. She's in Nicole's silversmithing class." Billie Jo looked at Nicole in mock shock. "You didn't tell them about Cleo?"

The Wolfpack started howling all at once. Cleo Jones! How could she have held out on them? They demanded to meet her immediately. Nicole explained that here in Santa Fe, she wasn't a movie star. She was quiet and private. Billie Jo backed her up on that.

"Remember that scene in *The Last Dance* where she does that striptease with her waitress uniform. In the back room after work? Well, that's when I knew I was gay. I went into that movie as the high school prom queen dating the quarterback and came out a lesbian. I wish I could thank her personally," Jane said, and now Nicole felt a little guilty for not wanting the Wolfpack to meet Cleo. But only a little.

"I'll tell you everything about Cleo over dinner. Let's get shopping so Billie Jo can go home!"

The Wolfpack oohed and aahed over everything at Zia. Very quickly, Jane amassed a small treasure trove of items to buy for herself and her daughter under the directive that it didn't "scream Southwestern," a phrase Billie Jo understood inherently. Tessa picked out a sophisticated necklace of three strands of beautiful turquoise beads, once Billie Jo told her the story of the young Navajo woman who created it. And Sarah bought a beaded dog collar, of course. For her part, Nicole let Billie Jo do the selling, watching her work with pride. And felt that same sense of pride that her friends were slapping down their credit cards to support the shop.

It was almost six, closing time for Marcos next door. Billie Jo would stay open to seven to snare the holiday shoppers. But on cue, as Nicole suspected, he came through the front door with sparkling wine and glasses for all. He couldn't have looked more handsome, in a charcoal-gray sweater, jeans, and a blue-and-black cashmere scarf loosely wrapped around his neck. His beard was trimmed and his eyes sparkled. He nodded at Nicole. "I thought I saw you come in here. Closing for the day and had a few open bottles to share. Bubbles, anyone?"

Tessa looked at Nicole, then looked at Marcos, then back at Nicole. "Yes, please."

The goodbyes at the airport on Monday morning were short. The Wolfpack was ready to get back to the rain and sleet of Portland with their authentic spices, cookbooks, art, napkins and tableware, jewelry, and red chile Christmas ornaments. Nicole was eager to lie on the couch and do nothing for the rest of the day. Of course, on the drive down, Jane had shocked them all by telling them that she had already made plans to return for a few performances during opera season in August because she'd met somebody at the hotel, and they would be meeting up again in July. "She lives in London but spends the summer here. She's a costumer for the Santa Fe Opera company. I met her at the spa. She's lovely. Lenore. Just lovely."

"Is that why you blew us off for dinner on Saturday night?" Sarah asked. "To be with her."

"Yes," Jane replied without apology.

"And did you go buy art with her?" Sarah demanded.

"I did."

"You dog, you." Tessa smiled.

Jane's revelation made Nicole thoughtful for a moment, knowing that Jane would be in Santa Fe next summer and she wouldn't. She would be back in Portland with her family, cooking and cleaning and wondering what to do with her life. And Jane would be here, listening to opera, soaking in the sunsets, and soaking up the margaritas. Nicole was jealous. "She sounds lovely, Jane. You deserve an opera-loving costumer named Lenore."

Quick hugs were exchanged at the curb. Sarah hustled in to check her bag, because of course, she had to check her bag. Jane had to check her painting, so she followed Sarah in. Tessa lingered, waiting for the other two to leave, then she studied Nicole. "You've got a lot of secrets, my friend. First Cleo Jones and then this Marcos. I'm not sure why you're not telling me the truth, but clearly there is something there between you and the bartender. It makes me think it's more serious than it should be. Keep it tight, Nicole. Be careful. Fun is one thing; feelings are another."

And with that warning, she gave Nicole a quick hug and walked into the terminal.

Chapter 25

Mendoza, Argentina
December

"Can I start you off with something?" asked the bartender in English, a young woman who Jason guessed to be in her late twenties by the smoothness of her skin and the tattoo sleeve on her arm, the sure signs of her age and generation. She wasn't beautiful, but she was striking—healthy, clean, dressed in a crisp white shirt and black pants, her hair twirled into a tight bun, oversize silver and green stone earrings setting off her eyes. (Nicole would have called them "statement earrings.") She had some sort of magnetism, that was for sure, because tearing his gaze away from the view of the Andes Mountains, a parade of giants higher than fifteen thousand feet, required something special. She had that something.

The restaurant at the Zuccardi Vineyards was one of the most visually arresting establishments he'd ever encountered. The room itself was a pleasing arrangement of blond wood, local slate, and glass. But the massive windows drew the eye toward the rows of grapes stretched out to the foot of the impressive mountains. Barren and lush at the same time.

Argentina had astounded Jason at every turn, and he was glad he'd let Sebastian talk him into spending a few weeks in this region. At three thousand feet and surrounded by the snowcapped jagged spine of the Andes, the Uco Valley made Napa look like a child's garden. It was home to innovative food, warm, handsome people, and some of the best Malbecs in the world. The last two weeks of drinking, eating, and absorbing the region had convinced Jason that there was a dynamite book to be written about the Mendoza lifestyle. Part cookbook, part self-help, part how-to manual. *Robust* was the word that came to mind when he thought of all of Argentina, but especially here. The people, the wine, the attitude. These people could make magic out of the hardest dirt and the coldest temperatures he'd ever seen in a wine-growing region. Like this woman in front of him, strong and sexy. There must be a book in that.

Jason found himself staring at her when she spoke again. "Need more time?"

"Sorry. Why don't you suggest something light to start with? I'm meeting Arturo for dinner in a half hour." He usually didn't name-drop the owner's name at a place like this, or any place, but he was meeting Arturo here at the bar. The bartender might get annoyed if he didn't mention it, like he was some sort of secret shopper here to rate her performance.

She grinned and got to work. "If you're meeting my father for dinner, I suggest you start with a large cup of coffee and a gallon of water. There will be plenty of wine in your future. You're going to need the caffeine to keep up and hydration to stay sober," she said, making good on her prescription and putting a black coffee and water in front of him. "I'm Julia, Arturo's daughter."

"I'm Jason. I'm a writer. Doing some research. Thank you for this. Is it too American to ask for cream?" Jason hoped his face didn't register his embarrassment. He'd been eyeing this woman with nothing like professional courtesy. And, of course, she was somebody's daughter. She could be his daughter. Jesus, he needed to get back on solid ground.

For him, the Five Hundred Mile Rule had only served to expose how old he had gotten in the last twenty-five years. And how completely off his game married life had made him. He was beginning to doubt if he'd ever really had any game in the first place.

With Abby, they found a collegial space where they could ride, dine, and screw with the same level of emotional engagement. But other than Abby, his radar had been way off and his desire to bother had been even further off. Was it really worth the effort? He shouldn't be checking out twentysomethings and, God knows, they weren't checking him out. He wanted to feel young again and all he felt was his age, every year of it.

Julia put the cream down in front of him. "Here you go. What do you write?"

Nothing. I write nothing except emails to my wife and even those I half-ass. I haven't written a single word of prose in four months. There's no spy novel, no thriller in me. Mainly, I read other people's books, which is not the same as writing my own books, Jason thought, but didn't say. Instead, he lied, "I'm working on a book about Argentina. I don't know what it is yet. A travel book? A cookbook? A memoir? Not sure yet."

"Make it a memoir. Then you'll put your whole self into it."

A nugget of wisdom from the young woman. He took a sip of his coffee. "How do you say *robust* in Spanish? I should know."

"You should know. It's *robusto.*"

"El café es robusto," he said, beaming like a kid who aced his Spanish vocab quiz.

"En Argentina todo es robusto," said Julia and then she turned her back on him to pour out another order for the waiter at the end of the bar. In Argentina, everything is robust.

That's a good book title, he thought as he took another sip of coffee and stared out at the mountains.

Chapter 26

Portland
December 2018

The joy drained from the living room the minute Jason's parents said their good nights and made their way to the guest quarters above the garage, promising not to get up too early on Christmas morning. "You have teenagers now. Of course, they won't wake up at the crack of dawn. But I miss those days," said Sandrine Elswick, also known as Zuzu to her grandchildren. Jason said nothing, but his mother's comment made no sense. He thought about the many Christmases his doctor parents had spent without his children, volunteering to be on call in San Francisco so they could go to Hawaii for New Year's. Even since retiring a few years before, they hadn't ventured north for the holiday. Still, she acted as if this were their grand holiday tradition. "What a lovely evening, Nicole. We were so happy to share it with you."

"See you in the morning," Jason said, his voice tight. He watched his parents, now in their late seventies, make their way across the covered walkway. It was a damp rainy night, the kind of night that made him glad he spent the extra money to build the covered walkway, a remodeling expense he almost struck from the list. It was Nicole who advocated for the simple roof, shielding guests from the inevitability of rain in Portland, citing safety precautions. ("I don't want to be responsible for your mother breaking her hip," she had argued. "It would be just my luck if she slipped, broke her hip, and had to rehab here for months.") He did feel better knowing his parents would stay dry and upright en route to their bedroom.

He wasn't sure what they were doing in Portland at Christmas in the first place. Last week, while he waited at JFK, he got a call from his mother about a last-minute change of plans. She announced that they were coming to Portland because, as his mother the psychiatrist said, she had "concerns" about Jack. "Let's not get into it over the phone. We'll see you next Sunday." And she rang off.

Jason had a theory about how she'd come to have concerns.

He turned to Nicole, who was clearing away the last of the Christmas Eve dishes and moving into the kitchen to prepare breakfast for the next day. "Is that what you wanted? My mother spending the entire dinner analyzing our sixteen-year-old son? That wasn't dinner conversation. It was a session with Dr. Elswick."

Nicole kept moving toward the kitchen, so Jason followed. She had her game face on. The tasks at hand were going to get done before she went to bed, no matter what conversation her husband wanted to have. It was nearly midnight. "I'm grateful for her professional opinion."

"Here's my professional opinion. Our son is a teenage boy who is testing every limit and sometimes he's an asshole. And sometimes he doesn't want to leave his room because he doesn't feel like it. Because that's what sixteen-year-old boys do. Test and provoke. He doesn't need therapy. He needs a job or a volunteer gig at a homeless shelter to put his life in perspective," Jason said, recorking the leftover wine and putting it in the fridge.

Nicole loaded the dishwasher like a woman with a mission. The action helped her avoid eye contact with her husband, which was key because she thought she might explode at his attitude. "Jason, you haven't seen the panic attacks, the tears when I ask him to do the simplest task like clean his room or brush his teeth. I can barely get him out of bed to go to school and you think a volunteer gig is the solution? You're never home these days . . ."

He started to object but she cut him off. "That's a fact, not a criticism. I'm the one trying to get him out of bed in the morning to go to school, not you. You're in San Francisco or New York. But I'm here. And something is not right with Jack."

Nicole was right, at least about the work piece. The acquisition of Stumptown by Kincaid & Blume and then his elevation to West Coast managing director of the parent company had resulted in weekly trips to New York or San Francisco to manage the business. And it would stay this way for the foreseeable future. The travel was a killer. He spent his weekends in Portland, but more often than not, he was working or reading for work or falling asleep on the couch because he was jet-lagged. He'd slacked off in the parenting department, but that was natural now that the kids were teenagers. They didn't need him as much and work did. Still, he knew his own son. He was lazy, not depressed.

But he needed to throw Nicole a bone. "Fine, if you think Jack needs help, let's get him help. But somebody other than my mother. I remember being analyzed every day of my childhood and let me tell you, it's not great. It's why I picked boarding school, to get away from her constant gaze."

"You know that your mother and I have had our differences," Nicole said in the understatement of the century. Her mother-in-law had never quite accepted that Jason had married someone like her, the daughter of a waitress and a "maintenance man," as she called her father. And the fact that Nicole and Jason had married at city hall followed by a reception at Hung Far Low was never mentioned, ever. Not even as a joke. Nicole let that get under her skin at almost every encounter, that feeling of not being good enough. "But your mother is a well-respected psychiatrist who specializes in adolescents. And she loves Jack and Chelsea as they are. She has a relationship with Jack that's very strong and grown-up. She never treats him like a child. Did you know they text all the time?"

Nicole herself was surprised to learn about the texting. Jack mentioned it in the car the other day as evidence that he was fine. He said something like if he had any issues, he'd ask Zuzu because they were always in contact. This news broadsided Nicole and made her jealous. But she was deeply concerned, so she encouraged him to keep up the communication. She firmly believed that the more adults in a teenager's life, the better. But this relationship she didn't expect. Why would he turn to Sandrine, snooty and scholarly Sandrine, over his own mother?

Nicole needed backup. She felt like she was losing Jack. She picked up the phone and called her mother-in-law, something she'd done about a half dozen times in her entire relationship with Jason. They usually communicated via email, the most impersonal way.

"I didn't beg her to come here for Christmas. She agreed to come because she had concerns based on some communication that she and Jack have had. I value her opinion because I have no one to talk to about this."

There it was. The accusation that always reared its ugly head when Jason and Nicole fought, the "you never talk to me" accusation. Jason was more open to conversation than 90 percent of the men his age. He knew that for a fact. What did Nicole expect? Nonstop conversation in the middle of a workday? Undivided attention the few hours of the week that he was home? "If this is about my new job, then say it. You don't have to hide behind Jack's alleged anxiety."

"Hide behind Jack? Is that what you think this is? About you? That's perfect. Just perfect." She slammed the dishwasher pod into the slot with a vengeance.

"What does that mean?"

"That you think everything in this house revolves around you."

"That's a lousy thing to say. I don't think that."

Nicole held her tongue because it was midnight on Christmas Eve and she still had presents to wrap. And she couldn't get into it with Jason about how his solution to every issue was that everyone else should change, except him. That could be for another time. "This is not about you. It's about Jack. And I need someone to see what I see and talk to me about how I feel because I have nobody. Not you because you're not here. Not Tessa, Jane, or Sarah because they have perfect kids who take five AP classes and are star athletes or academic decathlon champs. They don't want to hear about my average, anxious son."

"Jack is not average." Not Jack, who'd been the class president in middle school. Who wrote for the paper and was the Tin Man in *The Wizard of Oz*. Jack was sharp and popular, maybe not the greatest athlete, but he could hang with anyone, even the jocks. His Jack was not average. But he wasn't the same kid he was in middle school.

"I know that. But if you don't hand in the homework that's sitting at the bottom of your backpack, you don't get credit for it. His grades are very quickly becoming average."

"Is this about college acceptance?" Jason snapped, his hackles rising because he found no conversation among his parenting peers more tiresome than college acceptance. There was a place for everyone, even if it didn't rank in the top ten. Why his generation of parents found their own self-worth in their child's ACT scores or college acceptance record, he'd never understand.

"Of course not. You know I don't care where Jack goes. But until this year, I always thought that he would be fine anywhere, because he's Jack. And Jack is always fine."

"Because we're not getting caught up in the college admissions game."

"Says the guy who went to prep school and then a highly selective liberal arts college," Nicole countered. She got tired of hearing Jason pretend that status didn't matter to him. Status mattered to everyone. It was why humans didn't still sleep on dirt floors or in huts with mud roofs, because everyone wants to be a little bit better than the next person. What would make Jason happy is if Jack got into an Ivy League school but turned it down to go to Portland State. That was the right amount of "fuck you" for Jason Elswick. But it was the furthest thing from Nicole's mind. "Believe me, this is not about college acceptance. I worry about so much more than that."

"What does that mean?" Jason's tone softened, like he was listening instead of arguing.

"I don't want him to make one bad decision that's going to cost him the rest of his life. I know that sounds dramatic, but that's what happens these days. I don't want him to harm himself because he's having a bad day or take something some kid in a parking lot sells him because he wants to self-medicate. When we were in high school, we'd drown our sorrows in weak-ass pot and a six-pack of Raindogs. Today, these kids have access to so much more of everything, from the good stuff to the dangerous stuff." Nicole hit start on the dishwasher and moved over to the big farm table in the kitchen to finish wrapping presents.

"Jack hasn't talked about hurting himself, has he?" Finally, a note of genuine concern.

Nicole caught it. She looked at Jason and they connected. "Jack hasn't talked about anything. Which is why your mother is here. Why I asked her to be here. Please, keep an open mind."

"Do you want me to talk to him?"

"Do you know what to say?"

Jason shrugged. "I'm guessing it's not, 'Hey, buddy. What's up?'"

Finally, laughter. "I don't think so. Although, I bet he would appreciate a little more face time with you," Nicole said. "Why don't we see what your mother has to say? Together. Get her recommendations and go from there."

"As long as she doesn't turn her gaze on us. Like on our relationship," he said, making a gesture between the two of them.

"Don't worry. Your mother and I haven't grown that close in your absence," Nicole joked, cutting the wrapping paper square in half and in half again. She had to wrap four books for Chelsea and a new iPad for Jack, then she'd be done. "Remember, we're on the same team. I know things haven't been on track with us lately. We feel out of kilter. But we need to be aligned for the kids. They need us."

Jason let that sink in. Her acknowledgment that they hadn't been on the same page. Or in the same state. And on the rare nights when they shared the same bed, their lovemaking had been uninspired if it happened at all. He knew it and she knew it. And they'd get to that, get back to where they'd been a few years ago.

But first, they had to fix Jack.

Chapter 27

Santa Fe
December

The official closing time was five, but it was twenty minutes later when Nicole shut the door after the final customer on Christmas Eve, a well-dressed fiftyish businessman who'd arrived that afternoon from Dallas and needed something for his wife and three daughters, who were waiting for him at their family ski house in Taos. He'd been finishing up a deal and sent the family on ahead, but he wanted to make it up to them. He was the best kind of last-minute shopper: good taste and plenty of money. Nicole picked out individual items of jewelry based on his descriptions of each, including a modern multistrand necklace of semiprecious stones that she'd been eyeing for herself, created by a very talented local designer. It was perfect for his wife, whom the husband had described as "classic with a twist." In fact, she was sure that each of the four women in his life would open gifts perfectly suited to them.

But the second she shut the door after wishing him safe travels on the road to Taos, she collapsed. Every bone in her body hurt. Every muscle in her face ached from smiling and small talk. Every ounce of courtesy had been sucked from her heart and her brain. She almost started to cry.

She had spent the last six days on her feet at Zia, merchandising, hunting for inventory, restocking, and ringing people up. The store was so busy that the three of them, Billie Jo, Georgie, and Nicole, barely sat down. Lunch was half a turkey sandwich in the back and a quick walk around the block with Bardot before she was back at it. She washed champagne glasses in the back for the Sip n' Sparkle jewelry event a few nights ago. She even acquiesced to gift wrapping yesterday when Georgie asked for the afternoon off to volunteer at a party for underserved youth. Nicole had been working holiday retail for the last thirty years of her life and she'd never been more grateful to lock that front door. For the Zia Collective, it was a successful season, exactly what they'd need to make it through the slow days of January and February.

For Nicole, it was like a light bulb exploding in her head. This was what she was good at, this was her calling. The jewelry making was a hobby, a creative outlet she needed to tap into another side of her brain. But her life's work was retail, as shallow as that may sound to the outside world. It was picking out four unique gifts, the sale of which supported local artisans, so that four complete strangers would open those boxes and say, "This is perfect."

She'd come all this way to find out what she was good at all along.

She reconciled the receipts, locked the cash in the safe, triple-checked the lock on the back door. Coat, hat, gloves on. She traded her store clogs for her walking shoes, regretting for a second that she didn't have her car, but then remembered that her way home took her up Canyon Road, where the Christmas Eve tradition of the Farolito Walk would be in full swing with galleries and stores staying open late and showing off their glowing decorations. Cleo had told her it was a must-see, so she rallied her spirits before she collapsed on the couch at the casita. She leashed up Bardot and put on the fleece coat she'd bought the dog, a first for Nicole. In general, she was against clothes for dogs, but it really was chilly here and her minipoo needed the extra layer. No surprise, Bardot loved her bright pink fleece outfit and passersby loved her in it. Even amid the glowing lights, falling snow, and cobblestone streets filled with art lovers,

Bardot would be the belle of Canyon Road tonight. Nicole turned off the lights and locked the door.

It was snowing lightly. She took a deep breath of air, filling her lungs with the scent of snow and pine. It was a beautiful night. She had one more stop to make before she headed home.

"Merry Christmas," a familiar voice said.

She turned and saw Marcos locking up the tasting room. He looked exhausted, too. But still good. Still really good. She hadn't seen him in more than a week, by design.

The echo of what Tessa had said to her about fun versus feelings bounced around in her head, wheedling its way into her psyche. She decided to practice detachment, as the psychologist on her favorite podcast advised when discussing any toxic relationship. (Not that she and Marcos were toxic. The opposite was true.) In her quest for distance, her responses to his texts were vague and noncommittal. She tried to convince herself that the itch she scratched was satisfied and she and Marcos could go back to being friends, or at least, acquaintances.

But she was still glad to catch him before he left. "Merry Christmas to you. I was about to stop by. I saw your light on. Busy day?"

"I sold every bottle in the place. My father had to drive down from the vineyard with more cases of the sparkling rosé and the new red table wine we released last week," he said, walking toward her with a bottle in his hand. "I guess people are very thirsty in Santa Fe." He stopped in front of her, petted Bardot with affection, and then gave Nicole a kiss on the cheek. "I saved one bottle for you. In case your plans call for a bottle of red wine. And my special biscochitos, the official state cookie and Christmas tradition."

"Dinner tonight." She slipped the bottle and the baked goods into her backpack and pulled out a small black velvet pouch. "And this is for you. I made it, so no laughing and no returns."

He opened the drawstring and pulled out one of the key fobs she created in class with a charm the shape of the state of New Mexico, the classic logo of Santa Fe, and a stone. His was more rugged look-ing than the ones she had made for her friends. For him, she bought a piece of rare lime-green turquoise for the inlaid stonework. The color matched his eyes. "I can't believe you made this. It's amazing."

"Thank you. I think."

"You know what I mean. You're a woman of many talents." The snow was collecting on his hat and shoulders. She wanted to brush it off, to kiss him playfully. "What are your plans for the next few days?" he asked.

For one moment, she imagined having no plans but to be with him. To share Christmas and New Year's together like a normal couple in a new relationship, with long dinners, late mornings, and slow days of togetherness. Add in the romance of snow-covered Santa Fe and it would be a perfect week. Then she realized her foolishness. "Tonight, I have to stay awake until ten for an Inter-national Christmas Zoom with the family. One in Australia and one in Japan."

"And one in mythical Patagonia."

She hadn't wanted to mention Jason, which was childish. She nodded.

"I wish I could Zoom with my family. Instead, I must see them in person."

"You're terrible. Are you headed out there tonight? It's snowing," she said, pointing out the obvious.

"I am. Christmas Eve is a big deal in my family. It's a free-for-all of cultural traditions, from posole to tamales to hot dish. There's singing, reading Christmas stories aloud. Who knows, maybe some flamenco? More food. And we open the presents at midnight when the little kids are wired and the adults are really buzzed. It's great," he said, meaning it this time.

And a truth cracked open for Nicole. She had her life and he had his. Whatever they had shared was temporary. And over. As it should be. That was the deal she'd made with Jason, with herself.

Maybe this relationship with Marcos was mythical, too, like Patagonia. The knight who could dance and pour wine and make her feel like she was twenty-five again. That wasn't real. That couldn't possibly be real. Yes, this experience would become part of her personal mythology in time. Revealed to few, if any, that once upon a time she shared her bed with a young, handsome Spanish winemaker from Santa Fe. She took his hand. "You know I can't see you anymore. I mean, I can't see you naked anymore."

Marcos laughed. "I know. The string of nonsense emojis you sent in response to my *You up?* text was a dead giveaway. You literally sent me a ghost. You know that's not how ghosting works, right?"

"You millennials have so much to teach your elders." There were smiles and then a silence between the two of them as they stood and stared at each other for some time. *I could take it all back*, she thought. *I should tell him I changed my mind and invite him to stay in the casita over New Year's, the two of us in our bubble.* Why not? What was the harm in another few weeks of being with Marcos? This was so much harder than she thought it would be. Finally, Nicole said, "Thank you, Marcos. I had fun. All of it."

"I had fun, too, Nicole. All of it," he said, before he planted the lightest touch of his lips on hers. "Need a lift? It's no trouble."

"It's a perfect night to walk."

"Yes, it is. Don't miss the lights on Canyon, not that you could."

"I won't."

"Vaya con Dios, amiga."

"You as well, my friend."

Marcos walked off in one direction and Nicole and Bardot in the other. She wasn't sure who started to cry first, her or the dog.

Chapter 28

Santa Fe, Melbourne, Kyoto, Mendoza
December

Nicole checked herself in the mirror. It was the first time seeing her family in months and she wanted to look . . . how? She wanted to look like she'd made the right decision. Somehow energized and relaxed all at the same time. She wanted to come across like Cleo, she realized. A woman fully in control of her life and her emotions, which, surprisingly to Nicole, was the way she felt at this moment.

For the full Cleo effect, she let her hair dry naturally, added a light application of makeup and a swipe of lipstick, put on the gorgeous new earrings that Billie Jo had given her as a thank-you for her work, and spritzed on some perfume, even though only she would know. She layered an oatmeal V-neck time in months. Chelsea was spending the school break in Melbourne, and moisturized her décolletage so it would look soft, not crepey, on camera. She thought she looked good.

She set her laptop up in the living room; the candles and the fire glowed in the background. She snapped the small light onto the camera to brighten her face. Then she clicked the link ten minutes early in case her family decided to show up early. They didn't.

But at the appointed hour, the three faces popped up. Jason first, then Chelsea, and a few seconds later, Jack. Jason took over facilitating the call, as if this were a weekly global marketing meeting. But there was a difference in his manner. There was warmth, love, a sense of fun that had been missing for years.

Nicole, of course, teared up seeing her children for the first time in months. Chelsea was spending the school break in Melbourne, staying with a new college friend at her parents' colossal house along with two others from her program, a Kiwi and a Brit. She talked knowingly of the cultural differences between them, the various subjects they were each specializing in, and their plans for the week, which seemed to include more drinking and dancing than art and history. Somehow, in a semester in a foreign country, she had ditched her glasses for contacts, grown her hair long, and acquired the first tan of her life in the sunny Australian climate. "My friends make fun of how much sunscreen I wear. I'm still the palest person I know, but just a lot less pale than I was in Oregon." Fortunately, she hadn't adopted a temporary accent, like so many that went abroad, but she had developed into an excellent mimic and did the voices of all her professors. She hinted at a boyfriend, an Aussie named Conall whom she was going to see at a New Year's Eve party, but clammed up when Nicole asked more questions, offering her typical response to any query: "Mom. It's cool. You don't need to worry." She was having the time of her life and her blossoming made Nicole physically hurt because she was so proud.

Jack had taken the train from Tokyo to Kyoto, where he was staying for a week in a student hostel with two other friends from his program. In Kyoto, Christmas was celebrated in a nonreligious way, but with world-class lights and illumination all over the city. He said there were nonstop social events and Santa-san. He was overwhelmed by the beauty of the place and the kindness of the locals. His only issues were with the Instagram influencers degrading the sanctity of the temples with their nonstop photos. Jack also shared his opinions on Japanese beer, architecture, fashion, haircuts, street food, and movie theaters. He had developed theories on foreigners abroad, the positive impact of small homes on the climate crisis, and why the international version of *The Wall Street Journal* was so much better than the domestic version. He'd shaved off his scraggly beard, used some sort of grooming product in his hair, and traded in his hoodie for a blazer. He had gone from college kid to man in mere months. Nicole could have listened to him talk all night.

She thought back to those years in high school when she could barely get him out of bed and now, here he was, thriving in a foreign country. The patience, the energy, and the resources they had put into Jack's recovery from anxiety and depression had paid off. Her mother-in-law had been right: talk therapy, regular strenuous exercise, and a job in the evenings to occupy the hours teenagers usually spent alone in their rooms, ruminating on their misery. Nicole found a young therapist Jack liked and trusted and stayed out of the way, as she'd been instructed, even though it was killing her not to know every word that was said in a session. And an evening job scooping ice cream at the new Salt & Straw down the street was the perfect combination of mindless and social. As for Jason during Jack's slow recovery, he did a complete turnaround on his family time and took up rock climbing and snowshoeing with Jack.

Things didn't turn around overnight. It took two years of work for him to fully emerge during his senior year, finishing strong. Even now, she kept a worried eye on him when he seemed down or anxious, like during lockdown. Tonight, though, he was beaming, and she wanted to reach through the screen and squeeze him into a hug. She hoped Jason felt the same.

But it was her husband Nicole couldn't get enough of. My God, he looked amazing. Rugged but refined with a trim beard, his face lean and tan; even his shoulders seemed more relaxed, like his neck had lengthened, lightened. Maybe it was the weight of work or grief or the daily grind of the last twenty-five years lifted off him, but he looked like a new man. Her man, but wow. She listened to him describe the rides, the mountains, the glaciers, the people, and the food and wine with exuberance. His emails had been so dry, but now his storytelling was rich with detail and atmosphere. And he'd rediscovered his sense of humor—not the cynical observations that passed as comedy these days, but stories like the self-effacing tale of stripping down to his skivvies in a parking lot and then running through the hotel lobby nearly naked. Jack and Chelsea were in stitches. Nicole couldn't take her eyes off him.

"How's your book going, Dad?" Jack asked, but Jason brushed off the question.

"Enough about me. Let's get to your mother. I'm afraid the authorities here at the inn will shut off my internet any minute."

"What exactly are you doing there, Mom?" Chelsea asked, completely on brand for the self-absorbed college student she was. While Nicole had memorized every detail of her daughter's photos and texts, it didn't surprise her that even a child of Chelsea's capabilities would have paid only the slightest attention to her mother's actions. Of course, Nicole had filled them in on her change of plans and had posted photos of her casita, her studio, the glorious sunsets, even Bardot. Frankly, lots of Bardot. But none of that seemed to have fully registered with her children. In fact, her journey of self-discovery seemed to boil down to a single data point in Chelsea's eyes: "When did you go blonde? I don't miss the purple at all. This is more you. Your whole vibe is different. You're not even wearing black!"

"I like it, too, Mom," Jack echoed. "You look like Kristen Bell."

That was really a stretch. She was neither that blonde nor that young, but it was Christmas so she'd consider the comment her gift. "I'll take that comparison any day of the week. Thanks."

Finally, Jason chimed in. "I like it, too, Nic. You look good."

She was flustered, flushed. Was her husband flirting with her on the family Zoom call? The smile on his face said that he was. "Thank you. Something different."

The moment was broken the minute Chelsea yelled, "Where's the dog? Can we see her? Do we get to keep her?" On command, Bardot jumped up on Nicole's lap, delighted her new audience with her cuteness, and the whole conversation dissolved into one about the dog and not about Nicole. Which was fine with Nicole. She wanted to absorb everything she'd observed tonight about the people she loved.

Her husband, her children, who all seemed to have changed so much in four months. Was it possible she had changed as much as they seemed to have changed? Beyond the blonde hair, somewhere deeper. It was. She knew it.

And yet, the powerful feeling of love and gratitude that swept through her when she looked at the four glitchy faces of the video grid was so familiar. It was the same feeling she'd had when Jason walked into Needham's looking for a suit for Charlie and Clare's wedding. The same one she'd felt when they held each other's hands all the way through Jewel's set at the very first Lilith Fair or in front of the judge at city hall the day they got married. That explosion of joy she'd experienced giving birth to Jack and then Chelsea and watching them bloom. The same quiet pride in what they'd created when an impromptu family dinner turned into hours of conversation and laughter. She'd felt this way when Jack graduated from high school, healthy and happy at last, and when Chelsea graduated as valedictorian. And she'd felt this way with Jason a thousand nights, when they lay in each other's arms, after they'd made love.

"Oh shit, they really are turning off my internet! I just got a two-minute warning. And I'm the host, so you'll all be cut off. We'll have to say goodbye."

"Merry Christmas!"

"Love you!"

"See you in May!"

Nicole waited for everyone else to leave and the screen to go dark before shutting her laptop. No doubt about it, she missed her people. But she really missed her husband. Her person. She wished he was here with her right now.

———

Jason's screen went blank and his family disappeared. He closed his laptop and pushed the chair away from the small desk in his room at the Villa Mansa, a hotel off the beaten track that promised serenity and delivered. Was it serenity or was it loneliness? Tough call. All he knew was that the past hour seeing his family spread out over four continents on Christmas was the lowest moment of his trip.

What was he trying to prove all by himself in a foreign country making small talk with waiters and other tourists? He wasn't even sure he wanted to go to Nicaragua. That was Charlie's dream, learning to surf in a south of the border beach town, eating rice and beans and fish cooked on a plancha while drinking cheap beer and staring at the ocean. Was it too late to back out? His kids seemed to think that he was some kind of badass, with his beard, telling stories about motorcycling and mountains and being at the end of the world. He didn't want to disappoint them by abandoning his plans now, the writing and the surfing in a beach town on the edge of a jungle. But they'd learn sooner or later that he never was a badass, just a middle-aged guy afraid of going to work one day and never coming home—like Charlie.

All he could think about was Nicole. She was a whole different person. No, different wasn't the right word. She was a new version of herself, a vibrant, more relaxed iteration of the organized hard worker she'd always been. Her hair, the jewelry, even the goofy way she played with the dog made Jason stare. She looked confident, happy, and sexy, he thought, like she was in the right place at the right time.

Meanwhile he was floundering, killing time in this hotel until his rental in Playa Maderas started on New Year's Eve. The motorcycle trip felt like an accomplishment, a journey he needed to make, and the research trip for this Argentina book felt productive. But the next five months stretched before him like a giant question mark.

There was no novel and there never would be a novel. He wasn't a writer; he was a publisher.

He was somebody who made great writing happen, but not somebody who made great writing.

He knew if he told Nicole she would understand, make him feel like he'd accomplished enough already. He didn't need to accomplish more to feel complete. Better, yes, but not more.

Should he trash his plans and fly to Santa Fe and surprise her? Or is that exactly what he shouldn't do? Maybe Nicole looked so self-sufficient because she was. Maybe she didn't want him or need him there. Maybe she had somebody else. He pushed that image away. He couldn't wrap his head around Nicole with anyone else, so he refused to even entertain the thought. He could only think about Nicole in his arms, his bed.

Chapter 29

Santa Fe
Playa Maderas
New Year's Eve

Nicole's phone pinged as she was climbing into bed. For the last twenty-five years, after one disastrous New Year's Eve in San Francisco at a restaurant with an atrocious prix fixe meal they couldn't afford with friends they didn't really like, nothing made her happier than being home and in her pajamas by nine while everyone else was out making merry. Tonight was no exception.

Her neighbors, Albert and Peter, had invited her over for champagne and hors d'oeuvres earlier in the evening, a lively one-hour event where they gossiped about mutual acquaintances—especially Holly, who had texted Nicole she was in a "toe-tingling" romance with a younger man and still hadn't decided on "what to do with that dog." ("We'd take her in a second, you know we would," Albert the architect said, with Peter the third-grade teacher nodding.) She'd come home, sent out messages to friends and family with well wishes, took a short shower, and put on an old T-shirt and sweats. She was looking forward to watching *The Holiday* on her tablet in bed, once again coveting the coats in the movie. Then her phone pinged again. The thought that it might be Marcos flashed through her mind, warming her body. Would she rally if he wanted to stop by? She might. She had underestimated how lonely and alone she would feel without family during the holidays. Plus, she missed him, his body. She checked her phone.

It was Jason.

For four months, they hadn't exchanged one text, only emails. It had been a valuable lesson in self-restraint for her, not grabbing the phone and unloading to him in a text about something like the cold weather or the dead car battery or the fact that Chelsea's Australian bikinis seemed to be getting smaller and smaller. She felt like she was coping better with stress, relying on herself first, not looking outward for answers. Suddenly, this single text took on epic meaning. What could he want?

He was listed in her phone as "J" and his profile picture was from a wedding they attended five years ago, before the pandemic, before Charlie, before the sabbatical. He looked young, polished, his skin smoother, but not as ruggedly handsome as the other night. The text said: *Happy New Year.*

Even in texts, he still used capitalization and punctuation. Like a book guy. She hesitated to respond, trying to think of something clever to say, when another text came in: *Miss you.* That got her attention. None of his emails had expressed any sentiment, only facts. This caught her off guard. She responded right away: *Miss you too. You in Playa Maderas?*

He answered: *Yes. I'm hot and sticky and concerned about how cheap the tequila is here. I may have had a few shots at a bar. Did I mention I miss you?*

You did, she wrote, deciding not to add anything else to see where he might take this.

Jason texted: *I was thinking about that night in New York. Remember that hotel on Central Park South? The one we thought was going to be swanky, but wasn't at all? Remember us in that hotel?*

Nicole's whole chest and face immediately flushed. Oh yes, she remembered that hotel, once grand but now shabby, a place that catered mainly to tour groups and a few random patrons like Nicole and Jason, who scored free rooms with frequent-flier points, trying to save money for the business. Run-down and loud in the lobby, their room was on one of the few floors that had been renovated. It must be ten years now since that night. They had been at a book event downtown. She was wearing a Ralph Lauren black evening suit that she scored at a deep discount. It was a daring choice for her—with no blouse, only lingerie underneath, slim-cut trousers, and very high heels. But she knew that Jason loved that look. So much so that they cut out of the event early, swiping a bottle of champagne on their exit, and started making out in the cab on the way to the hotel, like buzzed twentysomethings, not parents of two on a forty-eight-hour work trip to the big city. Jason threw wads of money at the cab driver when he dropped them off. The elevator bank area was crowded with theatergoers coming home from the evening performances of *Cats* or *Phantom* or the *Evita* revival. Jason pressed his body against hers, oblivious to the stares of other guests. By the time they got to the room, it was clear that two things were going to happen: they were going to have sex and it was going to be fast.

For dramatic effect, Jason left the lights off but opened the curtain to reveal a spectacular view. The cityscape made them feel invincible. He literally gasped when she removed her suit jacket, revealing the black lace bra underneath. It may have been the best reveal of her entire marriage. No, for sure it was the best reveal of her marriage. Afterward, they ordered a couple of overpriced room service burgers, drank the warmish champagne, and made love again, slower this time. But still with the curtains open.

Oh yes, she remembered that night. She texted: *one of my top 5*
He responded: *You have a list?*
She texted: *you know I love making lists*
He answered: *Let's hear them.*

Nicole wasn't going to make it that easy. She was enjoying this too much. She responded: *not all at once. you'll have to wait for my weekly emails.*

Jason: *Like a countdown?*

She typed: *exactly*

He replied: *Torture.*

She answered: *good torture*

He texted: *The fireworks have started. My new landlord told me I had to watch them . . . because sometimes the embers land on the roof and my house could go up in flames.*

She typed: *please go!*

He ended: *Love you, Nic.*

She ended: *<3*

Nicole's whole body was on fire. She put the phone down and turned out the light. She hadn't thought about that night in years. Now she would. And all the other nights when being with Jason was exactly right.

For sure, too much cheap tequila was involved in that exchange. The fireworks were making his head spin. *Dry January starts tomorrow,* Jason thought. *Or at least, Beer Only January.* He had no idea that Nicole would respond like that. He'd been worried that she might be otherwise engaged, that she had found herself an Abby, but clearly not. He was surprised at how relieved he was that she answered right away, implying she was alone on New Year's Eve. And that she was playing along. Her response made his head spinning worthwhile. He wouldn't have had the guts to text her if he were stone-cold sober.

One night in town and he could already sense that becoming the drunk American at the beach bar was a real possibility here in Playa Maderas. Really, the place he had rented was Playa Maderas adjacent, a little outpost neighborhood two miles down the beach. The proper town of PM, as locals called it, had a whopping three restaurants, one decent beachfront hotel filled with young people seeking spiritual awakenings in yoga, surfing, and beer, and a legit grocery store, plus a few other amenities like a bakery and a laundromat.

In PM-adjacent, where he was renting, there was a cul-de-sac of beach houses like his, more run-down than in the online photo, owned by expats from various English-speaking countries, according to his landlord. Down the beach a bit farther was a crappy surf tourist motel, engulfed in the smell of weed, that seemed to be entirely occupied by people under thirty who hadn't combed their hair in months. (White kids with dreads, a Portland stereotype he was familiar with.) The only other prominent building in town was an establishment that served as bar, restaurant, post office, internet café, and market. He could tell that he'd be eating most meals at Pablo's Place, like he had tonight.

That depressed him.

The surfers on the beach were lighting off fireworks at random intervals. A giant bonfire was lit and some poor guy was playing Jack Johnson on a guitar, because that was the law in a town with a vibe like this. The crashing waves drowned out the singer occasionally, but not Jason's melancholy. Tomorrow, he'd pretend to start on his book. But tonight, his thoughts went back to that hotel in New York, that shining skyline, the way his wife moved in the black suit—and he wondered what Nicole was thinking, and doing, right now.

To: Jason
From: Nicole
Subject: #4

I'm calling New York Hotel #5, so the countdown continues with Halloween 2007 coming in at #4. Remember that party at Tessa's house for adults only, no children? You complained for a week about having to go because, and I quote, "Halloween is for children." I made you promise to go for one hour. And I told you to wear a retro suit and tie and go as Bruce Wayne from the TV series, which you agreed to do. But then I surprised you as Catwoman, your teen boy fantasy come to life, in that very authentic and very tight sparkling catsuit and the low-slung belt. Remember my full Julie Newmar wig, the kitty cat mask, and the long fake nails? I'm not sure we even would have made it to the party, except the babysitter showed up and we had to leave the house. All night long, I played my part and kept toying with you. We stayed long enough to guarantee that the kids were asleep when we got home. Let's say you liked my version of Catwoman so much, you had me leave on the mask and the ears in the bedroom. Think about that, Bruce Wayne. Meow.

xo Nic

To: Nicole
From: Jason
Re: #4

Good choice. Believe me, I remember that night. I also remember that I put on my cherished Nelson Riddle album of the TV series theme song and the lesser-known B side, "Nelson's Riddler," to accompany . . . us. Surprisingly inspiring, as I recall. My only critique would be your self-conscious use of the signature whip. You were so embarrassed. I'm sorry you had to return that suit. And I apologize for not being more enthusiastic about dressing up. You've always been way more into it than me. I missed giving you a night with Batman. Bruce Wayne is not the same.

To: Jason
From: Nicole
Subject: #3

The location: East Corvallis High School Parking Lot

The Date: Fourth of July, 2012

The Vehicle: A ten-year-old Ford Windstar

The Situation: That dreadful annual Fourth of July party my mother used to host when she was married to Bud, that guy who collected World War II miniatures and was part of that church/cult. And all his kids and grandkids and exes and stepkids and weird cousins would come and talk about Beaver football and their prepper manifesto. My mother pretended to like them even though it was obvious she had nothing in common with any of them, but Bud was union and had good health insurance, so she thought the marriage was worth it. At least our kids liked the Slip n' Slide and we never stayed the night.

The Details: My mother asked us in the middle of the party to go pick up some ice cream, which we did. Anything to get out of there for a few minutes. We went to the store and then were driving home past my alma mater, East Corvallis High, and I said, "I think I'm the only one in town who hasn't had sex in that parking lot." And you said, "Well, we gotta rectify that." And we did it in the back of our minivan, parked over near the entrance to the cafeteria.

The Music: You dug that Pixies CD out of the glove compartment, put on "Here Comes Your Man," and it was like being a senior in high school again. But so much better because you were you and not Danny Thompson, the guy I actually dated in high school with the saliva issues.

The Aftermath: We delivered three melted gallons of ice cream to my mother without explanation.

To: Nicole
From: Jason
Re: #3

Such a good choice. The minivan. The Pixies. The Danny Thompson reference. (Wasn't he the guy with the Camaro, though? Come on!) I had completely forgotten about the melted ice cream. Delivering that ice cream to your mother in that condition was probably the most irresponsible thing you ever did in your life.

We should make this an annual event. Now that your mom has moved on from Prepper Bud and his posse, it's safe to go back for the picnic if she still throws it. But I'd like to get back to that parking lot.

I'd like to add an addendum to this item vis-à-vis vehicles. Our attempt to couple atop that ATV at the Oregon coast was not as successful. Who knew the gearshift got so hot? Like on fire hot.

J.

To: Jason
From: Nicole
Subject: #2

Because it's my list and I get to make the rules, #2 is a group citation for Quickies Before Work. Too many to count over the years, but taken as a whole, some of our best work. Cast your mind back and I think you'll agree that these encounters add up to some good old-fashioned fun. And so efficient.

This one gets me going, baby.

xo Nic

From: Jason
To: Nicole

Me, too. Phew. We had some serious fun before 7 a.m.
   Jesus, I miss you.

                                        J.

Chapter 30

Santa Fe
Costa Rica
February

"Jason?" Nicole answered the phone with a question mark in her voice. She was standing in her kitchen, about to feed the dog, when the call came in. His photo and initial were on the screen, but she didn't quite believe he was on the other end of the phone. *Maybe #2 was just too much for him and he had to hear my voice*, she thought triumphantly. The last month, their correspondence had set her spirit on fire. She was counting down the days until she could see him in person, but at the same time she loved exploring their relationship from afar. Everything in her world felt altered by their new revelations. Her work at the studio reflected passion, confidence. Her mind was clear. The aches and pains of aging seemed to be on the back burner with the walking, the dancing, and the hot yoga she'd added in. She wanted to be at her best when they rendezvoused in May before heading to Asia. But she guessed he couldn't wait. "Is that you? You're going to have to wait for my overall #1."

"It's me. Listen Nic, it's my dad. He had a heart attack."

Suddenly serious, she asked, "Is he okay?"

"I spoke to my brother Chris. The situation isn't great. He was on the golf course when it happened, which is so fucking classic because he never golfed before he retired. People think doctors golf all the time, but all my father did was work. He worked for decades as a goddamn cardiologist and he never relaxed. Now he finally retires and gets the chance and has a heart attack on the eighth hole. Like way out there on the course," Jason rambled. Nicole could hear the concern and tension in his voice, but instead of expressing it to her, he went on a rant about golf. His relationship with his father had mellowed over the years. It wasn't perfect. There were still issues on Jason's end about never feeling good enough and his father's failure to take an interest in Jason's work. But there was mutual respect in terms of how each of them worked hard, raised successful kids, and stayed married, unlike Jason's brother Austin, who was on his third wife. "He's in the ICU."

"What is the prognosis?"

"Chris says it's really touch and go right now. He's had a stent put in and the docs are trying to stabilize him, but it can be very tricky to get the right combination of meds after an incident like this. So, it's wait and see for forty-eight hours," Jason reported.

That's when Nicole heard the distinct sounds of an airport announcement in the background. "Where are you?"

"I'm at the airport in Costa Rica. It's a couple of hours closer than Managua and they have more flights to San Francisco. I'm coming home."

"That's the right decision. You need to see him, be there with your mom." Nicole's own relationship with Sandrine had reached détente after she was so helpful in shepherding Jack through his anxiety. Sandrine turned out to be critical to her grandson's treatment and recovery, loving and knowledgeable. Also, a tremendous resource for Nicole to lean on. "She's probably a mess."

"She is. My brother said she's disoriented and struggling to comprehend what's happening. She's in a lot of denial for someone who has been married to a cardiologist for nearly sixty years," Jason said. "But what I mean is, I'm really coming home. I'm done with Nicaragua. I'm done with being apart. As soon as I hung up with Chris, I knew exactly what I needed to do. I called my landlord here and gave notice. I booked a flight. I got in a car to the airport. I'm coming home."

"Do you want me to meet you in San Francisco? I can come, Jason," Nicole said, even though she'd have to undo a host of commitments. She had projects due at school over the next few weeks and a paper. Cleo and Billie Jo were headed to Dallas and Los Angeles for their first trunk shows for the Zia Collective, finally executing that part of the plan post-pandemic, and Nicole had promised she'd work at the shop, along with Moon, the new hire who was a dream employee for Zia. Plus, there was Bardot, but of course Albert and Peter would take her if Nicole needed to leave. Why was she doing this to herself? Running through the list in her head again? She hadn't done this in so long—thought of all the reasons she couldn't do something instead of all the reasons she should do something. Jason needed her. "Give me a day or two and I can meet you there."

"It's okay. Let me get there and figure out what's happening. I'm going to stay with my mom and be there for her. I think for right now, it's best if it's only me."

Nicole wasn't hurt at all. Jason's family tended to close ranks on issues like this and usually that meant she was outside the circle, not inside. She was used to it. "Of course. When is your flight?"

"In an hour."

"Do you need me to do anything on my end? Call somebody? Arrange something like a car for you?"

"Austin's going to pick me up. Chris doesn't want to leave, which I understand. We'll go straight to the hospital."

"I'll touch base with Lucy in case there's anything." Her sister-in-law Dr. Lucy Chow, Chris's wife, was the dermatologist to the tech stars in Atherton. She and Nicole had bonded during one hot Elswick family vacation in Yosemite when they both refused to go into a cave because of claustrophobia, giving them two hours to talk about their love of skincare products. Ever since that day, they acted as communication directors for their two families, because God forbid the brothers contact each other to set up holidays or anniversary parties. Lucy always had gobs of free samples to offload on Nicole when she got to the Bay Area and Nicole alerted Lucy to special friends and family discounts at Needham's on her favorite designers. The derm was a clotheshorse. She was surprised she hadn't already heard from Lucy, but maybe protocol dictated that Jason be informed first. "Jason, I'm sorry this is happening to you. I'm sure this isn't how you wanted this part of your trip to end."

"I hate it here. I'm grateful to have an excuse to leave. Charlie would have hated it, too. Too many young Americans with too much money here for yoga retreats and thinking they fucking invented craft beer. And surfers are douchebags," he spat out. "I'll tell you more later. I think they're calling my flight. Love you, Nic."

She noticed he didn't mention the book and she didn't ask. "I love you, too, Jason. Call anytime."

"It's good to hear your voice."

"He's coming home, Bardot. You may have a new dad soon. I'm not sure how I feel about that. How should I feel about that, good dog?" Nicole said in the high, animated voice she used to talk to the dog. Nicole had a lot of one-sided conversations with Bardot, who seemed to understand it was her job to listen. At least until Nicole put the food bowl down.

How should she feel about it? She wanted to see Jason, of course, but did she want him here with her in Santa Fe? In December, she would have said no, especially because of Marcos. Even after she ended it with him, she needed space and time to be alone to absorb what had happened. Whenever she encountered Marcos—like at dance class the other night when he took her elbow or when he sat so close to her at the bar afterward that she could smell his scent—she felt the frisson of excitement between them. That hadn't disappeared just because she called off the physical part of their relationship. She couldn't imagine an encounter between Jason and Marcos where it would not have been obvious to Jason what had transpired.

But Jason was Jason, so much a part of her that ever since New Year's Eve, she had missed him, really missed him. *Yearning* was such a literary term, such a Jason word, but that's what she felt when she'd compiled her list and sent those emails, a level of intimacy and boldness unusual for her. That must mean something. But was it enough to end the sabbatical and have him move here? It was an open question.

"I don't have to decide today," she said out loud to the dog, who looked up at her after finishing her dinner. Maybe when they knew more about his father, she would ask Jason to come live with her until she finished her program. But she didn't have to commit today, she decided, as she put the rest of the turkey and rice she made for Bardot into the fridge. On the fridge door was a postcard from the O'Keeffe Museum, a quote from the artist herself: *I think it's so foolish for people to want to be happy. Happy is so momentary—you're happy for an instant and then you start thinking again. Interest is the most important thing in life; happiness is temporary, but interest is continuous.*

She thought of her friends and the conversation they had after leaving the O'Keeffe Museum, about the separate lives of the painter and her photographer husband. Was she like Georgia O'Keeffe, not wanting her husband to see the life she had created in New Mexico? Keeping Santa Fe as her secret? It wasn't that she didn't love Jason, didn't want to share her life with his. The communication from the last few months made it clear that their connection was still vital. But did she want to share this part of her life with him? That she didn't know.

Jason sat in the business class seat. He'd taken his credit card and practically thrown it at the ticketing agent, a dark-haired woman in her thirties looking crisp in her uniform, to pay for a ticket on the next flight to California. He must have looked desperate, and when he revealed why he was heading home, she found a ticket and gave it to him at the bereavement fare. Then she made a comment about how if his travels brought him back to Costa Rica, he should look her up, handing him her card. He realized he'd taken his wedding ring off months ago and should probably put it back on now that he was headed stateside. He thanked the gate agent and said he absolutely would, not wanting to seem rude. Now in his seat, he fished through his carry-on and found his ring tucked inside a zipped pocket, wrapped in a cocktail napkin from one of the many lodges he stayed at in Patagonia. A place where he'd slept with Abby, recollecting the evening fondly. That seemed like another time and place now.

He was headed back to San Francisco and then where? To Nicole. He'd go to Nicole. If she wanted him, if she'd let him. From the day he left Portland, he was always headed back to her, he realized. Just taking the long way home.

Chapter 31

Portland
December 2020

When the call came in from Charlie's brother, Jason was working in the guest room above the garage that he reconfigured into a home office, outfitted to the degree that he could manage more than a hundred employees in three cities via computer screen. He had upgraded the Wi-Fi, bought a standing desk, and taken one of the espresso machines from the empty Stumptown HQ. He called it his Pandemic Palace and there was nothing he liked about the place. He missed his people. He missed Smart Boards. He missed assistants, lunches out with writers, and drinks after work with colleagues. The only thing he didn't miss was the grind of travel. If he never ate another meal off a tray in his lifetime that would be fine. He was in the middle of a Zoom staff meeting when his cell rang, and the name Griffin Kendrick popped up on the screen.

He'd gotten to know Charlie's older brother over the years, of course. He was the CFO of a real estate development company. They'd gone on fishing weekends and ski trips and Charlie had even dragged them both to a Dead & Company show in Eugene a few years before, still trying to prove to them that the Dead was the greatest band of all time, hands down. ("Even John Mayer can't ruin the magic," Charlie had quipped, though they all knew he secretly worshipped Mayer's guitar skills.) Still, he and Griffin didn't have the kind of relationship where they picked up the phone and called each other in the middle of a workday. A Tuesday morning at 10:42, to be precise. Jason had a bad feeling. All this fucking Covid and there was Charlie in the middle of it as an ER doc, treating every person who walked through the door like a human being, even if they'd been out protesting mask mandates. Jason wasn't running the staff meeting, but he was the boss, so he logged off, because he could do what he wanted, and answered the call.

"Hey, Griff. Everything okay?" Jason said upon answering.

"No, man. It's not."

It seemed like an eternity after he hung up with Griffin before Jason forced himself into the house to tell Nicole, but it was only the length of the studio version of "Box of Rain," Charlie's favorite Dead song. Played once, then played again. It was the first thing Jason could think of to do for the guy he loved: play his favorite song by his favorite band. *A box of rain will ease the pain and love will see you through*.

Griffin said the highway patrol was piecing together what happened, but it looked like a single-car accident caused in part by morning fog and a slippery roadway. Exhausted and spent after twenty straight hours in the ER caring for the worst of the Covid patients coming into the hospital, Charlie took a shower in the hospital locker room to wash off all the germs, put on clean clothes, got in his BMW, and headed for home in Lake Oswego at about six in the morning, where he'd been isolating himself in the guest room for months to avoid exposing his family. Maybe he fell asleep or lost concentration, but something happened on the twenty-minute drive to the Portland suburb and Charlie's car went off the road and hit a tree head-on. He died instantly.

Griffin had asked him to go to Clare's side and be with her and the kids until he could get down from Seattle later that day. "I don't know how organized Charlie was about all his stuff, you know, like his will and shit. I hope he took care of all that," Griffin had said.

"Of course. Anything. Yes, I'll head there now," Jason responded, relieved to be assigned a task, something specific to do now. Because the thought of sitting with this reality was more than he could handle. He might never want to be alone with himself ever again, but definitely not now. How could he go through the rest of his life without Charlie? "Griffin, I'm so sorry for your loss."

There was a pause. Griffin was choked up. "I'm sorry for your loss, too, Jason." And he hung up. *How many more calls like that will Griffin have to make?* Jason thought.

When the song ended for the second time, Jason got up to cross the walkway to his house and tell his wife that the best man he ever knew ran into a fucking tree. For one second, one brief second, he wondered if Charlie had done it on purpose, just cranked the wheel to the left and driven that old Beemer into oblivion. He hoped not.

Such a long, long time to be gone and a short time to be there.

"What do you need me to do? Do you need me to drive you, Jason? I don't know if you should drive right now." Nicole's voice was shaking. She wasn't crying yet; she'd gone into action mode.

"I actually don't think you should drive," he said, speaking the truth.

"Poor Clare. And those kids. The twins are only in middle school. And Nico and Lily, they'll be lost without Charlie. He was the best father," she said. "What do you need?"

"Can you call my assistant Timothy? I just bailed on a staff meeting in the middle and now he's probably freaking out because I'm out of touch and I have Zoom meetings all day. Can you call him and tell him what happened? Tell him to clear my schedule for the week?" Jason asked, then added, "Please."

"Of course. Anyone else?"

"No. I'll call Martha in New York later," he said, referring to his counterpart on the East Coast. "Oh, tell Timothy no announcement email. I don't want eight million people replying all with their sympathy messages. Keep my whereabouts vague."

The tears were welling behind Nicole's eyes. She didn't want to cry in front of Jason or on the phone with his assistant. She needed to keep it together for her husband. For her friend. "Why don't you go change your clothes?" she said, nodding to the sweatpants he'd been wearing. "And text me later if there is anything I can organize for Clare. She doesn't have any siblings. She'll need me. I'm sure their nice neighbors will be all over food. I'm talking about . . . other stuff. Funeral details, if there even is one with this lockdown . . ." Her voice trailed off because the thought of trying to mourn someone like Charlie through a computer screen was too awful to contemplate.

Jason nodded, heading up the stairs to change, then turned to look back at his wife. She had her head in her hands and was sobbing. He turned away.

Chapter 32

San Francisco
Santa Fe
February

"I'm sorry to wake you."

It was after midnight. Nicole had fallen asleep reading, her light still on despite the hour. She had tried to stay up, thinking that Jason might call once he landed and had a chance to see his father. "I said call anytime. I meant it. Everything okay?"

"He's still with us but he looks terrible. I can see why my brother told me to get on a plane."

Nicole sat up in bed, working the pillow behind her back. "I'm so sorry. What are the doctors saying? His doctors, not your brothers?"

"That it's still a wait and see, but he's getting the best care."

"And your mom?"

"Better. She's coping better. She's still distraught, but she managed to take a sleeping pill."

"And you?"

"Disoriented. This is a far cry from Playa Maderas, but I'm glad to be here," he said, twisting around in the sheets to find a comfortable position. Then his business voice returned. "I'm ordering one of those mattresses in a box they advertise on podcasts tomorrow. I think this bed is the same twin I had in high school. I won't last another night in this bed," he said. "Nic, I have to tell you something . . ."

She was now fully awake and immediately her stomach clenched. *Please don't tell me anything. Please don't.* If she had brought about the end of their marriage with her stupid suggestion, she would never get over it. "What? What do you have to tell me?"

There was a long pause, then he started. "The book, Nic. My book. It doesn't exist. I didn't write a word. Not a single fucking word. I didn't even do that thing you see writers do in the movies and stare at a blank page with a blinking cursor. I didn't even try to write the novel I was supposed to be working on for months. Or my whole adult life. I had nothing in me."

"Oh, thank God," she said, starting to laugh with relief. "I thought . . . I thought it would be something worse. For us, I mean. Worse for us."

It took Jason a second to comprehend her meaning, but when he did, he replied, "Oh, no. Not terrible for us, just terrible for me." Then he started to laugh, too. "It feels so good to admit it to someone. I am not a writer. Not a writer. I must have read a hundred books. Franzen, Hemingway, Marquez, Allende, Morrison, Anne Tyler, Ta-Nehisi Coates. I finally read *The Sympathizer* and all of Sally Rooney's books. I went down a mystery rabbit hole, one after the other. I read for hours at a time. But I didn't write a single word."

"That's okay. Nobody's going to judge you because you didn't do something you've never done before."

"They will judge. But I have to be okay with it."

"Can I tell you something?"

"Please don't tell me you wrote a novel."

"No, never. Those emails will stand the test of time as my best written work. Here's my secret: I can't make a circle. At least in silver. I am a mediocre silversmith who can't make a bracelet to save her life. My idea for hammered silver cuffs with inspirational quotes was not only clichéd and overdone, but I'm also not skilled enough to execute the design. My bracelets looked like mutant handcuffs. And not in a sexy way. So, I'm making charms and pendants because they don't have to be circular. I almost quit the course in December," she said.

"I am so glad to hear this," he replied.

"Thank you. How kind," Nicole answered, feeling so at ease with the man on the other end of the phone. "Want to know the most tragic part? I discovered I am good at . . . retailing. Yup. Working in retail! Like I've been doing for thirty years. I am good at what I was already doing."

"Me, too! I put together six solid book ideas that someone else can write. And a few new ideas for brand extensions that I think are strong. I fired off a bunch of emails from the hospital waiting room to writers—real writers I know—to work on some of these pitches. Also, stuff I was doing before my midlife crisis."

"It wasn't a crisis," she said, her voice soft. "You weren't in crisis, just a bit bent out of shape. What you needed was a renewal. A re-up."

"A midlife re-up. Maybe that's another book idea," he said. Then asked, "And us? Is that what we had? A marriage re-up?"

She thought of Marcos, then swept the thoughts aside. She knew right then she wanted Jason to come to Santa Fe. "I think so. Don't you?"

"Yes. I do," he said, his voice tired now. "I have to get some sleep."

"Me, too."

"I'll talk to you tomorrow."

"Call anytime."

Jason turned off the light in his childhood bedroom. Despite the circumstances, he felt a thousand pounds lighter. He did feel renewed.

Chapter 33

Santa Fe
March

Roger peered over Nicole's shoulder in the studio. The piece she was working on, a variation of the charms she'd been creating all semester, was shaping up to be one of her most accomplished. Gary had asked her to make a New Mexico pendant with a heart in stonework and a dangling initial overlay for his "new ladylove," because that's the way Gary talked, like a guy who rolled off the Eagles tour in 1977 to spend a few days in a happening city. The pendant was less than an inch in diameter so the work had to be precise and sharp; the micro inlaid stones were clean and colorful. "Very groovy," her professor said.

"But not too groovy, right? I want it to look modern, not throwback-y." She had done some light hammering on the piece, giving the shape of the state a textured look. But the heart shape was polished. And the tiny letter "D" that hung from the bail that attached the pendant to the leather cord was in lowercase, a look Nicole thought was feminine and fresh.

"No. I like the design a lot. I know it's for Gary to give as a gift and that feels like a word he would say," Roger answered. "You know, the minute you walked away from hammered silver bangles and found your way into charms and pendants, you found yourself."

"Who knew it would be so hard for me to create a circle? It looks so easy, but it's deceptive."

"The key is that you knew when to let go of one idea and embrace another. Your pieces keep getting better and better and I don't think I've seen a lot like these in town. You may have found a professional outlet for your skills, if you can turn out more than one a week." Roger had spent a lot of time this term reinforcing professional practices, how much work a silversmith had to crank out monthly to make a living. It meant working night and day until you could create enough demand for your products to raise your prices.

"Thanks, Roger. I'm glad I stuck with the class. But I think I know that it will be more of a hobby for me than a career track. And the minute I realized the truth, I started enjoying the process more, and I got a lot better at the smithing. Imagine that?"

"What other designers say is that they work on commission. Which means 'occasionally when someone pays up front.' You can put that on your card: Nicole Elswick. Silversmith on Commission." They both laughed.

Roger had become a friend, as well as a mentor. In turn, she made some inquiries at boutiques in Portland about carrying some of his original designs in addition to his factory pieces. She had connected him to a very good store in Northwest Portland that would begin selling his work, after a successful Zoom meeting the owner, Roger, and she had. She was surprised how hands-on the selling process was, even for someone with Roger's portfolio of celebrity clients. It was a learning experience.

Just then, her phone vibrated in her pocket. She had told Roger about what was going on with Jason's father and asked permission to keep her phone during class, something he rarely allowed. She took it out and looked at the screen. It was Jason. "Can I take this? It's Jason."

"Of course. Outside."

———

For two weeks, Jason had called daily with brief updates when he had a moment and cell phone service, which could be hard to find inside the hospital. The calls were at random times and Nicole had made it a point to answer whenever he rang. His father was out of danger and now recovering from the heart attack and the subsequent angioplasty in a rehab facility in Menlo Park, close to his brother's house. As the medical news improved, the stress and tension of the first few phone calls after Jason's return had dissipated. Now they returned to familiar ground: the unending logistics of family life, especially when older parents were involved.

Dr. Michael Elswick's heart attack had created the cavalcade of changes that often happens in the lives of the elderly when medical issues arise: real estate issues, home health care needs, easy access for family members, financial revelations. Jason's parents, two well-educated, well-respected doctors who had earned a good living, were no different than most people's parents when it came to the realities of aging. The house they had lived in for fifty years in the Mission District was ragged around the edges. Their retirement income was not as much as expected. And, for two doctors who had access to some of the best health care in the world, they'd put off a lot of routine care over the years. As Jason said the other day, "The words *deferred maintenance* come up a lot, whether it's the house or their finances or their own bodies."

In the time he'd been in San Francisco, the family made the decision to move their parents out of the four-story Victorian in the city, into assisted living near Chris and Lucy's place in Atherton. The stairs were too much for the patient and the drive into the city was too much for the adult children. The house was the key asset to affording a place in one of the most expensive zip codes in America. But, once the medical decisions had been settled, all the doctors in Jason's family went back to doctoring and Jason stepped in to meet with real estate agents, sign contracts, arrange for movers, and hire painters and contractors to get the house in decent shape to sell.

And he spent hours helping his mother cope with all the changes, simply by being there with her.

"It's a good thing somebody in this family knows how to read the fine print in a contract. And a profit and loss statement. Doctors are terrible at all this practical stuff. My parents' finances are a mess," Jason said. It reminded Nicole of the months following Charlie's death, when he learned the same thing about his friend. He could save lives, but he could not balance a checkbook. Jason had stepped in then as now.

"What's your timeline now?" Nicole asked, standing outside in the freezing temperatures, glad she had grabbed her coat. "When do you think you'll be able to come to Santa Fe?"

"At least another month. The movers come next week, but it will be a few weeks before we get the place cleaned and painted. And I refuse to pay for a stager, even though Rufus the real estate agent thinks I'm making a tragic mistake. But no one's moving into this place as is, so why stage it? This whole thing will be gutted by some thirtysomething Googler," he said, his voice a mix of disdain and admiration.

"Listen to you. You sound like you're on an HGTV show. All that lockdown TV watching has really paid off," she said. "You know, I've already packed up two houses this year, ours and Holly's. Do you want me to come help?"

"No need. I want to see you, of course. I still need to know which one is #1 and I can't believe you won't tell me until we see each other in person. But the right moment is not when I'm sleeping in my childhood bedroom with my mom at the other end of the hall," he said.

"It's not a punishment; it's an enticement."

"So you say," he quipped. "You have school and the store. Finish what you started there. Let me deal with this on my own. We can all visit here this summer after we get back with the kids. When my dad is feeling better and my mother has adjusted to a small house and life. I told Chris we'd do that, spend some time here. I hope you don't mind."

"I think that's a lovely idea. It's been too long since we've been down there as a family." They still had their plans in place to meet the kids in the Philippines in May.

"It's been good to spend this time with my parents. I only wanted to kill my mother twice yesterday. That's way down from last week's average."

"It's a lot of changes for both of them. I'm sure they're scared."

"Yeah. Aren't we all?" he said.

"I've got to go back in. I'm freezing."

"Is that a silversmithing term?"

"No. I'm standing in the parking lot and it's twenty degrees. I'm literally freezing."

"Okay, Nic. I'll talk to you tomorrow."

"Tomorrow."

"Welcome back!" Nicole cried as she walked through the door of Zia. It was late afternoon on a Thursday night, but she'd gotten the word from Moon that Billie Jo and Cleo had returned and they were unpacking what merchandise was left from their first trunk shows in Dallas and Los Angeles, so she decided to surprise them at the store. She was greeted with hugs and high fives, but the biggest surprise seemed to be that she parked a car in front of the shop.

"You drove?" Cleo and Billie Jo said simultaneously. Then Cleo continued, "I didn't even really believe you had a car. I thought it was an elaborate ruse to get me to drive you home from class every week, preying on my guilty environmentalist sympathies."

"It's cold out!" Nicole argued. "Bardot won't leave the house, even in her pink coat!" It was true, the temperatures had stayed well below freezing for most of the week. The snow and ice that were charming and festive in December were miserable in March. She could understand why the locals who could afford to leave had fled south to their other houses in Mexico, or as one well-heeled woman at the coffee shop called it, "Old Mexico." Nicole kept her walking to short distances in daylight hours and went to hot yoga to warm up. "How was your trip? I mean, the Instagram posts were impressive, but did you really sell out in Dallas?"

Billie Jo took the question and ran, describing the enthusiastic shoppers in Texas and California, eating up all her storytelling about the mission, her artisans, and nearly every piece of jewelry they had brought with them. The emergency shipment of replacement jewelry that Moon and Nicole had put together and shipped to LA had also nearly sold out.

"The LA crowd all wanted special orders, as if buying something that day was akin to buying off the rack. But Billie Jo pivoted like a pro, taking special orders and design requests. I was so proud of her," Cleo explained. The warmth and pride in her voice were evident, not a drop of condescension. The two women had a mentor/mentee relationship that felt authentic in every way.

Billie Jo, the usually unemotional founder of the Zia Collective, practically blushed, then became teary-eyed and thanked Cleo for her support and faith. "I've learned so much from you." And then she looked at Nicole and said, "You, too, Nicole."

It was an emotional moment for all involved. Nicole felt a deep satisfaction at her small part of contributing to Zia, of being a part of the team to take Billie Jo's vision to the next level. Billie Jo could support her family with her work and promote artists who may not otherwise have had the ability to work full-time on their craft.

Cleo started to gather her things and then she turned to Nicole. "I have a huge favor. Could you give me a ride home? We Ubered from the airport together and I was going to take another home. But since you have your car . . ."

"It would be my pleasure."

———

The second she pulled her Tiguan away from the curb, Cleo was on her. "So, what's happening with the hubby?"

"Please, you don't really use the word *hubby*, do you?"

"Only in cases like this. I think of him as your made-up man."

"I assure you, he's real. As I told you, his father is out of the woods for now, but it will be a long recovery. But his parents have decided to do all the things they should have done five years ago: downsize, move closer to their adult children, and start taking care of themselves. Or at least, let Jason take better care of their affairs, so they don't have to cancel their Greek cruise in September, which is their highest priority, according to Jason. His plan is to be there another month and then come here."

"Thus ending the marriage sabbatical?"

"Yes. We'll be within the five-hundred-mile boundary if we're sharing Holly's house, so no shenanigans." She could have some fun with the arrangement now, even though it had occurred to her that she and Jason were still 1,149 miles apart and, technically, free to see other people. "It's already ended for me."

"Have you seen Marcos lately?" Cleo asked, making assumptions that Nicole didn't bother to protest.

"A couple of times at flamenco class. We're dance partners. Nothing more." That wasn't exactly true, but Nicole didn't want to go into it with Cleo. They were friendly, but they weren't friends. There had been too much heat between them to cool down to the mundanity of casual friendship. At dance class, they could touch and acknowledge the past in their movements, glances. On the street when they met, it was awkward. Only Bardot saved the encounters from being downright painful. She thought of a snippet of gossip from Clancy to share. "I heard he has a girlfriend. A gallery girl. Very beautiful. And the golden age of twenty-nine. May she stay that age forever."

"I'll be very interested in the reunion with your husband. This is a relationship experiment that really intrigues me because so many marriages are destroyed by affairs that turn out to mean nothing, but in the process the husband and wife can't reconcile. Your 'don't ask, don't tell' rule may be the secret to a long marriage. A secret I wish I had known."

"Don't wait for a Modern Love essay. This is between us. And Jason. And Marcos."

"I'm the only one you need to tell. A year from now. When you're back home, back to your old lives. I need to know how you feel then. Was it freeing? Or does not knowing eat you up?"

"I feel like you're preparing to play me in a movie."

"Your mother-in-law, maybe." Cleo laughed. "Take this exit, then a right." Nicole had never been to Cleo's house. Their relationship centered around smithing class and Zia. This was unknown territory, though Nicole doubted Cleo would invite her in and Nicole would decline anyway. Cleo looked tired from the travel, showing her age for once.

"I hope you can relax for the next few days. I'm sure that trip was a lot of being 'on' for you," Nicole said, hoping it came off as concerned and not ageist.

"Another left on Encantado and then up the hill. The house is about two miles from here," she directed. "Remember that first car ride home when I asked you to work with Billie Jo?"

"Of course."

"And look how that turned out. Very successful. For Billie Jo and for you, I think. Well, I have another proposition for you. How would you like to continue to work with Zia, even after you move back to Portland? Billie Jo is going to need someone to travel with her to do these trunk shows around the country. She needs an experienced hand to organize the marketing, the inventory, and—what do you call it, the actual selling? The, the . . . oh, you know what I mean . . ."

"The point of sale?"

"Yes. Point of sale. And it can't be me. I've been so happy to work with her and lend my name. But now, I'd like to step aside. The trips are too much for me. But you're young. If you were the behind-the-scenes person, it would be fabulous. You could work from Portland, but when the trunk shows happen four times a year, you could come to Santa Fe for a few days before, pack up everything, and then do the trips with Billie Jo. I think I've got one more in me, the New York show in May, but then I'd like to turn this part of the plan over to you. Billie Jo and I can figure out a compensation package for you. Or you can propose one. What do you think? Oh, turn at the next driveway. Follow the lights to the house."

"Got it." Like many of the most beautiful homes in the area, the profile of Cleo's house from the street was a one-story adobe-brown rambler, simple and not that impressive. As the car pulled into the circular gravel driveway, Nicole could see that while the front of the house was charming, the wow factor of the house would be the view of the mountains off the back side. She imagined floor to ceiling windows to take in the Sangre de Cristos at sunset. And she knew the interior design was magazine-worthy because she'd seen snippets of it in photos of Cleo in various publications, a corner of the timbered living room in one portrait of her, a blurred kitchen backdrop in another. Cleo kept her private life private. But she was letting Nicole in a little bit more with every conversation. And now, this job offer.

She waited to stop the car before answering the proposal, the satisfying crunch under the car wheels. "First of all, thank you so much. This is an amazing offer. It's so unexpected. Are you sure you don't want somebody here in Santa Fe? Somebody who grew up here and has that vibe to add to the authenticity?"

"If that person existed, then sure. But you're better because you understand what it's like to deal with people outside of our little bubble. No doubt, you've worked with high needs clients. I think, and Billie Jo agrees, that she can cover the Santa Fe credibility and you can make sure the other aspects of the business are functioning at a high level. You have a lot of assets, Nicole." They remained seated in the front of the car, heat on. The temperature gauge said fifteen degrees outside.

"I think it sounds like an incredible opportunity. It will keep me coming back here, but it will also get me out there," Nicole said, gesturing to the big wide world. "Can I think about it for twenty-four hours?"

"Of course. Need to talk to hubby?"

"Please stop. I'm begging you," Nicole said in mock horror. "No, I need to think it through for me. Do I want to piece together two or three jobs, this being one of them. Or work full-time somewhere in Portland. I'm guessing the first option will win out. But we still have college tuition to consider." And yes, she would talk to Jason, but for advice, not permission. "Cleo, why did you pick me out and offer me that ride home the first day of class? It was a leap."

Cleo moved around in her seat to get a better vantage point. "You reminded me of me. Isn't that how most people operate? You're drawn to the person who is most like you in a room. Your long career at Needham's told me you were loyal, creative, but also needed a job. You came across as someone who liked to work hard but took this big risk to come to a totally different city and start a new life. That's what I did when I moved to Hollywood. I wasn't from money; I needed every dime I made to stay afloat. I worked at the Bullock's on Wilshire at the makeup counter, watched all the fancy women and how they behaved in the world. I made a path for myself and kept working hard until it happened. Then I loosened up the rules a bit! Especially when it came to men. But I saw a lot of that in you, a hard worker who followed the rules, most of the time."

"Thank you."

"Plus, that store looked dreadful. A mess. Any help was better than no help."

"I appreciate the faith," Nicole said, sensing the exhaustion that Cleo was fighting. "I'll grab your enormous bag and meet you at the front door."

"Thank you, Nicole. So much better than an Uber."

Just then a figure opened the front door to Cleo's house, a woman much younger than Cleo. "That's Elena, my housekeeper. I texted her to have the bath ready and the kettle on for tea."

The two women hugged on the doorstep.

"I'll be in touch," Nicole said.

"I'm counting on it," Cleo answered, and Elena closed the door.

To: Holly
From: Nicole
Subject: Casita and Bardot Questions

Hi Holly . . .

I can't believe it's April already. The school year has flown by for me. I finish up mid-May and have a few questions with regards to the end of my stay at your beautiful house:

~ My husband is flying in from San Francisco this week. I mentioned that he might come stay with me at some point and now is that point. He'll be here for the rest of my stay in Santa Fe, then we'll drive my car back to leave with his brother in Northern California while we head to Asia.

~ Attached is the last of the spreadsheets re: Sincerely, Mimi. I think everything worth selling is sold. But there are some very lovely pieces of artwork left here. Also, a few really good antique rugs and some furniture. I think you'll be glad to have them. But if you don't want them, I can give you a list of galleries and resale shops here that will take them. I've already spoken to these places and they will come pick them up. But you should keep them.

~ I'd like to keep the online shop open for my own resale items. Do you have any objections to me using Sincerely, Mimi as the name?

~ Now on to my beloved Bardot. I would like to find Bardot a permanent home here if you have decided you don't want her. Because of our planned travels and homelessness until August, I'm not a good candidate, although I love her and will miss her. But Albert and Peter next door would be wonderful dog parents and would be honored to adopt her. I feel very strongly that you need to decide soon so that the transition for the dog will be easy. Feel no guilt, Holly. But decide soon.

Thanks, Holly. See you in May when we cross over!

Chapter 34

San Francisco
April

"Jason, you look amazing."

"Thank you, Olivia. I think not working has been good for my complexion," Jason joked to his Kincaid & Blume colleague Olivia Ko, a forty-year-old Stanford grad who'd been his second-in-command, a position she adjusted to after K&B bought Stumptown. They were lunching at Cotogna, a buzzy modern Italian place near the K&B offices, their first face-to-face meeting since the beginning of his professional sabbatical. Olivia had taken over some of Jason's duties in the interim; his counterpart in New York, Martha Morgenstern, assumed other parts of his job during his leave. Jason was surprised how easily he'd stepped away from the day-to-day duties that had consumed his life for more than twenty-five years. He thought he'd struggle with being out of the loop, not on top of all things publishing. But he found he rather liked life outside the loop. Other than a few emails about big picture business strategies and a few more about specific books or content ideas, Jason had let Olivia do her thing while he did his on his motorcycle. Did he miss work? He did, of course. But not as much as he would have thought a year ago.

Seeing Olivia here in the flesh, with that taut go-go-go look on her face and the constant glances at her phone screen, keeping up with multiple work conversations while she was supposed to be having lunch with him, made Jason wonder about going back at all. Of course, he had to go back. He was only fifty-one and in no position to retire. Kids in college, the new roof the house would need, a robust retirement fund—all compelling reasons to show up at work again next August 1. But he was beginning to think that his return might be more reluctant than refreshed.

"We've missed you. But you know how it is, the business marches on. I don't want to suck you back into a work conversation. You still have a few months before you're forced to reengage with all the gossip. Tell me about your trip and everything else!" Olivia said brightly, responding to a text in between sentences.

Jason gave her the short version of the Patagonia portion. He'd been working on his material, shaping the life-changing four-month excursion into a four-minute recap for the attention span challenged. He glossed over the surfing in Nicaragua portion, positioning the month in Playa Maderas as lazy beach time for reading books, which is what he ended up doing instead of learning to surf. And he finished with a brief report on his father's improving health, his mother's admirable adjustment to the new normal, and the whirlwind sale of the family house—keeping the part about it going for asking price and not a penny above to himself. There was a lot of real estate schadenfreude in the Bay Area and the fact that the house didn't spark a bidding war might make Olivia ecstatic. "And tomorrow, I'm off to Santa Fe to reunite with Nicole."

"You two! Role models! Marriage goals! The courage to spend nine months apart from each other doing your own thing and loving it. Clearly, you loved it. Look at you!" Olivia said between tiny bites of halibut crudo. She was the type who ordered appetizers as main courses and then took half home. "Oh, you remember that idea you sent me last summer about the Five Hundred Mile Rule? That's the book I want to publish. I have a writer working on it right now. I can send you the book proposal. Would you ever consider writing the foreword? Using your own experience?"

Jason took a few extra chews of his tortellini alla Norma. He'd forgotten all about his late-night drunkmail after the evening with Jen and Rich. The subject line? *Bestseller Right Here.* He'd outlined the concept of the Five Hundred Mile Rule in a paragraph and told her to find a writer. He'd sent it before Nicole had even told him about her plan to abandon Patagonia and flee to Santa Fe. Before they'd agreed to their own marriage sabbatical. Way before Abby. There was no way that Jason was going to confide in Olivia or anyone about what had transpired in his marriage. Or outside it. "We didn't do that rule thing. We did our own thing. I went to South America, she took up silversmithing. Nothing more."

He hoped he was convincing, but doubted it. Had Olivia told everyone in the office that Jason and Nicole were swinging their way through the year off? She must have from the disappointed look on her face.

"Oh, I guess I misunderstood your email. You seemed so enthusiastic that I thought you were going to try it, too. Well, no worries. I think it's still a sexy book idea. I was talking to Martha at the manager's meeting last month about how it could be the start of a whole line of relationship books for us. Everything is different about how humans interact since the pandemic and the explosion of social media and global connectivity. Those Gen Zers, they don't care about precedent or hierarchy. It's relationship anarchy out there. I thought, how about a series on rethinking relationships, from marriage to friendship to workplaces? Branded under the banner of Modern Relationship Rules, or something better. We're working on it. But put that on the back burner until you return. You're still on sabbatical, right? I've got it all covered. Enjoy all the beach reading in your future." She flagged down the waitperson and made him bend down so she could whisper into his ear, "Can I take the rest of this to go?"

———

The duo stood outside the restaurant on the corner of Pacific and Montgomery, the hub of historical Jackson Square. Olivia was headed back to the office, but Jason had nothing special to do that afternoon. The endless list of house-related tasks was complete, including the final inspection. The house would close next week. His parents were settled in their new living arrangements. And tomorrow he'd be on a plane to see his wife. He thought he'd wander the neighborhood, do some shopping at some of the trendy boutiques, maybe stop in at William Stout Architectural Books to browse the New Mexico section, pick up a design book or two and one of the classic Stout tote bags as a gift for Nicole. Tonight, he had booked himself a room at the Hotel Zeppelin on Post Street, a spot with a lively bar and decent food, so he wouldn't have to fuss much. Was that a sign of aging? The desire to not fuss? He was losing his edge.

"So happy to catch up, Jason. You're an inspiration. Really. Someday I'm going to have a life outside the office. But for now, just meetings, meetings, meetings," Olivia said. "My best to Nicole." The two had only met a few times so that seemed like overkill to Jason, but he supposed she was only being polite.

"See you in August," he said with a wave.

"That's a long time from now," she answered, a declarative statement that sounded vaguely threatening. "Ciao ciao." And she was gone, a half an order of cold fish in hand.

Jason had two thoughts: *Olivia Ko is gunning for my job*, and *I can never go back to that office.*

Chapter 35

Santa Fe
April

The countdown was on. Jason was arriving tomorrow, and Nicole was clearing her calendar so she could spend the first few days with him, not in the studio finishing her end of year projects. Or at the store finalizing the details of their arrangement for next year. Nothing would be more foolish than letting the everyday details of her life here in Santa Fe get in the way of her reunion with Jason. Was she still conflicted about their reunion? Maybe. She knew her stomach was in knots, a mix of nerves, excitement, and something else. Guilt? Caution?

The arrival of the prodigal husband was a topic of discussion among her friends. The Wolfpack had weighed in on the group text with all sorts of directives to shave, wax, tan, trim, and balayage. Tessa made wardrobe suggestions, most of which involved silk and lace, but Nicole was leaning toward cotton and cashmere. Sarah sent a few recipes for carob chip "chocolate" mousse with the curious message, "Ted and I enjoy eating these in the bedroom." Jane sent a short list of places where she could vouch for the couples massage package, which made Nicole realize that Jane had made some additional stealth trips to Santa Fe to see costume designer Lenore without telling her.

Of course, Cleo and Billie Jo had advice. Cleo suggested Nicole take a yoga class with lots of hip openers before the airport pickup and insisted that she dab several drops of essential oil behind her ears after her shower. "See Devina at Aromaland. Ask for the Cleo Trio. My personal blend. Magic!" Cleo stage-whispered.

Billie Jo's succinct advice? "Maxwell playlist."

She'd done most of the beauty treatments, booked the yoga class for tomorrow and the couples massage for later in the week, secured the essential oils, and compiled the playlist with a few other artists. In honor of their agreement, she'd gotten tested for STDs at Planned Parenthood, her first visit in decades, and the place still made her nervous and grateful. She felt physically ready to welcome Jason home.

But there was one more emotional task to handle: sell the flamenco dress from the show in December. In her mind, that dress would always be associated with Marcos, and that night, and it was too much to have to explain its existence to Jason. She had posted it on Sincerely, Mimi when her phone pinged. It was an email from Jason.

To: Nicole
From: Jason
Subject: My Top Five

It only seems fair that before I touch ground in New Mexico you have my Top 5 list. But unlike you, I'm going to give them to you all at once. Pour yourself a glass of red and take a seat, my bride.

#5 The Night in New York

We both agree. Please tell me you didn't sell that suit when we were packing up the house. Because I'd like to see you in that again. NYC next October?

#4 Our Honeymoon

Yes, going with a classic even though our honeymoon was hardly luxe. Remember our two-day honeymoon on the Oregon coast where the rain came down in sheets, the rental house smelled like mold and cheap floor cleaner, and we barely left the bed? It was the only getaway we could afford. (Your mom gave us a hundred bucks and my parents were too mad about the city hall wedding to contribute anything at all.) But that didn't stop us from doing all sorts of things to each other that were memorable, but also eating take-out chowder and watching Lifetime movies because it was the only channel we got. I don't know if it was the sex or the many movies about terrible things that happened to women who live alone, but it was a memorable forty-eight hours.

#3 You're Not Dave Matthews but You'll Do

I'll never understand your thing for Dave Matthews—the band or the guy. But I recall being the beneficiary of your lust for him after that show at the Aladdin in 2017. It was a fundraiser for refugees, so kind of grim, but that didn't stop you from getting all worked up when he sang "Crash Into Me" at that show. You did some serious crashing into me on the light-rail on the way home. How many times did we have to listen to that song when we got back to the house? (With that tortured line about hiking up your skirt . . . make it stop, Dave.) Not that many, as I recall. You were raring to go. Thank you, Dave Matthews.

#2 Lockdown Lunches

You know what I'm talking about. After the worst of it— Charlie and you losing your job and the kids being forced to come home—we found our little refuge in the Pandemic Palace. Every Wednesday for months, you'd make me lunch, bring it to my office, and we'd fool around on the couch. It was sweet and loving and the only good part of 2021. I miss your grilled cheese and tomato soup combo.

#1 You're Going to Have to Wait for This One.

See you in Santa Fe

Love you, J.

Nicole had done what Jason had instructed. She sipped the glass of wine, read his note four times, and teared up at the thought of those Wednesday lunches during those dark days. She realized all the prep she'd done, while well intentioned, was unnecessary. It wasn't about waxing or tanning or essential oils. Those lunchtime encounters were what the "for worse" part of "for better, for worse" truly meant. Neither of them was at their best, emotionally or physically. Jason had lost his best friend; the hole was unfillable. Nicole had lost her job, her Needham's family, her outside affirmation. While Jason's loss was tragic, both were unmooring, identity-shaking. The lunches stood in for therapy, for coping, for connection. Their need to physically connect was rooted in something deep: the years of being there, of listening and laughing, of sleeping side by side, night after night.

She put the cork back in the wine, shut down the computer, and looked at Bardot. "Come on, noodle. Let's go for our walk then get to bed early. We need to rest up. The sabbatical's over."

Chapter 36

Santa Fe
April

There was no pit of nerves in Nicole's stomach on this trip to the airport, only anticipation. When Jason came down the escalator to the arrivals level, instinctively she waved, and he waved back. He looked handsome, wearing a blazer, jeans, and a blue patterned scarf that she imagined he picked up in Argentina. It gave him the air of an international traveler. His hair was longer and there was more gray, but the cut was expensive. His face was tanner than usual, a sign he'd been spending more lunches walking the neighborhoods of San Francisco than at a desk. He carried a messenger bag over his shoulder and a canvas tote bag from a store in San Francisco she'd been to before, a design bookstore of some sort.

He kept his eyes on her, taking in her softer, more relaxed look. In Portland, when she wanted to take a break from her usual black wardrobe, she chose midnight blue. But today, she was in denim, soft brown suede, and a warm oatmeal wrap. She had on layers of silver necklaces, bangles on her wrist, and tiny drop earrings. Her boots were brown and worn in, like she'd spent a lot of time over the winter in them. The cutest dog he'd ever seen was on a leash in one hand and she held up a sign in the other. The sign said "Not Dave Matthews."

He strode right up to her. "I'm not Dave Matthews."

"Then you're the one I've been waiting for."

And then their lips touched for the first time in months.

———

When Jason stepped into the casita, déjà vu swept over him. He'd never been to Santa Fe before, never stepped foot in a house like this one, with thick walls, high beamed ceilings, a kiva fireplace, tiled floors. But it was the way Nicole had put it all together, with the antiques, the art, the mélange of textiles and colors, that was familiar. It reminded him of her little apartment in Goose Hollow, the one she lived in the night they met. How she had made a generic four-hundred-square-foot studio seem like her personal showcase with her distinct eye and understanding of exactly what she wanted. Here at the casita, even though the setting and the style were different, the sensation was the same: he was home. "This is beautiful."

"Wait until I light the fireplace and the candles. When the light dances off the walls, it's magical." She put down her bag, took off her jacket and hung it up on the pegs by the front door. She smoothed her jean shirt, filled Bardot's water bowl, fired up the playlist, and grabbed the matches to light the luminarias she'd splurged on for Jason's arrival. It wouldn't be dark outside for a few hours, the days lengthening in the spring, but she didn't care. "It's a little early to light these, but it's a special occasion. I think we can make an exception."

He wandered around the open living space, examining the paintings, the rugs, the textiles. Bardot followed him around the room, keeping an eye on this stranger. Nicole thought Jason seemed enchanted by the place, exactly like she had planned. When she finished with the lights, she said, "Do you want a tour of the property?"

"Only if we start in the bedroom," he said, coming up behind her and kissing her neck. She let him linger there, swaying her hips gently to Maxwell's "Pretty Wings" for a few measures. He responded by doing the same. Then she shimmied around to face him, ran her hands down his chest, and reached over his shoulder for the bottle of sparkling rosé she had on ice. He stepped aside to watch her pop the cork and pour. She'd gotten quite competent in her moves. She handed him a glass of bubbles. "Cheers."

"Cheers," he said, touching his glass to hers.

"Are you hungry?" she asked, putting out bowls of nuts, olives, cheese, and crackers, taking an olive for herself. "This is just for starters. I mastered steak adobo in honor of your arrival. I can throw that on the grill."

"I thought the whole reason you came to Santa Fe was because you didn't want to make dinner."

She smiled. He wasn't wrong. What she realized over the past months was it wasn't the act of cooking itself; it was the sameness of the meals and the drudgery of the dishes that had gotten to her. Preparing this meal for him would be a pleasure. "That was before I discovered the mysteries of red and green chiles. I'm newly inspired in the kitchen."

"I'm sure the steak will taste amazing later. How about the tour? The bedroom?"

"You must be tired if you want to start there," she teased.

"Not at all," he said, moving closer to her. "But I am very turned on. You have no idea what your denim-on-denim look is doing to me right now. It's like 1994 again." Nicole studied him like she had a secret. "What's that look for?"

"You guessed it," she said, putting down her glass. The song changed to Nirvana's "About a Girl" on cue, the acoustic version bringing back a flood of memories. They both listened to a verse, before Nicole said, "My #1 night."

He took in the music, her scent, the classic lipstick color. "The night we met."

She nodded. "The night we met."

"But we didn't sleep together," he said, pointing out the obvious to extend the moment. His hand found her hip and he liked the feel of the soft denim on his palm.

"We fell asleep in the same bed. After pouring our souls out to each other. I think that counts as coupling," she said. "And I spent the next three years thinking about you every night, in all kinds of ways. You were the boy that got away."

He pulled back, genuinely shocked. "You did? You never told me that."

"I didn't want your ego to get any bigger."

"You're very wise." He touched her hair, now lighter. Her face, now lined. Her lips, still red. He kissed her and she tasted like champagne and salt. "Can you guess mine?"

She shook her head. She had tried in the last twenty-four hours but failed. She assumed it would be something obscure. Or involve a good meal. Or an unusual location. "No idea."

"It's tonight."

"See, there's that ego. Pretty sure of yourself, huh."

"Well, I learned a few new things."

There was a deep silence between them, but no hint of discomfort, as he looked in her eyes. She held his gaze, beat for beat.

Finally, Nicole said, "I learned some new things, too."

And with that, they gave in to the moment. Together again.

Chapter 37

Portland
One Year Later

"Do you want a ride to the airport?" Jason asked as he made himself a second latte and watched Nicole whirl around the kitchen, doing the cleaning and organizing he told her earlier that she didn't have to do. But she was doing it anyway. His offer stopped her frantic movements for a few seconds, but then she resumed her tidying up.

"That would be great. Thank you," she said. She was headed back to Santa Fe, her second trip this year. In February, she'd returned, pulled together all the elements of the Zia Collective trunk show with Billie Jo, Cleo, and Moon, and then headed off to Dallas and Nashville for a week of successful selling as Billie Jo's sidekick. This time, Cleo was coming with them to New York. She would be there for PR value while Nicole and Billie Jo did the storytelling and sales. So far, the arrangement had worked out better than Nicole would have imagined in terms of compensation and satisfaction. Plus, the friendship between the women, including Moon, had continued to deepen and blossom. The multigenerational, multicultural exchange was a gift to Nicole, a true gift.

Plus, on the trip back to Santa Fe, she got to visit with former classmates, stop by El Farol to see Clancy, and take a flamenco class. She'd squeezed in a visit to the casita, now the happy home of Holly, who had returned from Vermont, mostly healed and healthy. She hadn't changed a thing about the casita, praising Nicole's design work, which touched Nicole. Holly was still not a Bardot fan, though, much to the delight of Albert and Peter, who welcomed the minipoo into their home with love, a new Ralph Lauren dog bed, and homemade treats. Roger even had her guest lecture to the new cohort of silversmithing students on the importance of retail merchandising. After the class, Raven joined them for drinks and enchiladas at The Shed. It wasn't the same as living there, but it was a way to stay connected to a city she'd come to love and the people she'd come to think of as family by choice.

She only thought of Marcos occasionally now. But he would always be a part of her Santa Fe fix. She'd even seen him one snowy night, watching from across the street as she closed up Zia. She had heard he was engaged to a woman, the Gallery Girl he had started seeing last year. And there she was, young and vibrant, climbing into his truck, laughing at something he'd said as he slid into the driver's seat, athletic and sure of himself. The scene was so familiar it made her heart hurt a little. That had been her sliding into the front seat of that truck, laughing and anticipating the night to come. But looking at the twosome now, the twenty-year age gap between the blonde and herself was a harsh reality check. Marcos and Gallery Girl had their whole married lives ahead of them; Nicole and Jason had slid into the phase of their marriage where the past was longer than the future. They had banked a wealth of emotional equity in twenty-five years and that would sustain them.

She'd have to report that to Cleo when she gave her the one-year follow-up, as requested.

Then she returned to the city she called home. Portland welcomed her back, green and lush. And wet. She'd missed all that moisture. She resumed her runs with the Wolfpack, sharing their lives as empty nesters as easily as they had shared their lives as new mothers. She hung out her shingle as a freelance retail merchandiser and picked up some regular clients, needing her services for everything from consulting to window design to holiday decorations. And in her free time, she banged out her silver charms, for friends, family, and on commission, as Roger had suggested. Turns out that the map of Oregon was even easier than New Mexico for a silversmith of her modest talents.

"I wish you were coming with me," Nicole shouted from the laundry room, pulling out a load of dish towels.

"I do, too. If you see Gary, tell him I'm still interested in his book idea," Jason replied, sitting at the breakfast bar, scrolling through emails on his laptop. "Thanks for sending me all the details about the graduation. I'll put it in my calendar."

"Graduations. I can't believe they'll both be done in June," Nicole said as she poked her head out into the kitchen. She was already anticipating the emotions of the double ceremonies in Eugene—one in the College of Arts and Science and the other in the College of Business—along with the anxieties of all the other potential family fireworks. "I'm so glad your father is well enough to come. I hope our mothers can figure out how to get along for the weekend."

"I'll take care of my mother if you take care of yours. And stop with the laundry. Finish packing. We should go soon. I can fold the dish towels."

She reemerged in the kitchen. "I'm stepping away from the laundry. I will tell Gary if I see him. Should I bug Cleo, too? Or are you going to let that drop?"

"I'll talk to him when I'm there for the literary festival in May." In the six weeks that Jason spent in Santa Fe last spring, he had found his people in town. He met with booksellers and librarians, local authors and chefs, and landed on the board of the newfound Santa Fe Literary Festival. He joined a hiking group, went to art openings, and bought a Panama hat from Montecristi Hats. He discovered a love of green chile cheeseburgers at Del Charro and Cadillac Margaritas at the Cowgirl BBQ. He managed to create his own relationships without stepping on hers.

But it was with Gary that he bonded for life. He was shocked that Nicole had failed to mention the great Gary Andrews in any emails. "He's one of the great touring musicians of all time. A legend," Jason had said at the time, after they ran into Gary at the bar at La Choza on a slow Tuesday night. At the graduation party for the students in Jewelry Design at Cleo's beautiful house, Jason and Gary had talked for hours, hatching a plan for a six-part podcast series on touring musicians that had come to fruition, thanks to Jason's new job. It was a big hit with critics and a decent hit with listeners. They were at work on another season. Jason tried to work the same magic on Cleo but she was more circumspect.

After Santa Fe, the trip to Asia with the kids, plus the extended stay with his family in the Bay Area, Jason took a hard look at his work life and decided to make some changes. His lunch with Olivia that day in San Francisco was the beginning of the end of his traditional career path, a trajectory that had always taken him forward and up. Now he craved sideways and out. As the end of his sabbatical neared, he pitched his bosses on a new job that was a lot like his old job. After ten years of managing a division in San Francisco while he lived in Portland, he wanted to go back to Stumptown and run his own imprint again. Going back to its original focus of travel and food, with a little music and celebrity thrown in. As he said in his pitch to the powers that be, "I want to find the Portland of every state, the Portland of every country. The place where art, food, music, travel, and creativity come together and define the city." He sold them on a multi-platform approach with books, newsletters, podcasts, and potential for TV. And they bought it. He was back at Stumptown full-time, the weekly travel and endless corporate meetings over. But the nonstop work and the overflowing creative energy still part of who he was.

It made Jason laugh to think about how he'd mocked the Stumptown founder, Neil Goldman, for his lack of ambition, only wanting to publish niche academic treatises on arcane subjects. Well, now he was Neil, except the subjects were cooler. His first projects included Gary's podcast and *Robusto*, the lifestyle book and cookbook about Mendoza, Argentina. The pipeline was full of projects, but he was pleading with Gary to write a memoir. Cleo, too. Both said they didn't want to spend the time talking about themselves—they'd rather talk about other people, other things. Jason was still trying to figure out how to make that happen.

Nicole returned to the kitchen, roller bag by her side. The dog looked nervous. They'd adopted Truffles, a chocolate-brown miniature poodle mix of unknown age and origin, from the Oregon Humane Society at the holidays. Mixed with what? Maybe a Wheaten? Or a bichon frise? Chelsea named her and Jack referred to her as a "mutti-poo." Most of their texts from their final semester in college involved details about graduation weekend (Chelsea) and asking for pictures of the dog (Jack). As far as Nicole and Jason were concerned, Truffles was the light of their life, a constant source of delight, activity, and mess. So much for not becoming the people who talked about their doodles all the time. The bulk of their evening banter was Truffles-related. At least she was a rescue.

When Nicole was out of town, Truffles went to the office with Jason. At night, Truffles patrolled the downstairs while Jason slept upstairs. Truffles had a big bark for a little mutt. Nicole reached down to scratch her soft, sweet ears. "You protect your dad, okay?"

Jason pulled on his jacket and a baseball cap and grabbed the handle of her roller bag. He called to Truffles to load up. Nicole did a last-minute check of her carry-on. Wallet, ID, laptop, lip balm. All good.

"Watch the dog," Jason said as he opened the door to the garage, but it was too late. Nicole was too far behind to grab her collar. The dog darted across the street where the neighbors were out front with what looked to be a real estate agent. A For Sale sign was being hammered into the ground in front of the house.

"Damn Truffles. Now we're going to have to talk to Rich and what's-her-name," Jason said under his breath.

"Jen. Her name is Jen," Nicole said, as if she could forget.

"Sorry about that. We're still working on her manners. She's just a people person," Jason explained while trying to corral Truffles without humiliating himself. The dog now perceived that she was in the middle of a very exciting game of chase and even someone with Jason's innate cool couldn't help but look foolish. Nicole stood at the edge of the property, adding to the chaos by calling the dog's name with no result, thinking that when she got back, they needed to get serious about some training for Truff. She hated being one of those lame dog owners who repeatedly called the dog's name as the dog did what it pleased.

And she hated being that person in front of Jen, the neighbor she had avoided for most of the last seven months since their return to Portland, save for a few waves from the front porch. Honestly, Jen hadn't exactly rushed over to greet her either. She resented that their sabbatical had given her something in common with Jen, who seemed to be fitter, tighter, and smoother since she'd last encountered her. The magic of surgery and injectables would soon run its course, Nicole thought, but until then, Jen was winning the aging game. Expensive athleisure was a good look on her.

She watched as Jason finally grabbed the dog by the collar, a beautiful purple, green, and red beaded collar from Zia. She called out to her husband, "Good work!"

Now that Jason had Truffles under control, he took in the scene with the couple, the sign, and the real estate agent. He had to say something, didn't he? "Don't tell me you're moving? We never got to have you over for paella. Nicole took cooking classes in Santa Fe and her paella could give yours a run for its money." Nicole recognized that he was desperate to get off their lawn, but it was hard to ignore the elephant in the ground, the fresh For Sale sign. She moved closer to him, hoping to bail him out with a line about being late for her plane. But Jason couldn't help himself. "Where you headed?"

Rich, who seemed to be aging in the places Jen was not—like the neck, the gut, and the hairline—plastered a big smile on his face and announced, "We're doing some downsizing. I'm headed to a condo on the waterfront."

"And I'm moving to Maui," Jen said triumphantly. "Making some life changes."

The real estate agent, a midlife mom in a quilted Burberry rain jacket, shrugged her shoulders and said nothing.

"And so it goes," Rich said in a complete non sequitur.

"And so it goes," Jason repeated like an idiot, a stunned idiot.

"We'll miss you," Nicole lied. "Best of luck to you both on your new paths. I have to get to the airport, so we'll say goodbye."

"Yes, take care," Jason said, tugging Truffles by the collar and hustling across the lawn, trying to regain his dignity.

"What the . . . ?" Jason said when they were both safely in the car, a used Volvo wagon they picked up upon their return, the former owners trading in the workhorse vehicle for a sleeker Tesla. "He's moving to some sad, divorced guy condo and she's going to Maui, looking like a Miss America contestant. And really, 'best of luck to you both on your new paths.' Where did that come from?"

"Just pull the car out and drive down the street. I don't want them to see me react," Nicole said. She was torn between laughing and screaming. The outcome was so predictable, but it could have been them.

"What do you think happened?" Jason asked as he hit the gas, powering the Volvo past the morose tableau of Rich and Jen and the For Sale sign, a matrimonial tragedy.

"I think one of those random hookups in the airport Sheraton finally took hold. She looked thrilled. Him, not so much." She almost felt sorry for the guy, standing there in his khakis and white sneakers, his bluster silenced.

"He looked like shit. No wonder I haven't seen them around in a while. Her car hasn't been in the driveway for months. I've been walking the dog so much, I've started to notice the comings and goings," Jason observed. "They blew up their whole lives."

Nicole shook her head. "I'm not so sure about that. Were they together long enough to have something to blow up? They didn't have a partnership. They had an arrangement from the start." There was no comparing the frivolity of Jen and Rich's brief marriage with the decades of work in Nicole and Jason's. At least, that's what Nicole thought.

"You're probably right," Jason agreed. His mind drifted to his time in Patagonia, an adventure that he sealed in a box, the full scope of which was his alone. He was no Rich and she was no Jen. He glanced over at his wife, silver hoops in her ears, putting on lipstick using the lighted vanity mirror in the sun visor, a feature she'd been so excited about at the dealership. Her lips were a soft rose. She flipped up the visor and gave him a questioning look. He flashed her a big grin and raised his right eyebrow. "They're not us, baby."

She shook her head, playing along. "No one is."

They drove in silence for a while, listening to the loopy raw vocals of Courtney Barnett, singing about mirrors and reflections. She watched her husband navigate the Fremont Bridge traffic as they crossed over the Willamette River. This bridge always seemed higher than it needed to be and made her palms sweat when she drove over it herself. But she could relax when Jason was behind the wheel.

"I hope you realize that we're going to be more than five hundred miles apart for the next ten days," Jason said, not taking his eyes off the road. "You know what that means, right?"

"I do," she said, turning to look at her husband of twenty-five years. "It means it's email season."

"I never thought of it that way, but yes, email season."

"Check your inbox tomorrow night."

Jason was trying to get over to the far-left lane to merge onto the highway out to the airport. Out of habit, they both turned and looked out the rear side window. It was clear.

"You're good," Nicole said.

Jason caught his wife's eye. "You're good, too."

Acknowledgments

One Saturday morning in the spring of 2021, I sent an email to my editor, Rachel Kahan of William Morrow, that simply said, "What do you think about a novel called *The Marriage Sabbatical*?" She emailed back right away: "I love it." From that scrap of encouragement, this book took shape, my third novel with Rachel. Without her guidance and belief, I wouldn't have had the guts and confidence to write this kind of story. Thank you, Rachel. I'm honored to be part of the William Morrow imprint and appreciate the support of Ariana Sinclair, Liz Psaltis, Ellie Anderson, and Amanda Hong.

Speaking of gutsy, thanks to my agent, Yfat Reiss Gendell of YRG Partners, who provides equal parts expertise and pep talks. Ashley Michelle Napier, who provides everything else needed from YRG Partners. Plus, great lunchtime brainstorming sessions. You both make the business of books fun.

Usually, I thank my husband, Berick Treidler, at the end of the acknowledgments. But with this book, it feels appropriate to thank him right up top so there's no misunderstanding that this is a work of fiction. After thirty plus years of marriage, with zero sabbaticals, I can say without a doubt that you're the one for me. Thank you for your unwavering support of my work and so much more.

I'd also like to thank my college pal and personal therapist for this project, Daniela Abbot, MA, LMFT, who provided insight, feedback, and gobs of reading material as I honed my characters around this plotline. Your contributions were invaluable. Early reader Lucinda Sill Morrison also has my thanks.

Thanks to my Santa Fe guides for showing me around town and providing insider details for the City Different: Mary Cardas,

Cheryl Palmer Keto, and Tina Richards. You made the city real to me and I hope you can feel that within the pages. And inspired the Wolf Pack gift baskets and Nicole's commitment to public transportation. Jeanne Foley Clark gifted me jewelry and insight into the silver trade. Thanks to Cheryl Papineau and her beautiful rental house that became the casita in the book. And to Ali McGraw, who my husband and I happened to run into in a small café in Santa Fe. (I was too stunned to speak, but he made exchanged pleasantries with the legend.) Because of that chance encounter with the iconic Ms. McGraw, the character Cleo Jones was born.

I'm grateful to my sisters Liz Dolan and Julie Dolan Smith along with brother-in-law Trem Smith for traveling to Patagonia and hiking through the wind, rain, sleet, sun, cold, and altitude so I didn't have to. I put my main character on a motorcycle because I couldn't bear to think about all that hiking.

Thanks to my Portland friends for filling in the memory gaps from my time there in the late eighties and early nineties, when the city was not nearly as Portland as it is now. I loved being able to re-create that pivotal time in my life in this novel. Cheers to Robin Lanahan, Sally Bjornsen, and Mona Mensing for providing the names of the early brew pubs and trendy restaurants to dot the city and for inspiring the Forest Park running group and the Irving Street loft apartment. As we always say on Satellite Sisters, you can't make new old friends. And to my former Nike colleagues and Wieden + Kennedy pals from back in the day, if you think you recognize yourself in the book, you're probably right.

I am always grateful to my community here in Pasadena, California, for supporting my work for decades. Thanks to the event planners from the libraries to the nonprofit organizations to the private clubs for welcoming me to luncheons, talks, and book clubs. I appreciate all the invitations. Cheers to local writers Naomi Hirahara, Kim Fay, Allison Gee, and Colleen Dunn Bates for being touchstones. Thanks to the staff at Vroman's Bookstore, especially

Jen Ramos and Gilbert Martinez, whose professionalism and enthusiasm have been invaluable to my career. And thanks to my friend Diana Nixon who has taken it upon herself to be my unpaid booking agent at various venues all over Southern California. You're the best, Diana.

A big thanks to @potato_the_toy_poodle on Instagram. Not only did this account provide hours of cuteness, it shaped Bardot's personality.

My Satellite Sisters community is filled with wonderful listeners and readers who have supported my books for over a decade. You have inspired me more than you know. I'm grateful to every Satellite Sister, Mister, and Smister who has shown up at a book event, preordered a copy, or posted on their social media. Thank you.

My extended family of sons, sisters, and brothers, cousins, nieces, nephews, and in-laws is very large and very supportive. I love you all. No free books.

A final thanks to readers for continuing to expand your worlds through the pages of a book. I'm grateful you've let me into your life.

About the Author

Lian Dolan is a writer and talker. She is the author of *Lost and Found in Paris*, *The Sweeney Sisters*, *Helen of Pasadena*, and *Elizabeth the First Wife*. She's written regular columns for *O, The Oprah Magazine*; *Working Mother* magazine; and *Pasadena* magazine. She is also the co-creator of Satellite Sisters, an online community for women. She graduated from Pomona College in Claremont, California, with a degree in Classics and now lives in Pasadena with her husband and grown sons.